This is a work of fiction. Name are the product of the author's imagination or are used fictiously. Any resemblance to actual persons, living or dead, events, or locales is entirely coincidental.

ISBN 978-1-7349634-0-3

Revised First Paperback Edition

For Mom and Pop

FIRELINE

ANTHONY DECAPITE

CHAPTER ONE

I was cooking up some fresh ink. Caleb was annoying the shit out of me by chipping at the paint on the wall. I knew the sound well, and knew I'd be finding little white flakes in my sheets for days. The metal slats squeaked from him squirming around on the top bunk, while I kept still on the bottom one. Each fighting our own battle in the war against a common enemy, the defining quality of our cell – not its cramped size or dull color or barred window, but time. It stretched on and on and on, and we both had our own ways to pass it.

I sat with my back to the door, holding a can of boot polish topped by a burning wick. The fingernail-sized flame was orange-brown and hypnotic, a fusing of light and heat, comfort and destruction, licking the air, whipped by it, reaching upward, spreading and retreating. A winding movement like nothing else in the world.

The wick burned down, wafting a smell like old-lady perfume tainted with gasoline. I blew out the glowing stub and opened the can of boot polish. The baby oil had done its job, burning the top layer of polish into soot that now lined the inside of the can. While white flakes fluttered down around me, I scraped the black powder into a paper bowl I'd made.

"Making ink here," I said.

"Not stopping you, Mace," Caleb said.

"Rather not have paint chips in it."

"Don't you like experimenting with color, *artiste*?"

The back of my right hand throbbed, tender from the unfinished tattoo stretched canvas-like across bones and veins. A four-pane window with a starry night sky inside it. It was going to be unique. Way more original than the hundreds of wolves, skulls, crosses, and spiderwebs decorating the cons of LAC. I had the window frame dotted out and half the night sky inked in. Blackwork was a bitch, and it'd be my focus today. The key to filling in the night was working in sections, inking tiny black circles. Too fast or too sloppy and it'd scar, pushing the pigment out. I'd leave spots of skin blank and the last thing I'd do is put in the stars with white ink.

People were bound to ask what it meant, and I'd tell them black was my favorite color, and that with the scattered pinpoints of light it'd make a badass contrast. What I wouldn't tell them is that the dark-light contrast played into the fact that some of my best and worst memories were from nights under the open sky. The snickering crackle of a juniper branch thrown on the fire; camping with Uncle Derrick. The rasp of a shovel against hard-packed earth; digging a grave in that field outside Victorville.

"Dude," I told Caleb, "it's hard enough trying to get this done with my left hand and make straight lines over the bones and shit."

"*I want to challenge myself,*" he quoted.

"It's already off to a bad start and I'm trying to fix the outline, which needs to be as black as it gets. You're not helping, all right?"

"Alright, don't get your panties in a twist," Caleb said, and stopped scratching the paint.

I patted down the soot with a paper towel, soaking up any remaining baby oil, then funneled the soot into a bottle cap. Adding a drop of water, I had ink.

My metal bunk groaned as I reached under the thin mattress and took out my homemade tattoo gun, which I was damn proud of. The needle was a sandpapered-down guitar string threaded through a pen barrel. It was fixed to a motor Caleb had swiped from a drill in the machine shop.

A rustle from the bunk above – foil – and a tapping of plastic – his binky.

"It's the middle of the day," I said.

A sharp intake of breath as he shot up anyway.

"Fuck off," he replied.

Caleb jumped out of his bunk and paced the cell like a cat in heat. The hell?

"Uppers now?"

"No, *Mom.*"

Caleb was tall, yoked, with a respectable crop of tattoos for an unaffiliated con. We both sported the same square beard, buzz cut, and iron shackle bicep tat. A signal to everyone not to fuck with the Jones brothers. The Aryan Brotherhood had shamrocks and swastikas. We had genetics.

Caleb wore the three years he had on me a lot harder. Bags under his eyes, scattered gray hairs in his beard, and nightmares that woke me up as often as him. I was pretty damn glad he was the one with the receding hairline. But Caleb made up for his age with a fire in his belly that I'd never really had. Motherfucker would shoot from his paper at lights out and wake up to run sixteen laps in the yard, hit the weights with me, win a couple books in a poker game, and then get another six laps in before Rec Time was over.

At the moment Caleb's fire was burning as nervous energy.

The buzzer rang for Rec Time, which was what he was waiting for. Our cell door unlocked.

Caleb took a towel from his cubby and unrolled it on the tiny countertop next to the shitter, letting his stash spill out. He scanned the small collection of commissary items and stamp books – the lunar-themed Forever stamps he had were top-notch currency. He finger-fucked the corners of the cubby hole to be sure. That was everything.

Caleb cracked his knuckles. Good thing he didn't do that during his poker games, or he wouldn't have those books. The knuckle pops told me he didn't have enough.

I rolled out of my bunk and flipped up my mattress, pulling out my own books and commissary items.

"How much you need?" I asked and held out a few books. We'd shared our losses and gains since I was 15, since the day I told Patty the social worker that the rubber-banded roll of cash taped to the bottom of the couch was my savings, not Caleb's illegal earnings.

Caleb hesitated.

"How much you need?" I asked again, indicating the stamp books.

Caleb waved them away and went for the commissary items instead. *Good, I ain't made of money,* I thought, relieved. I was low on commissary items, too: just a packet of sausage snack bites and a bag of chips.

He took both.

"If anyone asks, I didn't dip into your stash," he muttered. "It was all mine."

"Everyone knows we're on each other's count."

"Exactly. So if anyone asks, it was just my shit involved, all right?" Caleb scratched the scruff under his jawline.

"What are you into?" So secretive all the sudden.

"Forget it. It's not your debt, Mason."

"Fuck you. Your debts have been mine since tenth grade," I said, annoyed now. Not just secretive. Protective. Shielding me from something. Something he was ashamed of?

"You borrow for papers?" I asked. Caleb had always liked to get high, but he'd never had an outstanding debt because of it. *He's not an idiot.*

"Hell no. I'm not an idiot."

Like I said.

He filled his pillowcase with the goods and twisted it closed.

"Dude," I said.

"Stay out of this one," he said, and left.

Letting him get a head start, I ignored his demand and tailed him out, my blue CDCR uniform blending into the dozens of others as Facility B's prisoners streamed from their cells. He seemed like he was in trouble, and I had his back whether he liked it or not. During Caleb's first stint in prison, I'd picked up the slack and done jobs for his boss, Quincy Reed. And he'd more than returned the favor when my sentence started some years later, when the A.B. were using their fists and feet to milk me for send-ins.

"Mace!" A familiar voice called out to me, and I looked over to the Rec Room. It was Rubio, a heavily tattooed *La Raza*. He sat by the TV with Baker, a thickset white dude, and pointed to a wide spot on the couch he had saved for me and Caleb. Rubio and Baker were the other members of our four-man car – the name in here for a group of inmates that had each other's backs.

I nodded thanks but kept after Caleb. He weaved through the mass of inmates funneling into the Rec Room and kept on towards Facilities.

I followed him to the kitchen door. Someone had left the side door propped open for him. He looked around and ducked in. Snagging the door, I slipped in after him.

It was a large, industrial space dominated by brushed stainless steel. Dim, with the silvery surfaces distorting the light of a single fluorescent left on over the stove. The countertops were stacked with bags of pre-cut meat, veggies, and cheese. There are no knives in a prison kitchen.

Caleb used the handle of a skillet to break open a locked cabinet. He pulled out individual peanut butter packets and dumped handful after handful into the pillowcase.

What the hell?

"We in the smuggling business now?"

Caleb straightened, frowning. He turned to me, quiet for a moment. The goods crinkled as he twisted the pillowcase.

It's not that big a deal, I thought. Ripping shit off is why we were here in the first place. Me for the Benz job. Max sentence because I held my mud. It kept the heat off Caleb, but he arrived at LAC not long after seeing me limp into the visiting room covered in cuts and bruises. For him, it was a burglary of a tech company in Silicon Beach, private security everywhere. He'd picked it to make sure he got caught. If stealing from the kitchen was our new hustle, I didn't know why he'd keep it from me.

"It's not business. Fuckers are keeping meals from that fish, Andre," he said.

Andre. The fish – a new inmate – was a quiet black kid, no older than 20, and had been here less than a month. Last week, Caleb had brought him over to lift weights with us.

"The kid has no car and no connections. A perfect vic. He's being taken advantage of," Caleb explained. "Trying to keep him out of all this fucked up shit. Kid's got a chance."

"Why? Who gives a shit about some random fish?"

Caleb sighed and shook his head. "He reminds me of you," he said.

I didn't get it, and tried to read Caleb for answers. He wouldn't meet my eyes. What'd he have to be guilty about? I'd be a cold, bloody pulp in the shower drains if he hadn't shown up. *Does he mean the field outside Victorville?* That was over ten years ago.

"It's just a little help," Caleb added.

"It's some real bitch shit," a gravelly voice behind us said.

We turned to see the owner of the voice, Grayson Graham, coming in the door with C.O. Ulrich at his side.

Graham was a brick shithouse of a con. At least 6-foot-6, arms as big as my head, tree trunk legs, and a barrel chest. His pale, freckled face was clean-shaven, and his reddish-brown hair was cut in a high-and-tight. He cultivated a soldierly look, and everyone in his car followed suit. On paper, Graham was the picture of rehabilitation. Level I, Group A, top-notch Prison Industry worker. And with shady fucks like Ulrich watching his back, I could see why that picture stuck. In reality, Graham ran the contraband business, was tight with the A.B., and word was he killed Mike Williams, who they found bled out in the showers a few months ago.

Ulrich was skinny, white, and mean. He'd been a correctional officer for almost as long as I'd been a con. He took his baton out.

"How about a safety check," Graham growled, and it was not a question.

Ulrich walked up to me and my brother as a chill snaked down me, turning my legs to jelly. My tensing stomach somehow kept me upright. I knew Graham had a few guards watching his back, but I didn't know he was the shot-caller.

I glanced at Caleb. We were supposed to interlace our fingers on the back of our heads. He glared at Ulrich, who hefted his baton meaningfully. Caleb glanced at me, and as if that settled it, put his hands on the back of his head.

I could almost feel the heat of Caleb's rage as Ulrich frisked him.

"The brother, too."

I put my hands on the back of my head and the corrupt piece-of-shit ran his hands down my body. The way my heart was hammering, I was surprised he couldn't feel it. Ulrich nodded at Graham.

"Clean," he said. Instead of going back to Graham's side, he stepped behind and to the side of me, making me even more nervous. Which was the whole point.

Graham wore latex gloves on his hands – no fingerprints – and his right hand was a loose fist, his index finger and thumb extended slightly. Hiding a shiv.

Caleb saw it, too – his eyes were flicking over Graham's right hand, Ulrich with his baton, and the exit.

"Why you coming between me and my fish?" Graham asked.

He meant Andre, and it all clicked. Graham wasn't intervening because of his contraband business. Graham, with his kitchen job, was the one *keeping* food from Andre. Probably running an extortion game on the kid.

"Nobody knows I'm feeding him. Your rep is safe," Caleb said. Making the case that if no one knew about Caleb's charity, no one could question Graham's power to punish and extort without consequence.

"I asked you a question," Graham said. "You stepped between me and my vic. Why?"

Graham kicked the door stop out and let the door slam behind him. Sweat trickled from my armpits, the room suddenly claustrophobic, and I couldn't help but glance at Graham's loose fist with the shiv I couldn't see. Ulrich's utility belt clinked as he shifted his feet, and he was close enough for the sulfur stench of his coffee-breath to waft over my shoulder. Only two people could help us, Rubio and Baker, and right now they were probably laughing hysterically over a *Maury* paternity fight.

Caleb stood straight and solid. I couldn't see a bead of sweat on him. He stared right at Graham, defiant.

"The kid is starving," Caleb said.

"And?"

"Dude's just trying to keep his head down, He's got no connects, no car, and he didn't do anything to you," Caleb said, voice rising. "Conning a man is one thing, extorting him is another."

Dammit, Caleb.

"Got a fucking Boy Scout here. You're supposed to look out for your own. You're supposed to protect your kin," Graham said, pointing his chin at me.

Caleb's posture faltered. Now his forehead was glistening.

"How much do you want?" I asked. "We can hook it up."

Graham flicked a finger. *Crack!* My knees buckled as Ulrich bashed them with his baton, and my shins banged the floor. Caleb stooped to help me – Ulrich shoved him back into place. I staggered to my feet with shockwaves of pain pulsing from my kneecaps.

"Not talking to you." Graham said.

"It's true," Caleb said. "We can make it right."

"No, you can't."

He launched himself at Caleb, and the shiv slid between his fingers and into his grip.

I sprang forward but Ulrich yanked his baton against my throat, slamming me back.

Caleb swerved to the side, but Graham was *fast*, and Caleb

weaponless.

A ribbon of blood splashed on the floor – Caleb took a slice on his forearms; he was using them to block Graham's swipes – *Whap!* Caleb sidestepped and punched Graham in the face, then jabbed him in the ribs and danced away from a thrust.

I grabbed the baton, pushing to get it off my throat, but Ulrich's pull was stronger, his grip tighter than my clawing fingers, the cold fiberglass smashing against my Adam's apple and making spots devour my vision as I sputtered. I kicked and pounded at Ulrich behind me, but he just pulled tighter.

Caleb grabbed a mixing bowl to use as a shield and Graham laughed. Then came at Caleb like his first attack had been a warm-up, dodging the bowl and plunging the shiv into Caleb's arm and slamming him onto the floor. The bowl clanged away, and a lead lump dropped in my stomach. Caleb wiped sweat from his brow, smearing blood across his face.

My brother – the tough one, the fighter – was outmatched.

It was more suffocating than the baton on my throat. Vision blurring, heart thundering, I threw my weight into Ulrich and ran backwards as fast as I could.

Whack! Ulrich's head smacked a wall and the baton slipped off my throat. Heaving in air, I spun to face him. His head wobbled, eyes glazed over. I kicked him in the crotch, watched him fall, then kicked the son of a bitch again.

Graham stood over my brother. I dashed to the kitchen drawers and wrenched one after the other – all locked. *Need a weapon.* Caleb kicked out, but Graham just danced out of reach. The lead lump in my guts jolted. Caleb dragged himself away –

Graham stabbed his ankle and yanked him back with the shiv. Caleb's scream razored through me and a strangled howl erupted from some deep, primal place. Jerkily, I forced motion into my jelly legs, running and diving into the bastard, slamming him to the floor. Pounding my fists into him, everything went away. Except his raw skin. His nose crunched deliciously against my knuckles. Exhilarating. Blood running down his face.

Graham rolled me and he was on top.

There was a snap on my stomach, like a rubber band. Again on my side, beneath my ribs. Then on my inner thigh, and there was a grating scrape on my hip bone.

Slippery warmth spread below my waist. I looked down – my uniform was in shreds and soaked with blood from gashes skipping down my body. As soon as I saw them, the pain hit. It was sharp and *deep*, so deep I was nauseous. I couldn't think.

A glint – Graham's blade coming straight at my face – *shlick* – it went through my palm and out the back of my hand, the shiv grip catching on the muscles.

Saved by reflexes. I'd thrown my right hand over my face. Fresh blood dripped in my mouth – *tastes like copper* – and the pain sent shockwaves through my body as he pushed down and I pushed up, the shiv wavering inches from my eyes.

An angry shout. Caleb pushed Graham off me and the shiv skittered across the tile. Caleb flung himself on Graham, fighting like an animal. The slashes on both of his arms and his foot spackled the floor with blood, but the wounds didn't look deep. *Thank God.*

The silver surfaces around me blurred. Losing focus. Legs no longer jelly, going numb.

Ulrich shambled over. Arms and baton hanging limp at his sides. In shock.

"Do something!" Graham roared.

I lurched toward them – *too late*.

Ulrich cracked Caleb on the head with his baton and he crumpled. Scooping up the shiv, Graham pinned Caleb face-down and stabbed him in the back.

An implosion in my gut. The monster stabbed him again and again. My chest was collapsing in on itself as I stumbled over and grabbed Graham's wrist.

I couldn't hold him for long. The room spinning, my strength slipping away. I slid in the swamp of blood fed by my wounds, by Caleb's. *Keep it together, Mason.*

Graham ripped from my grip and slashed – leaving a jagged red line and stinging pain across my chest.

Caleb didn't seem to be moving, and it didn't seem to matter. Everything was fading.

Ulrich pulled me off Graham and held me back. I was too weak to resist.

Then, white as a sheet, Caleb pushed off the floor. *He's alive.* I gulped in air – I'd forgotten to breathe. He looked at me and his eyes went wide. Did I have the same wide eyes staring back at him?

Caleb lurched, ripped Ulrich's security card off his belt, and slipped and stumbled to the door. *Don't leave me.* My brother swiped the card on the red square by the door. They grabbed him, but he stretched and kicked and pressed a button.

An ear-piercing siren went off, its shrieking pulses bouncing off the stainless-steel surfaces. Graham winced and covered his ears.

Not leaving. Setting off the alarm.

Graham flayed Caleb's back and let him slam on the ground.

He didn't move. The sight sucked the air out of me. *Get up.* My vision clouded, darkness creeping in at the edges.

Graham threw down the shiv, took the security card from Caleb's limp hand and swiped it, pressing buttons, trying to turn off the alarm.

"Won't work. Has to be shut down from the hub. Fuck!" Ulrich shouted.

"How much time we got?" Graham snapped.

"Less than a minute."

Graham gave the card back to Ulrich with a disgusted glare and raced out with Ulrich running behind, boots squeaking and squelching.

The alarm was shrieking but I barely noticed it as I crawled over to Caleb. He was face down in a pool of blood. Lightning bolts of pain torched my body as I reached out and turned his face to mine. His eyes were closed. I thought I heard ragged breathing, could swear his back was rising and falling.

I reached out to feel his neck for a pulse and the world fell away.

CHAPTER TWO

An ache, deep in my belly, deep in my chest. Radiating out, it stroked a pounding headache into being and forced me awake.

There was no bunk above me, and Caleb wasn't there. The bed I was in was *too soft*, with a headrest angled so I was wasn't lying straight back. Bulky, cream-colored cases and big buttons – an array of electronics that looked straight out of the 80's. A tube in my wrist.

Hospital.

My thoughts came at gridlock pace, out of joint and smothered by a whispering fog. *Drugs.* I reached for a bed handle and searing pain ripped through my body. My hand was a block of concrete and my insides were snared with jagged rebar, stabbing parts of me I never knew existed. Even breathing was agonizing. The only movement free of torture was turning my head to find I was alone.

Caleb. Last I remember, he was breathing. *Wasn't he?* Bloody, but breathing, and if *I* was alive, then…

"Hey," I said, my voice a ragged croak. No response. I wasn't strong enough to talk over the beeping and whirring medical devices. I tried to shout, my voice cracking, lungs tugging at the throbbing wounds in my gut, "Hey!"

The door opened. Something familiar: a man in a correctional officer uniform. Hispanic dude with a bored expression. He took a good look at me and pressed a radio button on his chest.

"Jones is awake."

One of us is, I thought. *Where's the other one?*

"My brother."

The C.O. stared at me. Not from confusion; he clearly understood what I was asking. He grimaced, as if not sure what to say. Or what he was allowed to.

"Where's my brother?"

"He didn't make it," he said, finally. "I'm sorry."

The room spun. He probably misheard me.

"I mean Caleb Jones," I ignored the pain speaking caused. "Looks like me, but taller. He's probably in another room." They'd have to take us to the same hospital. Wouldn't they?

"He's not. You need to –"

"There's been a mistake," I said, voice rasping, words catching. *Maybe he's in another wing… or in surgery… Between the CDCR and hospital bureaucracies, who the hell knows?* I took a breath and summoned as much force as I could: "Go check."

His eyes flashed. Inmates don't talk to C.O.s like that. I didn't give a shit.

"There's no mistake, inmate," he said, leaning on his C.O. authority like an asshole.

"Caleb Jones. Go check."

"He was DOA. I saw the body."

No.

There wasn't enough air. *Not. Possible.*

"Show me."

Anger flashed across his face again. Then he sighed.

"I'll run it up the chain. It takes some doing to get you cleared to leave the room. Liability, security concerns."

Security concerns? I couldn't even move. There was sympathy in the C.O.'s eyes, and that was the scariest thing of all. If a C.O. felt bad for a con, then what he said might be true. But it couldn't be.

I had to see for myself. I looked at the C.O.'s nameplate.

"Please, Officer Galvan."

Galvan hesitated.

"Please."

Galvan rolled me on a gurney down the hallway and the hospital ceiling passed overhead, the tiles and lights blurring together. The hospital's freight elevator lurched as it started down, and it made my body feel like it was ripping in half. Another hallway. The ceiling dimmer, the air colder. The wheeze of something like a massive fridge door opening, and he rolled me into a room gray and white and cold.

My heart threatened to burst out of my chest as he pushed me next to a steel examination table with a frosted-white body bag on top.

"Can you?" I indicated the body bag with my eyes.

Galvan made a disgusted face and stood back as he unzipped the body bag and pulled away the plastic down to the stomach.

I looked at the face and something inside me twisted, making my eyes ratchet over the rest of the body. Stab wounds. Deep, red, unbleeding. I didn't linger on those. The "This Will Pass" hourglass tattoo. The sword and shield tat. The iron shackle bicep tat, the same one I had. *Goddammit.*

The face again. Between the buzz cut with its receding hairline and the square beard.

Goddammit.

I reached out and touched Caleb's shoulder. Cold and clammy. The skin had no give.

I fell hard back on the gurney, my insides lurching like the elevator had. The air was being squeezed from my lungs.

Something smelled metallic as warmth spread across my abdomen – my gown soaking with blood.

"Son of a bitch. Ripped your stitches," Galvan said.

Cobwebs collapsed over the C.O.'s agitated face, and everything went dark.

H ours or days later, I was awake with fresh stitches and a full tray of food over my bed. A nurse stooped over me. She was a short Filipino woman with a sweet smile that I wanted to wipe off her stupid, kindly face. She told me her name, but I didn't give a shit.

Her world was behind frosted-glass, a separate place. I was in the LAC kitchen.

Ulrich cracking Caleb on the head with the baton.

Graham ripping his back open with the shiv.

The two of them running away while he bled out on the floor.

The flash of each cut, the metallic taste of blood no longer there, the shrieking ring of the alarm – all more real than the nurse and the hospital room.

She said something about vitals and put a thermometer stick in my mouth. "Under your tongue, please, under your tongue." I bit the plastic stick and wrenched the handheld device it was attached to out of her hands, it cracked on the floor. Then spat the stick out for good measure.

The nurse clucked, then inflated a band I hadn't even noticed her wrapping around my arm. It squeezed, beeped, and deflated.

"Your blood pressure is pretty high."

I sensed the nurse moving around in the vague and distant place. Taking off the armband, sweeping up the broken thermometer pieces. She touched my hand, and I granted her a glance. She pulled a tray filled with food over my bed. How long had that been there?

"You need to eat," she said. And then stood there staring at me, waiting.

I could understand the words, but they had no weight. Her frosted-glass world didn't matter, what she said didn't matter, but she wouldn't go away.

"Not hungry," I said. I detected the emptiness of my stomach, but it was in her world. I was with Caleb as he laid face-down in a warm, red sea. He turned cold and pale and stiff while I did nothing to save him.

"You've been here almost a week."

I didn't know how that was possible.

The nurse looked at me sympathetically, her face breaking through the distance and murk. It made me goddamn sick.

"I'm sorry for what happened to you." She paused. "You're lucky to be alive."

Luck had nothing to do with it. I was alive because Caleb pulled the alarm, and he was dead because I couldn't protect him. I should be the one in cold storage.

Avoiding the nurse's eyes, I tore a bit of bread from the sandwich on the tray and chewed. It got her to leave, and I spat out the bit and pushed the tray away.

I had a vague sense of being moved around, surrounded by surgical masks, and a blue blanket billowing over me. Voices. Lights. Then darkness again.

I woke up in a fog. It was different than the painkiller haze I'd been in before, but definitely drugs. My stomach was numb.

Something was tenting my gown around the abdomen. Pulling up the hem, I saw a plastic washer anchored in the skin above my belly button, and protruding from it was a tube with a syringe-looking plastic cap. In the drug fog, it took a full minute to realize what it was.

Feeding tube. Those sneaky bastards.

I can be sneaky too. I'm a fucking con.

I pressed the button to elevate the incline of the headrest. Better leverage. I tugged on the tube, and the anchor tugged on my skin, firmly in place. The movement stirred my abdomen, but there was no pain.

Pulled harder. Still in place, too weak. Not even a sting as the endcap slipped and tore the stitches on my right hand. Blood flowed freely from my palm. So warm. As the tube slid through my weak, bloody hands, I got an idea. Looping the tube around the head-rest rail, I smacked the button and made the headrest go completely horizontal.

With a wet pop, the plastic washer shot out, and bile gushed out like pus from a popped zit. I chuckled, satisfied exhaustion spreading from my core.

Maybe now I could just slip away. I closed my eyes.

And heard the beep of the EKG.

Had it always been beeping? I wouldn't be able to slip away if this thing went off. I didn't need them rushing in and bringing me back.

I strained for the wired sensors taped on my chest and yanked them off.

A flat alarm tone erupted from the EKG.

Shit. Ears burning, face slick, I slapped the sensors back on, and the EKG went back to its steady beeps.

A hospital is a hard place to slip away.

Cobwebs crept into the edges of my vision. I looked at the yellow-brown fluid spilling from the hole in my stomach and a wave of nausea rippled through me.

What are you doing, Mason?

Graham killed my brother, and I was lying here feeling sorry for myself. Caleb ran to pull the alarm with his dying breath to save me. I was sitting here trying to reach my dying breath, like a fucking bitch.

All Caleb had done was stand up for a kid who couldn't stand up for himself. And Graham killed him for it.

I didn't have to die. I could live to kill Graham.

Before darkness swallowed me, I buzzed for the nurse.

Yes. I would live to kill Graham. It was an exhilarating idea.

CHAPTER THREE

It was humiliating. Me, getting lifted and shifted by the short Filipino nurse, somehow stronger than she looked, listening to the slosh of the bedpan as she took it to the toilet and flushed it. Her giving commands in a gentle tone that only made it worse, using metaphorical kid gloves on top of the latex ones she wore as she literally wiped my ass. I couldn't, and it was hard to imagine anything more humiliating.

I distracted myself by taking stock of my injuries. After getting the doctor's chicken scratch on my chart translated, I'd connected the long list to the sharp pains throughout my body. *Punctured internal and external obliques, punctured small intestine, lacerated iliopsoas, transverse patellar fracture.* The list went on. Wasn't masochism. Naming each pain gave me a hill to climb. Some control. I had to rebuild the house of Mason to take down the house of Graham.

A knock at the door returned my thoughts to my humiliating circumstances. The nurse had one strong hand on my hip while the other powdered my keister. She said it was to prevent bed sores, but it just made me feel like more of a baby.

"The patient needs privacy. Give us a few minutes," the nurse shouted, finishing up and rolling me back into place. I watched her take off the gloves. Graham had worn a pair just like them when he sliced me and Caleb up. A professional butcher.

The nurse threw away the gloves, washed up, and cracked the door. She was a bit flustered by the person on the other side, but I couldn't see who it was. She told the person to wait and closed the door again.

She made a big show of adjusting my sheets and tucking me in, then leaned in and whispered to me, "I was at the nurses' station, and one of the sheriff's department guys was hitting on my friend…" Jesus, why the gossip? *Am I her buddy now?* "What happened to you and your brother… they've got nothing to go on. No fingerprints, no surveillance footage. I thought you should know."

C.O. Ulrich had covered their tracks. More than the information itself, I was stunned by the nurse telling me it. I'd been such a dick to her.

"Why are you telling me this?"

"When we have patients like you, some cops come in here and make us do labs they don't have warrants for. Push us around, you know?"

Fucking right I do.

"This guy seems like one of those," she said, then tapped her nose and bustled away.

I couldn't remember the last time someone had done something for me without asking for something in return. I wanted to say 'thank you,' but I hadn't paid attention when she told me her name, and before I knew it she was letting '*this guy*', a man holding a badge, into the room.

The man with the badge was short, mustachioed, and wore wireframe glasses. The badge was for the Special Services Unit, the prison detectives. He crossed the room and extended his hand.

"Special Agent Brown, SSU."

"Can't move too much, sorry." It was nice to have an excuse not to shake hands with a prison pig. Special Agent Brown dropped his hand.

He pulled up a chair next to me, extended the tray over the bed, and unpacked an In-N-Out bag on it. He took out a Double-Double burger and chomped out a large bite, slopping juices on the tray. It smelled damn good.

"Hope you don't mind," Brown said, "been running around all day, never got lunch."

I nodded. I knew this game.

"How are you feeling, Mason?"

"Shitty," I said.

He smiled sympathetically. "I'll look into getting you an increased dosage on the painkillers. How does that sound?"

"Like bullshit, since I'm already maxed out and you're not allowed to sway doctors' decisions." Did he think I was stupid? Just because this was my first prison sentence didn't mean it was my first interrogation.

Brown frowned.

I reached out – a shooting pain torched from groin to chest – and upended the In-N-Out bag. A second burger, still in its wrapper, plopped on the tray. The punctures and lacerations riddling my guts made even the most basic movements agony.

"Next, you're gonna say how bad hospital food is, and that you can hook me up with this burger after I answer a few questions. How about we skip that."

"Fair enough," he replied. He stopped eating, wiped his mouth with a napkin, then each individual finger. "Tell me about your brother's drug use."

"I don't know what you're talking about," I said reflexively.

"We have a toxicology report."

I shrugged, which made my chest sting. *Lacerated pectoralis major and minor.*

"You didn't have any drugs in your system, though. Must really wear on you to have an addict for a cellie, even if he is your brother."

"Caleb had his shit together." The fuck was his game here? Trying to turn me against my brother?

"So, what was the dust-up about? The prison contraband game?"

I said nothing, and Brown continued.

"The pillowcase of food. Great way to make money on the inside. Territorial, though. Is that how you ended up here? Your brother go too far trying to pay for his drug habit?"

My blood boiled, and I didn't respond.

"You're not a snitch. I get it. I can put you in P.C. where you'll be safe."

"Sure. I love hanging out with child molesters." *Fuck protective custody.*

"I want justice for your brother."

I almost thought the dedicated look on Brown's face was genuine. But all pigs and C.O.s care about is lording their authority over people. And SSU agents were just jumped-up C.O.s.

"The only way to get that justice for him is for you to tell me what happened," Brown said.

Not true. There are different kinds of justice. That's why the molesters are in P.C., after all. To keep them safe from prison justice.

This guy was manipulative as hell, but maybe he did really want the truth, maybe he'd even believe me. I'd never once snitched, but there was a first time for everything.

I could roll the dice and tell Brown everything. Rest my future on the hope that he'd take the word of one con over a fellow correctional officer, that he could actually build a case and convict Graham for murder and Ulrich as an accessory. Even if that somehow happened, Graham wouldn't get the death he deserved. California hadn't executed a con since 2006, so Graham would just stay in the prison system where he was already a king.

And if I snitched, I'd be dead before the case got to court. There'd be no one left to avenge Caleb. I'd never once snitched, and I would *not* start now.

But I needed to know what'd happened since I'd been in the hospital. Had Graham and Ulrich been charged? How well had they covered their tracks?

The rusty smell of blood filled my nostrils – Graham and Ulrich ran out of the kitchen, boots squelching as the world collapsed. The shiv clinking on the floor.

"You want justice?" I asked. "All you've done so far is talk shit about my dead brother. What do you know? Who are you going after for ripping him apart?"

"I don't usually provide that kind of information to a person of interest," Brown said.

"Person of interest? You think I'd kill my own brother?"

"Oldest story in the world. Ever heard of Cain and Abel?"

"If I'm your best lead for what happened, you must not be very good at your job," I said.

Brown's mustache twitched, and the line of his jaw hardened. He took off his glasses and wiped them with a cloth. A uniformed C.O. would have punished me for that one, but he had thicker skin.

"Give me another option to explore," he said, putting his glasses back on to stare at me.

I was floored. He couldn't really be considering me for Caleb's death, could he? There had to be something, some detail that proved I didn't do it. As if 28 years of brotherhood wasn't enough.

I kept thinking of the moment Graham and Ulrich ran away with the alarm blaring. My brain was trying to tell me something, but what was it?

Off my silence, Brown shrugged and nodded at the door. "I can leave, and we can charge you. Without more evidence…" he shrugged.

Without more evidence, the gears of justice would grind me into hamburger.

I'd be no use to Caleb on trial for his murder. I heard the clinking of the shiv again. Saw Graham's latex-gloved hands, just like the nurse's.

That's it.

"I'm no forensics expert, but I think you already have evidence that rules me out. You get the shiv that was left behind?"

A narrowing of his eyes told me yes.

"Bet it didn't have fingerprints on it," I continued. "Not even a half-print or smudge. Because the killer wore gloves. Now, when you found me next to my brother on the kitchen floor, was I wearing gloves? You think after getting stabbed half a dozen times, I was able to somehow take off and get rid of gloves, *without leaving a trail*, before passing out in a pool of my own blood?"

Brown scratched his nose and looked at his notepad.

"Yeah, fuck you," I said.

Brown rapped the tray with his knuckles and jabbed a finger at me. "Watch it. You're still an inmate," he growled. The tray grazed my knees, sending a shockwave from the kneecap split in two by Ulrich and wired back together by surgeons. I white-knuckled the bed rails to keep from shouting.

"Write me up then."

His mustache moved like an inchworm on a twig and he looked up at the ceiling. Was it stupid to antagonize him? Probably. But my brother was dead, and I couldn't even wipe my own ass. I had a shield of pitifulness.

A long silence followed.

"I can only work with the information in front of me," Brown said, his tone apologetic.

I didn't buy it, but I think he was done going after me.

"That's why I need your help," he continued. "Tell me what happened in the kitchen."

"You're the ones with cameras," I said, drawing in slow breaths, my throbbing muscles tensing. There were at least 10 of them in the kitchen and the hallway outside it, and they should've shown him everything he needed to know. Should be an open and shut case. But the nurse said they didn't have footage, which meant Ulrich used his access as a C.O. to get rid of it. The butcher's understudy.

If the nurse was right, the California Department of Corrections and Rehabilitation was as dirty as I thought, and Brown *needed* my testimony to make a case. If the nurse was wrong and he *did* have the footage, what good was a convict's testimony?

"I want to hear it from you," Brown said.

The nurse was right, I could see it in his eyes. Prison pigs. Dirtier than the shit-covered farm animals they're named for.

I pasted on a smile and tried not to grind my teeth. "I'm sorry. I think… I think I blacked it out somehow," I lied. "I remember breakfast that morning… then the next thing I remember is a gloved hand, the shiv falling, and my brother on the floor."

Brown stared at me and took a deep breath.

Did he buy it?

He glanced at my EKG, where my heart rhythm pulsed in green peaks. Was it faster than before? '***80 bpm***.' The same number I'd seen for days. Brown frowned, unable to find leverage in the reading. My tensed muscles loosened a mite. For the first time in days, my body had done something right.

"You can remember why the murder weapon has no

fingerprints, but you can't remember who attacked you? Don't play games with me," Brown said.

"You came in here playing games. Trying to tempt me with fast food, acting like you can hook me up with better meds when you can't, and then pretending I'm a person of interest to push me into snitching. I lost my brother and a lot of blood, and if I say I blacked out..." I shrugged; it sent a stinging jolt through my stomach, "Well, maybe you should look at what your cameras saw instead of relying on my faulty memory."

"Let the C.O. at the door know if you 'remember' anything," Brown said with a guilt-tripping glare.

He bagged all the outside food and left with it.

I pulled the medical tape off the back of my right hand. Crooked train tracks of stitches held together the sides of a red ravine where the shiv had come out. The wound was right in the middle of the unfinished tattoo, distorting the window frame and splintering the night sky. Ruined. I stared at it, wondering what pissed Brown off more: me stonewalling him or the stink of corruption from the missing footage.

Though he'd play manipulative games to get it, Special Agent Brown had the self-righteous halo of someone who wanted the truth. I doubted he'd make me a suspect, but it was no victory. I was as empty-handed as him. I knew nothing about Graham and Ulrich.

CHAPTER FOUR

A month later, I was back at LAC. Stuck in its dedicated Health Care Facility, a completely separate building. I couldn't get a bead on Graham or Ulrich. Muddled by opioids, I nose-dived through razoring pain, sour sweat, and a ratchety wheelchair that chunk-chunk-chunked as it went. I slept but didn't rest, waking from nightmares I couldn't remember.

Another month after my return, I walked again. It was strange, though. Now that I could crutch myself around, actually move, there was an empty space that followed me everywhere, a weight on every limb. Trudging through a colorless maze everywhere I went.

I imagined bashing Ulrich's face in with a baton and slicing Graham apart with his own shiv. It kept the empty space from crushing me, a spark plug blasting a charge through my nerves and igniting heat in my muscles. I was still alive, alive so I could complete a mission.

Step one was rebuilding the house of Mason. Step two was getting intel on my targets. I'd get help from Rubio for that. Baker had been released on parole while I was in the hospital, making Rubio the remaining member of our car. First, I had to get the doctor-prescribed drugs that'd keep me moving. Did that count as a step? *Let's call it One-B.*

The HCF pharmacy disbursal room was a lot like those on the outside, with the waiting room full of chairs and magazines. Except in this one, the staff and drugs were behind a barred window, and the patients in line were hardened criminals. Or at least, they used to be. Stretching from the window was a line of diabetics and old cons with bum tickers. And of course, me, painfully crutching forward each time the line moved.

Speakers in the ceiling played *'Pour Some Sugar on Me.'* Kinda weird, but at least it wasn't muzak. Suddenly I was in the back seat of Mom's car, on one of the road trips to Aunt Jenny's, me and Caleb rocking out to another Def Leppard song. I couldn't remember which one.

How'd it go?

With *'Pour Some Sugar on Me'* playing, I'd never think of it.

The pharmacy nurse, a chubby brown-skinned man, said "next," and I was up. At the window, he shoved two paper cups under the reinforced glass.

The first had one 800 milligram ibuprofen horse pill and a single Band-Aid-like patch the size of a postage stamp. Suboxone to help with the opioid withdrawals. The hospital and HCF had pumped me full of all kinds of powerful shit, and this was supposed to keep me from becoming an addict. I stuck the suboxone patch on my shoulder and washed the ibuprofen down with the water in the second cup.

The pharmacy nurse nodded me off and called for the next inmate patient.

I crutched away, stacking the empty cups together and crumpling them.

Near the door was the Bucket Man, a short, stocky Hispanic inmate with a friendly smile. A splotchy apron covered his inmate uniform and he wore long gloves and galoshes. 'Bucket Man' was the prison industry job where the prisoner took a cleaning cart around and mopped up people's messes – blood, urine, semen, you name it. The prison point system was something else. Stay out of trouble, play nice with others, and you'll keep your points nice and low. Get down to almost no points, and they reward you with literally the shittiest job on the inside.

This Bucket Man stood with a cleaning cart to take empty cups, and he helped everyone who had trouble moving. He supported a con with a cane whose hand shook as he tossed his empty cup and took him to the door. Next, he took the cups from an inmate who had an arm in a sling, and that's when I saw it.

It was quick, barely noticeable – a smooth sleight of hand – swiping a false bottom off the cup and depositing it in the rubber lip of the trash can while dropping the empty cup in the trash.

I kept moving and inspected my own cups. One of them had a false bottom with three extra suboxone strips were taped to it.

My eyes flicked to the camera in the ceiling. The Bucket Man's placement was perfect – his back blocked the swipe from its line of sight. Why'd he even slip off the drugs right then at all? He could just let the patients unknowingly dump it and collect it from the trash later. *Wait...* Probably because they inspected the trash bags for just that kind of thing later.

Smart hustle. It required a man on the inside – the pharmacy nurse or someone else who worked in there, but still, impressive.

The Bucket Man didn't need to know that I knew, though. Leaning on my crutches, I fumbled to put the false bottom back on the cup – right as the inmate with a sling left, exposing me to the Bucket Man.

His friendly grin disappeared, and in the same moment, he twisted the plastic handle off the end of the mop, revealing a razor blade set in serrated plastic. He made a tiny cutting motion: *'Don't say shit.'*

My heart went from zero to sixty and hot beads of sweat popped onto my forehead, bleeding into my eyes. Not just on-edge, on the verge of panic.

What the hell's wrong with me?

Without thinking, I smacked the mop away, and it fell underneath a chair.

I hid my panic and glared at the Bucket Man. Before he could react, we were interrupted by a commotion at the front of the line.

"What the fuck? Hey, guard!" A white kid at the front of the line called for the C.O., pointing to the pharmacy nurse. The C.O., a stocky black dude, came in from outside. Powell, his nametape declared. The white kid showed C.O. Powell a cup with the false bottom peeled back, revealing extra pills taped to the actual bottom.

C.O. Powell didn't mess around. He hit a button and the

door slammed closed, an automatic deadbolt ringing as it socked in place. Powell threw back his shoulders and addressed all the inmate patients in the room; about fifteen of us including the Bucket Man, "Everyone against the wall. Hands on your heads."

Complaints burst out immediately. "Yo, I can't even move this arm, man," one inmate said, and others chimed in with their own injuries.

"Suck it up," Powell said, and the inmates moved.

I went to the wall, the Bucket Man's eyes burning a hole in my back. Putting my hands on my head, my body had no support and a hundred tiny daggers stabbed from my thighs to my gut. Gasping, I slumped back onto the crutches. I didn't give a shit what Powell said.

I heard Powell addressing the pharmacy nurse: "You, stand up and keep your hands off your desk."

I glanced over as Powell went inside the pharmacy station. Papers rustled, drawers opened and shut. Minutes later, the C.O. came back out, apparently finding nothing.

"You too, offender," Powell said to the Bucket Man, who'd stayed behind his cleaning cart. Low points or not, he was still an inmate. "Two arm's length between every one of you."

Bucket Man abandoned his cleaning cart and stood against the wall next to me. Between the blade and the hidden drugs, the dude had a lot to hide.

Suddenly, I had leverage.

Powell began patting each of us down.

"That was just a warning. You don't say shit," the Bucket Man said, the desperation in his voice a lot more obvious than he would've liked.

"I'm on a lotta drugs, man, I'm liable to have a slip of the tongue," I said.

"Shit man, what do you want?"

I just smiled and let him sweat it out. Me and the Bucket Man were last in line to be frisked, and a moment later, C.O. Powell was patting me down. Of course, I had nothing on me.

Powell frisked the Bucket Man and found nothing, but he wasn't done. He looked in the mop bucket; nothing but dirty water, crouched down to look through the cleaning cart; nothing.

"Dump the trash can," Powell ordered.

Out of the corner of my eye, I watched the Bucket Man carefully hold the lip and upend the trash can, keeping the drugs inside the lip as all the empty cups spilled out on the floor. Powell spread them out with his foot, then put on latex gloves and sifted through.

Nothing but empty cups.

The mop laid in the shadows of the chair next to me. *I can use it.* With a show of pain worthy of a Daytime Emmy, I stumbled into a crouch, blocking Powell and the Bucket Man's line of sight with my body. The razor blade set in plastic was actually one half of the mop handle, its cover the other half. I popped the blade attachment off the stick and swiped both pieces into my underwear, using the hem of my shirt like a glove. Hoping to keep the fingerprints intact. The Bucket Man was wearing gloves at the moment, but I doubted that was the case when he built this weapon. *Leverage.* Using the mop for support, I staggered up and handed it to the Bucket Man.

The Bucket Man's eyes flashed at the disappearance of his

blade, but he kept his silence with Powell standing next to him. The C.O. glanced at the mop, which now looked completely ordinary, then looked over the room and shook his head.

"Offender. Report to SSU," he called to the whistle blower. The young dude looked proud of himself, and I was disgusted. No fucking integrity, these kids.

To the Bucket Man, Powell pointed at the scattered cups.

"Clean this up," he ordered, and snapped on latex gloves. Then, Powell carefully placed the only false cup he'd found in a Ziploc bag.

The Bucket Man glared at me, and I flicked my eyes toward Powell in response. He caught my meaning. "Name," I demanded.

"Ortiz," he said.

Powell sealed the bag and marched out the door.

"You're gonna come see me," I told Ortiz, and crutched as fast I could in Powell's wake. Insurance for a safe exit. I looked back, and Ortiz nodded at me as he fixed his cleaning cart and picked up the cups. On the one hand, I'd saved his ass by keeping Powell from seeing his weapon. On the other, I had the weapon in my possession. Dude owed me *and* I had leverage on him.

L ater, he came to see me in the HCF dorm to find out just how much he owed me. I'd stuffed the toilet in the dorm-cell next to me with paper towels, making it overflow, and after a couple hours of bitching from the neighboring inmates, Ortiz the Bucket Man came to clean it.

Ortiz walked with a jaunty swagger, head and shoulders

bobbing down and side-to-side. "Yo, you ain't have to do *this*," he said, dismayed at the mess. He dammed the flow with his mop, sighed, and took off the long gloves he wore so he could chew on his nails.

His bare forearms displayed a canvas of tattoos. A well-inked but cliched-as-hell spiderweb on one elbow that represented time in prison. A shop-quality '213' in bold numerals, declaring his stomping grounds with the SoCal area code. Probably in a gang. The most interesting piece, one I couldn't interpret – a skull with a rose growing out of the mouth. Clearly had some personal meaning, it was too bad the line work was so weak. I could've done way better.

"You heard of a con named Grayson Graham?" I asked, cutting to the chase. Muscles cramping from the day's crutching, I forced myself to my feet, leaving the crutches on the cot. I was weak but couldn't show it.

"Where's my shit?" Ortiz asked in reply.

His mop-handle blade was concealed in the EXIT sign over the dorm door.

"Somewhere C.O.s will never see it if you help me out. So. Heard of Grayson Graham?"

Ortiz glowered.

"Yeah. Graham's people took over our hustle," Ortiz said. He cupped and connected his hands to make an 'S', the sign for the *Sureños*, a Mexican Mafia-backed gang.

For as long as anyone could remember, the *Sureños* had controlled the LAC contraband hustle. Until a year ago, when Graham and his people entered the game. Blood was spilled, bodies dropped, P.I. jobs shuffled, and suddenly everyone had to go through Graham to get their drugs and phones. That made Graham our common enemy. My pulse quickened, but I clamped down on my excitement. I needed to come across as calm and in charge.

"He the one that did this to you?" Ortiz asked, motioning to my crutches.

Pretty smart for a shit-mopping nail-biter. Or maybe it was an obvious conclusion to jump to. A twinge of paranoia raised goosebumps on my arms. I'd never get Graham if I couldn't keep this quiet, so I ignored Ortiz's question.

"You're going to keep tabs on him for me," I said.

Ortiz backed up, stunned. "Keep tabs. For how long?"

"Until I say. Once I got what I need, you get your weapon back." Caleb had always been the bulldog who barked what was what and people obeyed. Now I had to be the bulldog.

"Look, I need a little something to line my pockets if this is gonna be a long-term thing."

"You kidding me?" My body tensed, stomach muscles stinging in response. Ibuprofen wasn't enough. "I kept Powell from seeing that blade. I could've shown it to him with a swipe of my foot, but instead I did you a solid."

"You call blackmailing me a solid?" Ortiz cocked his head but narrowed his eyes, comically quizzical and angry at the same time.

"I'm *real* sorry for not returning the blade you pulled on me."

"Aight, fair enough. But Graham's a bad dude. Trust. And my peoples got enough problems with his already. I ain't trying to get on his radar unless it's worth my while."

My rage must've been showing, because he was quick to speak again.

"Hold up, hold up, don't piss your panties. I got you. I'll find out where he is, what he's up to. Quick eyes-on kinda thing. And I'll hit you up on this."

Ortiz slipped me a cell phone, and I tucked it in my underwear. "Good," I said.

"Anything beyond this quick eyes-on, we need terms. Deal?"

"Deal."

We fist-bumped, and I hoped it meant something to him. There was a risk of Ortiz telling Graham I was keeping tabs on him, which would ruin everything. But a favor for Graham was a betrayal to the *Sureños*, so it was a small risk. The bigger danger here was the *Sureños* themselves. I had Ortiz's weapon and it *might* have his fingerprints on it, but there was a chance they'd just kill me and let it stay hidden.

The muscles in my lower back twitched from standing for the past few minutes. To hide it, I put on Ortiz's gloves and sat next to the toilet I'd clogged, taking the tension off my back as I fished out the paper towels. Together, we cleaned up the mess I made.

When Ortiz was gone, I sank onto my coat. Something in my body creaked.

I'd be stronger in time. All the stitches were out, the throbbing pockets inside me on the mend. Had to rebuild my muscles, and then I'd be ready. If Ortiz came back with details about Graham that I could exploit and I was recovered, I could do it. *Couldn't I?* The flop-sweat panic that come over me because of Ortiz's blade wasn't normal. It wasn't me. As for killing Graham... *Was that me?* On the outside, I'd roughed up rivals and made threats. In the yard, I'd stood ground and thrown down. But I'd never killed.

If blood had to be spilled, Caleb was the one to spill it. The brass knuckle tune-up of the shipping container snitch. Strangling the crocodile-jacketed double-crosser on the Benz job that landed me here. That crimson chaos with the meth dealer. Caleb was a sledgehammer and I was an idea man.

Now, I had to be like him. I had to come down hard as iron to crush his killer.

F ive steps unsupported," Joe commanded. He was a clean-cut, 20-something black dude and was my physical therapist. I stood between two waist-high parallel bars in the Health Care Facility's physical therapy room. It had cushioned tables and chairs, exercise machines, kettle bells, medicine balls, and resistance bands. All the standard PT equipment and no C.O.s.

Or there weren't supposed to be. When I gripped the parallel bars to steel myself for the steps, I saw Ulrich standing in the entry corridor. His eyes hooded over, watching me. Caustic bile boiled up my throat. That copper taste on my tongue, rust smell in my nostrils. The world fell away and the only thing left was him smacking his baton on Caleb's head.

"You got this. Five steps unsupported," Joe said again.

Sucking in deep but shaky breaths, I brought the world back into focus. No blood on me, no ripped stitches or open wounds. Still the taste and smell of it lingered. I'd only taken three steps unsupported since walking again, but I had to show Ulrich I wasn't down and out. I nodded at Joe and let go of the parallel bars.

One. Goddamn that hurt.

Two, Three. Sweat trickled down my face.

Four. I got this.

I lifted my foot for five, shaking. I grabbed for the bars, slipped, and fell on the floor. The throbbing stab pains deepened.

"It's all right, I got you," Joe said, helping me up.

Ulrich smirked, and my face burned. The sweat poured heavier, salty in my eyes, and my heart drummed rapid-fire. My body shaking from a hurricane of fatigue, rage, and panic.

Joe helped me to a cushioned table, laid me down, and went to get some ice. Ulrich put on a professional face and intercepted him, pointing at me. Joe frowned, whispering something.

Ulrich barked something about "the investigation" and Joe let him by. The butcher's apprentice marched over and stood at the foot of the table. The nearest patient was an old-timer across the room, out of earshot if Ulrich spoke quietly.

But he did not speak. He just stood there and hooked his thumbs in his belt.

Was he here to taunt me? Hurt me? Finish the job they started in the kitchen? I glanced at a camera in the ceiling, heart pounding in my chest. Even if it was on, its recordings could be erased. They did it before.

Joe was still here, holding an ice pack and reading a chart, and so was the old-timer, who stretched on a medicine ball. *Witnesses,* I reminded myself, but it didn't slow my heartbeat.

I sat up, the familiar pain of movement rippling through my body, stared at Ulrich, and said nothing.

"You're being very quiet," he said.

Still, I said nothing.

"That's good. Good for your health."

The message was clear. Not talking was the reason I was still alive after returning to LAC, and continued silence would keep me alive.

A feverish fantasy played in my mind – me caving in Ulrich's face with a kettle bell. Then I'd be cuffed and on trial for murder. And worse, Graham would know he was next. Blind rage wouldn't get me what I wanted. Plus, I could barely walk without crutches, much less jump up and swing a kettle bell.

Gotta play the long game, I thought.

I put on a face I hoped looked defeated and simply nodded.

Ulrich walked away.

The knee-jerk panic dissolved, a deep calm washing over me. Without knowing it, he'd shown me my mission was the only way. He wanted me to be afraid, but his warning just made me more eager to take him and Graham down. And when his time came, he wouldn't get a warning.

A polite cough brought me out of my reverie. Joe stood over me, brimming with positivity.

"C'mon. We got ten more minutes. Let's get some resistance bands sets in."

"Let's not," I said, holding myself upright with excruciating pain.

"Jones…"

"Call it a day, Joe. Take the ten for yourself."

This was the only place in all of LAC where I could tell a prison worker to fuck off without a beating, and I was taking advantage.

"Suit yourself. Let me help you out." Joe grabbed my crutches and supported me himself on my way to reception, where a guard would escort me back to the HCF dorm. Wild. *I tell him to fuck off, and he comes back with kindness.*

In the privacy of my dorm-cell, I checked the phone from Ortiz. A text said he was headed to meet me. I was surprised that he had news already – maybe his people weren't going to kill me.

Ortiz came to my dorm, and when we made sure no one was in earshot, he spoke.

"Graham ain't in LAC anymore."

I couldn't believe it. How the fuck was it possible? Early release? Retrial? Escaped?

Then I thought, *It's a trick*, and said, "Prove it."

"Look," Ortiz said, and showed me a picture he'd taken with his phone: a prisoner transfer form that showed where Grayson Graham had been assigned:

'CDCR Conservation Camp #21: La Cuenca.'

Conservation Camp? Where had I heard that before?
I only had to read further, where it said:

'Volunteer fire/hand crew duties.'

I couldn't believe it. The murdering psychopath had been approved for a spot on an inmate firefighting crew. It was the most respectable and sought-after job an inmate could get.

"The camp, La Cuenca, I looked it up. Central California," Ortiz said.

Graham was hundreds of miles away. Was he trying to steer clear of any possible heat? To steer clear of me?

Central California. I was locked up in the largest prison in Southern California. I had thought the biggest hurdle would be getting into another cell block to get at him. But this? This was the worst possible news.

How in the hell was I going to get Graham now?

"Good news for your crew," I said, finally.

"Naw," Ortiz said, "He's got plenty of dudes on the count to keep his house in order, and they all got juice with the C.O.s. The kind of backing this motherfucker has, they get a whiff of movement from my peoples and the hats and bats will be out in full force. Check this: when he was in front of the UCC, a no-shit firefighter showed up to be a character witness for his ass. Some dude named Sean Wolfe."

The Unit Classification Committee was the board of LAC officials that approved security levels, job assignments, and transfers.

Still holding onto the hope that it was all bullshit, I kept reading the transfer form. It only got worse in the notes section, which was full of hand-written comments from the reclassifying official:

'Outstanding disciplinary record.'
'Committed to rehabilitation.'
'Inmate Graham belongs on the fireline.'

Outstanding. Committed. Belongs on the fireline. Like he was some kind of goddamn hero. It made me sick to my stomach.

"Son of a bitch," I said. It was the only thing I could say.

I held out the phone Ortiz had given me. He'd done what I asked. There was no follow up, no terms to be discussed. Nothing to be done. Nothing that *could be* done.

Ortiz must've seen it on my face.

"Sorry, man," he said, and he seemed genuine. He pushed the phone back at me. "You keep that."

Prison is a strange place. Kindness, because it so rarely comes about, shines all the brighter for it.

"Thanks," I said, and slumped into my bed.

Ortiz nodded and left.

I was alone, and the free, valuable piece of contraband just made the despair that crashed down on me so much worse. Because there was nothing I could do with it.

How do you get revenge on a man with connections on both sides of the law? Someone who's doing the most respectable job an inmate can get and hundreds of miles away?

You can't. I didn't have the resources to farm out a hit on a man like that.

It was over.

CHAPTER FIVE

Christmas ribbons became blood became fire. I woke up, sheets slick with sweat, heart hammering, the sensation of burning flesh lingering on my skin. An idea forming in my mind.

Crackling with nervous energy, I did sit-ups like Caleb used to do first thing in the morning. Got to 11 before tearing pains stopped me. *Not bad for a guy who can't walk.*

If Graham thinks he's out of reach he's got another thing coming. People die fighting fires all the time. Why not Graham? Being on an inmate fire crew is a dangerous job. And accidents happen to even highly trained, professional firefighters.

I could make it look like an accident, and that would protect me from retaliation. Graham killed my brother and got away with it. The best possible revenge would be to do the same. I'd make

Graham meet his end on the fireline, and I'd make it look like an accident.

I rolled over, put my palms on concrete damp with sweat, and pushed. A searing pain shot from groin to chest and a deep twinge cramped my scarred right hand. My fingers throbbed crimson, in sharp relief to the pink-white scar winding through the mangled shadow of the tattoo. Not ready for pushups yet. Refusing to slump onto my stomach, I propped myself on my elbows and locked into a plank. The jolt in my torso dulled, my flexed stomach muscles taking the load.

I'd only just started physical therapy, but I knew what I had to do. *I'll get on the fireline if it breaks me.*

T ime to rally the troops. Troops was a bad way to put it, though. Me and Caleb's car was small: the two of us, Isaac Rubio, and A.J. Baker, who was now out on parole. It was down to just me and Rubio.

I had months to go in the HCF and no legit reason to see an inmate from Facility B, so I paid off a flexible C.O. to bring Rubio to the yard during my doctor-ordered Vitamin D time.

Rubio raised a lanky, thickly tattooed arm, scratching his head in agitation as he walked over to me. The C.O. nodded and walked away. When the coast was clear, I told Rubio what we needed to do.

"You and me are getting on a fire crew to take out Graham."

He had always been a good soldier. Caleb would say what needed to happen, and Rubio would nod and go make it happen.

He didn't do that this time. Instead, he looked at his feet.

"Without Caleb…" he began, and never finished.

I couldn't believe it.

"You're supposed to be on the count for us. You want people to think you're no good?"

"Nobody's gonna think that 'cause everyone knows you're busted up. How you gonna be on the count for me? A dust up would be over by the time you limped over."

"I'm getting better. I'll be one-hundred soon, watch me."

"Bro…"

"Bro? Don't 'bro' me when you're leaving me high and dry," I said. *Fucking coward.* He wouldn't stand up unless he had Caleb to stand behind.

"I'm trying to do you a favor. Man, you're *alive*. And you're holding your mud, so you're not a threat, and to the boards, you could be a comeback kid. Keep it straight and narrow and heal up. Before you know it, your points are gone and you've got an early release."

Doing me a favor? 'Comeback kid?' Bullshit. He was scared or selfish or both. Fighting to keep my voice down, I asked, "and what about Caleb?"

Rubio sighed and looked around, as if he'd find the words he needed floating in the LAC yard. "Caleb was like a brother to me," he began, and quickly added, "I know he *was* your brother, but… he was the shot caller. Your shot caller. Now you can call your own shots. And all I'm saying is… don't be stupid. Don't waste that."

Asshole was trying to dress it up like he was doing me a favor, like it wasn't a betrayal. There was nothing else to call it.

"Get out of my face," I said.

"I'm trying to –"

"Get the fuck out of my face."

Rubio stepped up to me as if to fight. Then he shook his head, pity on his face.

I watched him walk away. I could barely walk, much less take his no-good ass down. I was soaked with sweat and my hands were cramping around the handles of my crutches. As the hot anger cooled, the empty space returned.

My feet were too damn heavy, my body too. Even the air settled like lead in my lungs. The empty space was swallowing me up. I hadn't just lost my brother and best friend. I'd lost the only person I could truly rely on. We'd had each other's backs for so long that I'd become dependent on it.

Rubio was an asshole, and I was a child.

I won't be dependent ever again, I resolved, fighting through the heavy space. Until it was done, I would not have friends, not even allies. Everyone I met would be an obstacle to overcome, or a pawn to leverage until my checkmate against Graham.

That's the only thing that matters, I told myself, and thought about the day I would put all this shit back on Graham and Ulrich's doorstep. These thoughts were kindling in the smoldering fire keeping the emptiness at bay.

I had some pawns I could leverage, I realized, and the idea I'd been nursing began to grow into a plan. I took out the phone Ortiz gave me and pounded out a text to him.

'Got a deal for your people. Need to talk terms with your shot-caller ASAP.'

CHAPTER SIX

I t would take three lies to get on the fireline. I stood before four LAC officials looking at me over laptops and paperwork. A uniformed CO, a health administrator in a tweed pant suit, one of the LAC social workers, and the case manager – a pencil pusher in business casual. This was the Unit Classification Committee reviewing my submission for placement on an inmate crew.

The health administrator chewed on a pencil, squinting at me like a chalkboard equation she couldn't quite crack. "And how does what happened to your brother affect your decision?" she asked in an affected British accent faker than Madonna's. That and a smug head tilt told me she thought it was a brilliant question. It wasn't. Prior to this submission, Caleb's murder was the most recent event in my file. I was prepared for a question like this.

"It's the reason I want to go out there. I want to put it behind me…" I began.

"You running from that trouble, son?" The C.O., Major Elliot asked. He was a stern black guy I'd seen only during big announcements.

"No sir."

Toward it, actually.

Six weeks ago, Ortiz had got me a face-to-face with his shot caller, Serrato. The man was tall, his face riddled with acne scars, and he had only two visible tattoos. Weird for a man in his position. Then I heard his voice – a chilling rasp – and I realized he didn't need ink.

"Talk. And don't waste my time," Serrato had said.

I tossed Ortiz's mop handle blade on the table, a gesture of goodwill, and said, "I'm going to kill Graham. With your help."

Serrato leaned into the single light of the HVAC machine room. One of the *Sureños'* last bastions at LAC. Didn't have a lot of real estate these days, which was why they needed me.

It took some convincing, but Serrato was smart enough to see we had a mutual interest in seeing Graham dead. They couldn't afford a war with him, of course.

"That's why we make it happen out there. On the fireline," I told him.

"Dangerous work, that shit," Serrato said.

"Exactly."

We made an alliance. Serrato would give me the *Sureños'* support and resources to remove Graham from the equation, giving them the opportunity to surgically change the guard in the contraband game at LAC. There was one catch.

Ortiz would be with me to make sure I didn't fuck them over.

As of the day of my UCC hearing, Ortiz had been approved for fire crew duties. It gave me some confidence that the *Sureños* were able to push him through. They were serious and capable.

I had to be just as capable. I made eye contact with every person on the UCC board. Good manners were fucking exhausting.

"What I mean, ladies, gentlemen, is that I want to move on. Finish out my sentence in a way that helps others."

This was the first lie, and I needed them to believe it if I had any hope of getting to Graham.

"And yet you didn't you cooperate with the investigation," Major Elliot said. "Doesn't sound to me like a man who wants to help others."

Motherfucker had years in this place. He knew damn well why I couldn't cooperate. I swallowed the rage bubbling up and reached out to that familiar empty space. I let its weight drape me, so the miseries that came with it could prove my case.

"I'm… very lucky to be alive," I said simply, feeling my sinuses swell and my throat tighten, making my voice croak. "Losing my brother… changed me. Placement on a fire crew is a privilege…"

The social worker gave me a sympathetic smile, and I fought a twist of guilt in my gut. *Why should* I *feel bad?* These people had no idea that the man who killed Caleb was on a fire crew, that they had already failed their most basic duty as the UCC.

I shouldn't have any issues trying to dupe them into doing it again.

I cleared my throat.

"It's an opportunity I don't take for granted. I appreciate your time, and I hope you can give me a chance."

The next morning, I got the news.

Approved for duty, pending a physical fitness test.

T he second lie was to my physical therapist, Joe, and Dr. Chu, the woman with the ability to declare me physically fit for duty.

"I'm back to 100 percent," I told them.

I was 75 percent at best. Shards of pain lingered all over, like barb wire embedded in my body, especially in my right hand. Through Ortiz, I had fentanyl for the pain, muscle relaxants for range of motion, and Adderall for focus. I hoped it'd be enough.

We stood on a 50-yard stretch of heat-waving concrete behind some administrative buildings. In the shade stood a pullup bar, orange cones, and tires for agility drills.

"Fire crew duties are strenuous, and my test will be strenuous," Dr. Chu said. "Do you consent?"

"Yes."

"All right. Move all the equipment into the sun and we'll get started," she motioned to the pull-up bar, orange cones, and tires.

500 pounds later, pain already cutting through the fentanyl, the real test began. Laps, sit ups, pull ups, zig-zagging around cones, dancing through the tire holes.

Sweating, dizzy with pain, I ran up to Dr. Chu with all my drills complete. Joe whooped and high-fived me.

"One more thing," she said, and opened the gate to a guard tower with six flights of stairs to the top. She handed me two 20-pound dumbbells.

"Don't forget these."

I almost collapsed just looking at the stairs.

Then I saw Caleb, with most of his blood on the floor, running to pull the alarm.

I yanked the dumbbells from Dr. Chu and heaved my way up the stairs.

When I came back down, I stood in front of her, no strength left. Only purpose keeping me on my feet.

"Pass," Dr. Chu said.

I waited for her to walk inside, then dropped to my knees. Joe raised his hand for another high five, and I slapped it with a smile. *I did it.*

"Proud of you, man," he said, and gave me a bottle of water. "Be sure to keep up with your stretches and core exercises. You'll be doing this stuff every day in training."

Every day. The thought made me dizzy.

I'd arranged for Andre to meet me in the HCF dorm, where I'd spend the days until I shipped out for training. Andre was a low-point ass-kisser who'd already nabbed himself a highly prized laundry job. It had taken some doing to get him here today, but he couldn't refuse me.

I'd only met him once, when he hit the weights with me and Caleb. Wide eyes on a boyish face. A jaw lined with razor bumps, except for his chin, which had a laughable tuft of hair. Maybe 19 or 20, and this was probably his first stint. Andre was in that time where he'd either stay an inmate or become a con.

'*He reminds me of you,*' Caleb'd said. *How?* Was it the old dig about me being 'soft?' Andre definitely didn't strike me as tough. Or was it his situation? Like Andre, I'd been on my own when I first came to LAC. Wasn't in a gang, didn't have a car. Couldn't join a black or Mexican gang because the A.B. would murder me for betraying the race. Wouldn't join the A.B. because they were racist assholes, so they targeted me, and I paid 'em off for as long as I could, send-in after send-in, until my second month when I couldn't pay anymore and they beat me within an inch of my life.

Andre brought me back to reality by answering the question I forgot I'd asked.

"I'm getting by, now that Graham's gone," he said.

"It won't last," I told him. "Ulrich's got it out for you," I continued. "Once I leave LAC and he's happy I'm not talking, he'll bring down the hammer. Gonna be even worse than when Graham was around."

My third lie. Ulrich didn't give a shit about Andre and wasn't about to stir the pot with anyone related to what happened in the kitchen. But I couldn't leave LAC until the butcher's apprentice paid the price.

"I'll keep my head down, then," Andre said, avoiding my eyes. "I'm better off without a car. Rather stay out of…" he cleared his throat, "whatever you brought me here for. You know, stay clean."

Self-righteous piece of shit.

He was the reason Caleb was dead. "*Fuckers are keeping meals from that fish, Andre… It's just a little help,*" Caleb had said. "*You're supposed to protect your kin,*" Graham had said, pointing his chin at me, and Caleb had sagged, his body betraying his fear. For *me.* And for that little help, Caleb had been ripped apart.

I didn't waste time, managing to spit out words between clenched teeth.

"My brother died trying to help you," I said. I couldn't wrap my head around Caleb risking so much to protect this nobody. Caleb came to LAC to protect *me* from the A.B. I'd been ashamed – *I'm a weakling who needs his big brother to save him* – and relieved – *I might actually survive this* – and livid – "*Now you're a target, too!*" It at least made sense. I was his brother.

'He reminds me of you.'

If that's why Caleb stole food for Andre, was that why he wanted him to stay out of the game? Had Caleb been ashamed of me? My insides lurched at the thought.

Andre hung his head and ran his hands through his nappy hair.

"Your brother was a good dude," he said finally. "I didn't ask him to do what he did, or even know why he did it. And I'm grateful. I am. For real, man, I'm sorry for what happened."

His eyes were glassy, and I looked away.

"Sorry doesn't mean shit," I said. "Sorry isn't what I want to hear from you."

This high-minded bullshit was a luxury of the young and naïve, a quality of someone who'd never had to make the hard choices. *Stay clean? You're knee-deep in my brother's blood.*

"It's all I got. I can't do nothing for you. Your brother wouldn't want me to," Andre said.

"How the fuck would you –"

"He told me," Andre said. "When he found out what Graham

was doing, first time he snuck me some food. We talked. He told me his story, I told him mine. He said that he fucked up when it came to you, but I'm young enough to change." I blinked hard, stunned, and the kid shook his head. "Didn't give me any details. Just that he should've done things different with you back in the day."

Back in the day. When he told me I was like Andre and couldn't meet my eyes, Caleb *had* meant the field outside Victorville. My brother's Robin Hood routine finally made sense. *'Should've done things different.'* Twelve – no, thirteen – years gone, and I could still smell the stale manure, and a trace of the rage that'd burned through me that night heated my face as I stood across from Andre. I'd been ballistic at Caleb for dragging me into his mess – my insides seesawed – and apparently he'd regretted it ever since. That night was my first step into the outlaw world.

What happened that night didn't matter now, and neither did Caleb's reasons for helping Andre. *Sorry, Caleb.*

"He told me to stay out of the game," Andre continued. "Best thing I can do for your brother is what he told me to."

The little shit had a spine, I'd give him that. Didn't make him worth my brother's life.

"You can't stay out of the game if Ulrich keeps you locked up during mealtimes, or throws you in solitary just for fun," I said. "Or he gives you a cellie serving life, a real psycho who doesn't give a fuck about anything and thinks you're pretty."

There it was. The wide eyes of fear.

"He can make your life hell. And he's going to, because you're one of Graham's vics."

"He's a C.O. What the hell am I supposed to do?" Andre burst.
I told him.

CHAPTER SEVEN

Me and Ortiz left for training in a week. I'd hammered the plan into Andre's head, got a new phone and a cable for it from the *Sureños*, but I still hadn't received the malware from the Moldovan. Before I left LAC, I had to see this done.

I'd stayed up nights racking my brain for the right way to get Ulrich. Even considered an anonymous tip – it's still snitching – to get SSU on his ass about corruption, but Graham could get a whiff, and though he had plenty of enemies I couldn't risk him suspecting me. Thought about killing the skinny bastard. Beating him to death with his own baton, making him choke on his own baton, throttling his windpipe with his own baton. All variations of the same theme, clearly. Killing Ulrich wasn't the way either. A dead C.O. would bring an investigatory tornado I couldn't escape.

And Ulrich was just the butcher's apprentice. Only the butcher had to die.

I was on my fifth lap around the patchy grass of the HCF yard, running even though I hated running. Unless you're chasing someone or someone is chasing you, what's the point? Never understood why Caleb liked it. Maybe he didn't. Maybe he ran every morning for the same reason I was running right now, to burn off restless energy because he had nowhere else to put it.

All I could do was wait for a message from the Moldovan.

It was the exchange with Agent Brown that'd inspired me. He'd offered to put me in protective custody so I'd snitch for him, and I'd flung it back him; no hanging out with child molesters for me. That disgust was one of the few things people like me had in common with non-criminals. Civilians, police, correctional officers, politicians, pretty much everyone *but* the sickos themselves thought they were deviants. It was a life-ruining black mark, and fitting payback for helping Graham kill my brother.

For all the shitty things Ulrich was, he wasn't a child molester – as far as I knew. I'd used the phone Ortiz gifted me to reach out to an old friend from the dark web, a Moldovan known as *Balaur*. I'd bought from Balaur before, on the outside. He was my go-to provider for transponder clones, keyless entry authenticators, fresh identities – all the stuff that Caleb looked down on when he first brought me into the business. He loved the hands on, hardcore shit. I had to drag him kicking and screaming into the 21st Century.

As I ran, Balaur was two days overdue on the malware he owed me. It was a descendant of Purple Haze, an NSA cyber exploit stolen by hackers that used operating system vulnerabilities to take over computers. I could just see Caleb smirking at what I was doing. '*Nerd.*' Balaur was customizing the program so that when it took over Ulrich's office computer, it'd turn into a cesspool of sick shit. An entirely new internet history, a set of downloads stretching back a year, and a series of outgoing messages. Possessing the sick shit was a criminal act on its own, and the outgoing messages were the nail in the coffin to make sure he'd get caught.

This lovely place, California State Prison, Los Angeles County, was on the outskirts of the city of Lancaster, which had four city council members. One of them, Marvin Nicholls, had a preteen daughter named Erica active on *GabJab*, the trendiest social media app. As a wannabe 'cool dad,' Councilman Nicholls had *GabJab* too.

The messages from Ulrich's computer would say '*To Erica*' but they'd end up in the Councilman's *GabJab* direct message bin. As if Ulrich had mistakenly sent the suggestive DMs to the dad instead of the daughter. Real reason? I wanted the Councilman's full wrath to descend on Ulrich without exposing the girl to perversion. I'd be damned if my fake victim, an innocent girl, became a real one.

I shuddered, nauseous at even the thought of the things that would be in those messages and on that computer. But what else could I do?

A stitch throbbed in my side, but it was because I ate a sandwich ten minutes ago and not because of the wounds in my abdomen. Progress. Pressing my hand to my abdomen, I pushed on. Duct-taped to my thigh, underneath my track pants was a new phone Ortiz had slipped me – *the Infiltrator,* I was calling it. If Balaur messaged me, I'd know right away, so I might as well keep running.

When the malware was ready, I'd download it to the Infiltrator and then hand it over to Andre with its USB cable. As a laundry worker, Andre dropped off dry-cleaned uniforms in a bunch of C.O.'s offices – including Ulrich's. Andre would plug the phone into Ulrich's computer and let it unleash the whirlwind.

13 laps later, I limped from the yard a sweaty mess with no messages received on the Infiltrator. It was Tuesday, and Andre said Ulrich got his dry-cleaning back on Wednesdays – tomorrow night. And next Monday, the bus would be here to take me and Ortiz away. Ulrich needed to get arrested before I left. I had to see it with my own eyes. His wide-eyed confusion and hopeless fear.

After a shower, a message from Balaur was waiting for me, with a link to the download. *Finally.* In my HCF dorm-cell, I started the download. 1% every two minutes, like watching paint dry. I couldn't get on the Wi-Fi, of course, and I obviously didn't have a great data plan for my contraband phone. The possibility of detection by a cell activity scan was even worse. The C.O.s used to run those scans every month or so, now it was every couple of weeks. Had to risk it, though.

My stomach churned. I'd had bubble guts for days and had run out of antacids. A lot of risks with this plan. It was simple in and of itself – download malware then upload it on Ulrich's computer – but damn dicey. Buying, from a foreigner, a program stolen from the NSA in order to smear a state employee. If caught, it'd be one helluva federal case.

I waited for the download to finish. Waited for lights out. Waited for morning, for Andre to wheel his big, blue laundry bin into the HCF.

His boyish face was focused on his feet when he entered, pushing the wheeled bin. *Good.* He knew not to make eye contact, not to talk to me, to avoid tipping off anybody watching and to keep the video surveillance footage clean. His forehead was shiny. Nervous. As for me, I was sure my jittery muscles would rip out of my skin if they weren't attached to my bones. *Me too, Andre.*

The handful of inmates in the dorm-like HCF lined up at the entrances to their berths, dirty uniforms and linens wrapped up in the large bed sheet. Hefting mine, the weight of the phone and USB cord inside wasn't even noticeable. For Andre's sake, I forced a casual pose as I tossed my laundry in his bin. He wheeled past and I turned away, seemingly focusing on a motorcycle magazine. With my peripherals, I watched Andre shift around the laundry bundles, noticing a pillowcase care tag torn into two flaps. My mark. *Package inside.* With the squeak of a sticky wheel, Andre was out the door.

Tonight, the kid would either free me to pursue Graham or doom me to federal prison. Again, all I could do was wait. The glossy magazine was shaking in my hands, so I rolled it up and started drumming a twitchy beat on my knee.

Too much of it was out of my hands. The Moldovan's malware, Andre's sneak-level, the councilman's response. Was there a better way?

The rest of the day went by slow and the night almost sleepless. The one hour of shut eye I had ended with a nightmare where my teeth fell out.

The next morning, Andre came through the HCF with clean, folded stacks of white and blue, a vein on his temple pulsing and a scowl on his face. *Shit.* Still, I forced caution and avoided his eyes as he tossed my stack in my cell. This pillowcase tag was cut in a diagonal, making a tiny triangle. The malware had been uploaded to Ulrich's computer.

Everything in my body loosened, like crumpled foam returning to its original shape. Andre was gone before he could see the smile on my face. He was probably pissed at what he went through last night. *Think that's stressful, kid? Try watching your brother get shivved in the back.* Andre had done his part without getting caught, at least. Now it was time for Ulrich to get caught.

T he rest of the day passed, then all of Friday, Saturday and Sunday without word from Serrato, or Ortiz, or the guards. "I ain't heard a thing, man, stop asking," Ortiz said Monday morning as four C.O.s escorted the two of us to the gate. A van waited there to take us to our training camp. It was the eleventh hour.

Maybe the Moldovan's malware hadn't worked. Or maybe it'd worked just fine and the warden was sweeping it under the rug over the councilman's objections. What kind of father would let that happen?

Then came one of the most satisfying sights I'd ever seen.

Ulrich, in bracelets, fighting deputies as they pushed him into the back of an LA Sherriff's Department cruiser.

"Unbelievable," one of the C.O.s said, watching one of their own get arrested.

"Fucking sicko," another one said. "Let 'em have him."

Guess word of his crime had already spread through the C.O. grapevine.

A smile spread across Ortiz's face as he saw it, too, and I motioned for him to cut it out. We didn't need the C.O.s escorting us to notice our glee. Didn't need Ulrich to see *me*, so I moved to walk behind Ortiz.

It took everything in me to keep from crowing with victory. Climbed out of a lake of blood, fought through months of physical therapy, lied to the officials who could make or break my future with a stroke of a pen. All of it led here, to the first payback.

The skinny, mean bastard didn't look so mean right now. Just skinny and scared. Pale, jerky, with the darting eyes of a rabid weasel. *Good.* Ulrich took orders from a cold-blooded butcher. Tried to strangle me and keep me out of the fight. Cracked my brother on the head and watched the monster rip us apart.

The deputies finally got him in the cruiser, slamming the door shut.

Got you, you son of a bitch. Maybe he could survive in protective custody. Maybe not. I didn't care either way. Ulrich was done.

One down, one to go.

CHAPTER EIGHT

And your honor graduate, Mason Jones!"

With whistles, applause, and a few catcalls rising from the seated inmates, I crossed the grass and shook hands with the smiling Sierra Conservation Camp Commander. He pulled me in front of the camera guy and held up my training certificate with his free hand.

I forced a smile. I was supposed to be proud, but I was impatient. Ready for my mission.

"Good job, Mr. Jones," he said, and nodded me onward to the short line of CDCR and CalFire muckity-mucks behind him.

Me and 43 other inmates were gathered in the outdoor basketball court of Sierra Conservation Camp, where all inmate hand crews were trained. It was a flat plot of land with stark white buildings and serpentine blacktop baking in the sun.

A training officer began calling the names of the rest of the inmates. As instructed, they rose row by row and proceeded in an orderly fashion to accept their certificates from the commander. Before coming here, I'd never seen inmates show this much discipline – willingly. After two weeks of intense training, they weren't about to screw up their chance to serve out the rest of their sentence outside of prison. *Their* only worry was finishing their sentence.

What's that like?

Ortiz stood up with the rest of the row and gave me a chin nod. I nodded back. He was here, but I was still alone. He had to answer to the *Sureños,* but it wasn't just that. He also had their support, their brotherhood. Brotherhood was no longer an option for me. Did I need Ortiz for the mission? Definitely. So much depended on his *Sureños.* But for them it was business. They needed Graham gone and Ortiz wanted to move up the ranks. If my murder mission failed, their lives would go on. I couldn't.

Going down the line of shiny-collared officers and shaking hands, I stopped myself from rushing through it. Nothing *I* could do would get me out of SCC faster. Besides, I had to maintain my façade as an exemplary inmate. I didn't bust my ass to become honor graduate for shits and giggles.

I'd taken my cue from Graham and become great on paper. If a vicious killer could do it, so could I. Since the day I had made the deal with Serrato, I'd turned myself into a rehabilitation success story. *Yes sir, no sir, three bags full, sir.*

I met the eyes of everyone in line, smiled, and thanked them as they congratulated me. My last stop was a CDCR officer with two stars on his collar and a Clint Eastwood squint, Associate Warden Hearst. I remembered him from our arrival at SCC.

"*You're here because you knew it was time to change,*" Hearst had begun.

That'd been a shitty day. Not because of the 6-mile ruck march to introduce us to crew life. Hiking up and down a roller coaster of forested hills with a 50-pound pack had been no-joke incredible. I didn't know if it was the woodsy smells, outstretching greenery, or straightforward sweat, but I was surprised to find I loved it. What had made that first day shitty was Hearst's speech.

It had been here in this courtyard. There we were, shipped from prisons all over the state, sweating in the late afternoon sun. It must've been in the mid-90s.

Instinctually, I hated him. He was a pig. And when he began his speech like that, I knew it would only get worse, because it was the same bullshit I'd fed the UCC.

"You're here to become a better version of yourself. If that's not why you're here, if you're here to cheat the system, I'll show you the door, no questions asked," Hearst said. "I'll even give you a ride back to the prison you came from."

As if Graham had done this to become a better version of himself. Getting lectured about cheating the system when they let a murderer in their ranks.

Incompetent hypocrites. I was feverish with rage.

Most nights I couldn't sleep. Every plunge of Graham's knife into Caleb replaying in my mind. So I thought of how I'd do it. One fantasy involved the drip-torches the pros used for prescribed burns. I imagined uncapping the tank and dumping its fuel all over

Graham, then pushing him into the fire.

I wouldn't, though. I wasn't the monster. Death was enough. It didn't have to be gruesome, or even painful, as much as he deserved that. It just had to look accidental and be final.

"You need to want this," Hearst continued. "Because you're going to work alongside heroes. You'll be right there in the thick of it with them. 24 hours on, 24 hours off, on, off, until the fire is dead. And then the next fire. It's not easy. But you'll be a part of something bigger. Doesn't matter that you're in orange and the men and women next to you are in yellow. Together, you're a team that saves lives."

Saving lives.

What I planned to do was the opposite. My stomach turned thinking about using *this* work as the means to the end. But it was the only option Graham had given me when he ran from LAC to La Cuenca Conservation Camp with his boots still bloody.

The butcher deserved it. My stomach settled.

I missed the conclusion of Hearst's speech, only picking up fragments. Commending us for being selected, some horseshit about "digging deep," believing in ourselves, and looking out for each other.

Ortiz and I had caught each other's eye at that. Sure, it was a business arrangement, but at least I had someone to watch my back.

"Good luck," Hearst had finished.

Two weeks later, here I was shaking his hand.

"Outstanding, Jones," he said, tapping the certificate where it said Honor Graduate. "I expect good things from you."

Wiping a murderer off the face of the Earth would be a good

thing.

Training was over. It was time to kick off the mission.

After the ceremony, the inmates were milling about the blacktop, congratulating each other, meeting with their women and their kids. A family event. If pigs or C.O.s had planted bugs, the clamor of voices and the rattling of AC units would make for some jacked-up audio.

While everyone else was slapping each other on the back, Ortiz and I sat next to an AC older than God, planning.

"Sooner or later, there'll be a fire big enough that crews from both our stations get called in to the same base camp," I said.

'It's always fire season in California.' Instructors had drilled this into us during training. Wildfires burning all the way into Christmas and starting up as early as February. Bad news for homeowners and insurance companies. Good news for me, because it meant it was only a matter of time before I was reunited with Graham.

"Disguised as a pro firefighter, I isolate Graham from his crew and lead him away from camp and into our trap," I continued. The *Sureños* would provide the professional gear disguise.

For a big fire, there would be hundreds of responders involved. 30-plus fireline inmates. 50-plus pro wildland firefighters. With crew sizes that big, it would be easy for Mason Jones to disappear during his rest shift and reappear as a pro firefighter. A pro firefighter can move freely in and out of camp. A pro firefighter can pull an inmate for a special assignment.

"Hold up, hold up. What about Pete? Comes across friendly.

Knew a white dude named Pete once, super chill."

Ortiz was obsessed with deciding on the name for my alternate identity.

I ignored him: "So that'll be our first step when we get to a big fire. Finding a spot away from base camp where we can corner him. Maybe put his back to the fire. There are a couple of ways we could make it look like an accident."

"Pete is someone you can trust, you know? The last name, though, that's gonna make or break it."

"Dude, focus."

"I'm focused. You're on steps X through Z. I'm on step A. You need an identity,"

"It's a minor detail," I said, patience wearing thin. Caleb hadn't cared about little details, and that'd given me the freedom to handle them how I wanted. Ortiz had ideas. It was annoying.

"Naw, man, it's everything. Trust. A good name will make people trust you," he said, stern. Hard-Ass Ortiz had replaced Chill Ortiz and wanted to make it clear he was in charge.

I never got in pissing contests with Caleb. We had a rhythm. A rhythm he led, sure, but now I had to. Establishing who was the alpha wolf was about more than ego. *My brother, my mission.* I wasn't about to let an outsider tell me how to run it.

I played along, hoping it would shut Ortiz up.

"Okay, whatever. First name, Peter…" I began.

"Peter? Jesus's main bro? Pete-*err?* It's all stuffy and formal. Just *Pete.*"

Even while being a hard-ass, he couldn't resist being a wise-ass.

"Worlds apart. Huge difference," I said.

"Fuck you, but there is. So we're going with Pete. Pete is friendly and trustworthy, so the last name needs to be strong. A tough white-boy last name."

"It's a fake identity that I'm using two times at the most. First time, finding the spot to set the trap. Second and last time, doing the deed. Let's focus on the actual fucking plan."

I stared at him for a while, not wanting to let him have this one. He was *not* the shot caller here. But his words wormed into my head, and I had a flash of inspiration.

"McLean," I said. "'Mac' is very white bread, 'clean' like I got nothing to hide, but together, it's tough. McLean is someone you'd follow into battle."

"Which is what we need Graham to do," Ortiz said. "McLean… I like it."

"So psyched to have your approval."

"What's your problem, man?"

The problem is that I don't work for you, I thought. He damn well knew that, swinging his dick around like this. "I made the deal with your shot caller, not with you," I said, as if he actually needed a reminder.

"What we're doing is an *investment* for my people. If you act the fool and put that investment at risk, you and me gonna have problems."

"You're my handler," I paraphrased.

Ortiz's stern shot-caller face disappeared, and he grinned. "Naw, man, we partners."

I knew it was bullshit, but I could bullshit with the best of 'em. I brought my fist out, and we pounded.

"You got it man. Partners," I said. *You're a pawn to leverage.*

It was nothing personal, but Caleb was the last partner I had, and no one would ever replace him. This thing with the *Sureños* wasn't ideal, but ideal went out the window when the CDCR let a murderer join the ranks of inmate fire crews.

Ortiz wasn't even a bad dude, for a gangbanger. He'd shown that when he gifted me the phone at LAC... maybe. Were there any real gifts in prison? Could have just been a down payment on a future favor. Was it kindness, or maneuvering?

Doesn't matter, I reminded myself.

What mattered is that I had to manage this husky man-child so I could get what I needed from his people. I needed to make him *feel* like a partner, at least.

I watched Ortiz begin chewing his nails, brow furrowed.

This was going to be tough.

If vengeance was easy, everyone would do it.

CHAPTER NINE

Me, Ortiz, and five other inmates fresh from SCC were sardined into a transport truck headed to my new base of operations, Mountain Home Conservation Camp.

Graham was at La Cuenca Conservation Camp, and us getting assigned to a separate home camp was all part of the plan. I know there's that saying about 'keeping your enemies close,' but when your plan depends on your vic not recognizing you, it's better not to give him the chance to see you on the daily. Amazingly, Ortiz and I had agreed on the '*actual fucking plan*.' In broad strokes, at least.

Step One: Get the Disguise.
Step Two: Isolate and Trap Graham.
Step Three: An 'Accident' Happens.
Step Four: Clean and Dump Disguise.

Crammed next to a bunch of dudes, I thought of those trips to Aunt Jenny's again. The tune of the Def Leppard song was *right there*, but I couldn't bring it to the surface of my mind. Me and Caleb would sing it together, and it was pissing me off that I couldn't remember.

How'd that damn song go?

The truck rattled as it went over rutted mountain roads, and I grabbed the seat to keep steady. Blinding pain shot from my right hand, blanking my mind, and when I regained my senses, I found myself panting like a dog. Ortiz looked over, eyes wide. I probably looked like shit. I waved him off with my good hand.

I shuddered, remembering the *shlick* of the blade, the shiv handle catching on muscle and the shockwaves of pain as Graham pushed down. It hadn't fully healed.

I tried to stretch out my right hand, loosen up the muscles, but the shooting pain wouldn't let me. I tried to make a fist, and that was just as agonizing. The only position I could keep it in was a loose, claw-like half-fist.

Figures. Graham and Ulrich had given me a broken kneecap, a cut across my chest, two stab wounds in my abdomen, and one in my *pelvis* – but it was the stab to my damn hand that lingered.

I got Ortiz's attention, and raised my eyebrows in question.

He knew what I was asking, and shook his head, showing open palms.

No drugs.

The pain in my hand, as bad as it was, was a small price to pay – a little bigger without drugs though.

"Your brother worth all this?" Ortiz asked with a light-hearted smile.

"He's my blood and my best friend. Yeah, he's worth it," I said, not light-hearted.

"You two always super tight?"

"What's it to you, man?" I didn't want to dredge this up, especially not with him.

"Just making conversation. If you wanna sit in silence with the pain…"

Guess I couldn't fault him for trying to distract me.

"We weren't always tight. Most of the time growing up, I hated him. You have any brothers?" I asked.

"Not by blood," Ortiz said.

"Right. Well, older brothers like to beat the shit out of you. Me, I got my revenge the only way I could – by ratting him out when my mom wasn't high. The snitchiest snitch you could imagine. It just made him beat on me even harder." He was always so much stronger. "Never could fight back, really. It just made it more fun for him, a game I could never win. When I was fifteen, a sophomore, our living situation… was kinda in flux."

The truck kept bouncing along the rutted mountain road, and I gripped the seat with my good left hand, not just to steady myself, but because focusing on that pushed the pain to the back of my mind.

Ortiz nodded for me to continue and perched his chin on his fist, like the statue of the thinking dude. Or like you see shrinks doing in movies. Was he psychoanalyzing me? I didn't care. This memory was worth dredging up.

"I wasn't in the game then, but Caleb was and he had some

cash coming in. And this social worker, Patty, came to inspect the trailer my brother bought. She found his money stash taped to the bottom of the couch. 425 dollars. Patty thought it was exactly what it *was* – dirty money. But I told her it was mine, came up with this story about how it was everything I had saved since starting my job at…" what was the name of Julio's shop? *Oh yeah,* "… Amigo Compucell. Told her I didn't trust Chase or Bank of America or Wells Fargo, and that with all the break-ins in the neighborhood, I had to hide my money. Kids at school knew about my job, so the best hiding spot was under the couch rather than my room.

"Patty bought it." The loyalty I felt for my brother right then, I'd never even known it was there. Caleb looked at me different after that. Literally. After Patty left, that pinched glare he reserved for me, like I was a bug to be quashed… I never saw it again. With actual warmth on his face, Caleb had said, '*Thanks, bro.*'

My throat got thick and my eyelids swelled up, threatening to spill. *Not here.* Not in front of Ortiz and a bus-full of cons. Sniffing and clearing my throat, I couldn't stop my voice from cracking as I continued. "He stopped beating me up. And I promised I would never snitch again, about him or anyone."

"That right?"

"Yup." I smiled. That was the day my asshole brother became my best friend.

A high-pitch whine of brakes, and we all lurched as the truck slowed and made a U-turn. The cab window of the truck opened and the C.O. in the passenger seat called out.

"Inmate Jones."

Had he seen me in pain? No way they would turn this thing

around on my account. I got up and went to the window.

"We're being re-routed to help with a brush fire. Pass the word," he said.

"We don't have any tools or turnout gear," I said. We were all still in our thin, scrub-like inmate uniform.

"They'll issue you gear on-site. The fire's not dicking around, so neither is Incident Command."

It's always fire season in California.

The C.O. hefted a 24-pack of water bottles onto the windowsill.

"Pass the word to the other inmates, get 'em hydrated, get 'em ready."

"Yes, sir. Uh, why me?"

"You were the honor grad in your class, weren't you?"

I nodded.

"Then go, and lead with honor," he said with a smirk.

I took the water bottles, which required two hands and sent waves of pain through my right one. Ortiz noticed and helped me take it to the group.

He could be surprisingly thoughtful. But I was just an investment. I dropped the sentiment like a bad penny.

"Listen up, guys," I said, and told the other inmates what was going on.

An hour later, we knew we were getting close. The campfire smell got heavier and heavier in the truck. How big was the fire? Big enough to need multiple crews? An inmate crew with a murderer in its ranks? Goosebumps tickled across my arms.

Finishing a water bottle, I crinkled the plastic in my good hand. The crackle was satisfying.

"You think you can handle this? Without the moral support?" Ortiz asked.

"I'll be fine," I said, bullshitting myself as much as him. I could end up doing a full shift – *24 hours* – of hard labor without painkillers. "That's not what I'm worried about," I added. Worse than the pain was the possibility of Graham seeing me before I was ready. The idea was that I'd never actually be face-to-face with him. I'd gone clean-shaven as a precaution, but that was only half of it. The firefighter uniform and breathing mask was the key. The disguise made me official, trustworthy, and most importantly, able to order an inmate around. And I didn't have it yet.

Water dribbled from a tear in the plastic bottle clenched in my fist. Releasing it, I watched it expand into a misshapen blob.

"Call your guy," I said. "Let's get the uniform today."

"*Or* we just be sure to stay away from Graham's crew, if they're even on this fire. If we see him, we make sure he doesn't see us. And by 'us' I mean 'you,' 'cause I'm nobody to him. Trust, man. It's too soon and too risky."

"I disagree, partner." I crushed the plastic bottle in my fist again. A poor man's stress ball.

"We agreed, *partner,*" Ortiz scowled. "The plan is to get it on a work project once we get set up at Mountain Home."

"The bigger risk is him recognizing me. That's why we need the disguise right away," I argued. Was I being paranoid? The C.O. had said it was a brush fire. Maybe it'd be just us and a pro crew, no other inmates. There were almost 200 inmate crews in the state. What were the odds he was there? *No, Mason.* Plan for the worst. Not paranoid. Smart.

"We still have to work a shift, and he could see you then as Inmate Jones. *If* he's even on this fire."

"True. And if he did, we'd have to move up the schedule, right? And if we gotta do it sooner, we *need* that damn firefighter uniform," I said.

"Fuckin' A. You're a goddamn bulldozer, but… shit."

I held my tongue as he started thinking aloud.

"We're going to our first fire and ain't even been set up at our home camp first… this could be a crazy fire season," Ortiz said, stating the obvious. "We need to be ready in case things change on us again."

Exacta-fucking-mundo, I thought.

"I think that's smart, bro," I said, burying my nose in his asshole.

"I'll get my connect up here. We'll do it today."

The brakes squeaked and the truck came to a halt. We had arrived.

I sat there, waiting. No one moved. They were waiting on *me,* I realized.

"Let's go," I said, and jumped out of the truck.

I landed on a road cutting through a steep, forested hillside. Up the road a gated McMansion community overlooked green fingers of land splotched with dead, gray trees and dry, yellow grass. There was a fire engine parked down the road, and professional and inmate crews were chopping trees and hosing down growth in the woods along it.

Not just us and a pro crew. Counted about 30 inmates, which meant two crews at 14 men a pop. I couldn't pick out any faces from here.

The fire was 300 yards below us, and it was majestic. The flames flowed in beautiful waves, bursting with yellow sparks, and sporadically shot up pillars of fire. Like something from the damn Bible. The blaze crackled from forest-carpeted valleys, sending plumes both black and white that bled into a brown haze covering the sky above.

A professional firefighter, distinguishable by yellow Nomex tops and bottoms, stuck a shovel in the ground and came over as the other inmates massed around me. He took off his helmet and shook each of our hands. His mustache was thick, his hair short and gray at the temples, and his face had a Midwestern look to it, stocky but strong.

"My name is Mark Hallenbeck and I'm your fire captain today," he told us, and started handing out tools. Chainsaws, McLeod scrapers, and shovels. I rocked back and forth on my heels, unable to stand still. "Normally, crew position is determined by need and availability at your home camp. We don't have time for that."

Hallenbeck sized me up and picked up a Pulaski axe. Named after the forest ranger who designed it, the head had the axe blade on one side and a horizontal blade – an adze – on the other.

He shoved it into my permanently half-open right hand – I bit my tongue to bury a shout of pain.

"Congrats, you're a Pulaski," Hallenbeck said.

I was hoping to be a Dragspoon or Swamper, the least labor-intensive positions, but at least I wasn't a Sawyer handling a chainsaw. I wouldn't be able to handle it with my hand like this. My chest tightened. Would I even be able to handle Pulaski?

Hallenbeck gave Ortiz a Pulaski axe, too. Some good luck today, at least. We'd be close together. In moments, all six of us graduates had tools. And nothing else.

Ortiz looked at me, as if asking '*What now?*'

And yesterday this motherfucker was acting like he was in charge.

"Sir?" I piped up to Hallenbeck.

"Relax, we got your turnout gear," Hallenbeck said, anticipating a different question than the one I was going to ask: *What camp are you from?* If it was La Cuenca, that camp's inmate crew could be here – Graham could be here. "Damarius!"

At his shout, an inmate and the biggest Black man I'd ever seen opened the back of a flatbed truck and threw down a pile of orange clothing. Tops and bottoms made of fire-resistant Nomex fabric. Damarius motioned at three other inmates, and they climbed into the flatbed and began unloading helmets, backpacks, gloves, canteens, goggles, and fire-resistant boots.

"You can help," Damarius said to me and the rest of the fish standing there. His voice was a calm, deep rumble. Being told what to do was a relief because this was all happening damn fast. I nodded and waved our group over to help unload the turnout gear.

"There are 20 sets, and six of you. Better find the right size. This fire has a bad habit of flaring up," Hallenbeck told us.

Fighting fire with random gear that might not fit. *Seems safe.*

Must've read my mind, because he said, "Don't worry. This job, slip and falls or contact with equipment," Hallenbeck mimed fingers getting cut off, "are way more likely than burn injuries." He was deadpan but had a twinkle in his eye.

What's with this guy?

"These four here," he nodded at Damarius and the other three inmates, "the rest of their crew has rejoined the free world, and good for them. Bad for the folks of West Hills." Hallenbeck pointed at the McMansion community. "This gentleman, Damarius, is the First Sawyer and senior crewman. He will establish your hookline. You will do what he says, and you will do what I say. Get suited up. You have five minutes."

As my group picked through the mess of gear, Damarius told us our positioning and I looked over his team. Graham wasn't in *this* crew.

"You two Pullers," Damarius motioned to two inmates from my truck, "will be behind me and the Second Sawyer, Baby Einstein…"

Baby Einstein had a big, doughy face and looked like a big, dumb idiot, so I had a feeling his nickname had been well-earned.

Ortiz smirked at me and I couldn't help but smirk back.

"Pulaskis, you're with Steve," Damarius pointed Ortiz and I to one of his team, an average-looking beanpole of a man. He tapped our axes with his as we joined him, waggling his eyebrows. Damarius continued with the others. Hallenbeck pointedly checked his watch.

"Sir, what camp are you from?" I asked Hallenbeck while pulling on Nomex pants. Seemed like an innocent enough question.

"La Cuenca, why?" he replied.

Fuck. Graham *could* be here. There were about 26 other inmates out here.

I tamed my face muscles and didn't dare exchange looks with Ortiz. This was bad. And my mind was blanking on a lie to tell Hallenbeck.

"You got a boyfriend you wanna meet up with, Jones?" Ortiz teased.

The stumpy prick was quick-witted, I had to give him that. And it gave me the seconds I needed to come up with a lie.

"Hoping to get a glimpse of the Malibu crew, actually," I said. The Malibu Conservation Camp inmates were all female.

"Those haggard bitches?" Steve chortled. "Goddamn, how long you been locked up, man?"

"Okay, Skeevy Steve. Like you wouldn't hit the worst beast outta all of 'em," retorted a balding man shouldering a McLeod rake hoe, earning laughs from Baby Einstein and Damarius.

"Don't mind Skeevy," the McLeod told me. "He got his name when his bunkmate caught him jerking it to tentacle porn."

Apparently, 'Skeevy' Steve giving me shit was ironic.

It gave me a strange sense of comfort. Not because Steve was a pervert, but because even out here, inmates still had pitch-perfect prison nicknames. The only constant in an entirely new world.

"You better be done, ladies. Time to get to work!" Hallenbeck shouted.

We threw on the rest of our gear and followed Hallenbeck and Damarius into battle. I was already sweating. Not from the heat, but because I had to furtively study the face of every inmate in the forest. I didn't see Graham. Still, I drew my cloth face-shield tight to keep him from seeing me first.

CHAPTER TEN

Charcoal slivers flew from my Pulaski axe blade, roiling the dust cloud mushrooming from the charred stump in front of me. Another chop and the stump groaned, opening its cream-colored grain like the pages of a book. The grain looked white against the burned-black bark, a strangely satisfying contrast. The same contrast I'd seen with the others' teeth inside their ash-dusted faces. A few of those smiles had been on our crew earlier today, but after six hours only one remained. At my glance in his direction, Ortiz grinned and mimed fucking a split stump with his Pulaski handle. For at least the seventh time today.

Still, I couldn't help but laugh. Ortiz was a 13-year-old in a grown-ass man's body. As grown-ass as a stumpy cholo can get. A stumpy cholo that happened to be a member of a deadly cartel-backed gang.

I raised my eyebrows at him, and he gave the smallest of nods – that meant his man was ready. A *Sureño* runner, parked only a few miles away, ready to fly in a drone with my packages. We just needed a chance to slip away. My job was getting in the way of my mission.

I went back to chopping my stump, and he went back to his.

It was about three in the afternoon and our vantage point, now dubbed Anchor Point Blackhawks, offered an amazing view of the fire. A range of hills, with a black scoop out of half of them, bordered by a hot orange wall. Right now, the wall wasn't expanding. Winds were low.

I looked at the firebreak I'd scraped out with the others while biding my time. It was a ten-yard-wide strip of dirt clear of everything that can burn. The other inmates of our crew were spread out in front of and behind me, intent on the work.

They looked tired, but they were busting their asses, working with some kind of satisfied rhythm. I didn't get it.

It was at least 95 degrees out, the sky was cloudless, the sun was merciless, and my helmet band was soaked through, no longer keeping salty sweat from stinging my eyes. I had Nomex outerwear, a helmet and goggles, fire-resistant boots, a fire shelter, a first aid kit, and two canteens on me – over 60 pounds of gear, and every ounce of it weighed down my throbbing muscles. The campfire smell had lost its appeal five hours ago, when the pain in my right hand kicked into high gear and the smoky air started making my throat raw.

Grinning and laughing, a nearby pro crew shoveled and picked the smoking remnants of a prescribed burn, ashes clouding their jolly faces. "Having fun now!" one crowed. "Beautiful day," said another. One guy whistled a Motown tune. The Seven Dwarves whistling while they worked.

These people are batshit.

I had never worked this hard in my life. That was the point of what Caleb and I did. Boosting luxury car transports, cloning VINs, getting them on a freighter, that took elbow grease for sure. But this was medieval peasant shit.

Looked like we were a few yards away from completing this firebreak. That meant break time, and that meant a chance to get up to some trouble.

Captain Hallenbeck called for a break, and I kept my eyes and ears open for an opportunity. Hallenbeck went to talk with another CalFire fighter, Lieutenant Nelson, who'd been working the area since we arrived.

I relaxed on a log near them; ready to sponge up some intel. The rest of the crew took off their helmets and orange jackets, found what shade they could, and guzzled water. Ortiz laid out, using his helmet to shield his face, but tipped it up so he could see me. Waiting for my cue.

For what seemed like hours, Hallenbeck and Nelson shot the shit about wives and babies, boring me out of my skull, until they were interrupted by a voice on their radios:

"Wind tunnel effect in a draw east of Anchor Point Avalanche. Anyone available to kill spots?"

Nelson eyed the La Cuenca crew.

"Can we get your guys on ember patrol?" he asked.

"They need this break and they're due for a meal," Hallenbeck said.

"Your crew," Nelson said. "But we got some citizens ignoring evac calls and hunkering down."

As if it was our job to protect idiots from their own idiocy. Still, this might be my chance.

"A little spot fire might change their minds," Hallenbeck said, unswayed.

Hallenbeck had been driving us hard from the moment we stepped out of the truck, but he seemed to have a good head on his shoulders. These CalFire guys weren't half bad, despite being batshit.

"Doubt it," Nelson replied. "They're 'It's up to God' people. A spot fire could leave us with some very crispy idiots *and* turn the tide back against us. We need to maintain this containment."

"Let's do it, Captain," I chimed in. "This ain't no union job. Let's work."

A chorus of shouts and insults came from the rest of the crew.

"Hey, the sooner we beat this, the sooner we get to go to our camp," Ortiz chimed in.

The balding McLeod snorted. Stocky, olive-skinned, and baggy-eyed, I'd learned he went by Vito. Real clever, that nickname. "Couple of guys in the woods ain't gonna turn the tide," Vito said.

I looked at Damarius for support.

"You never know," he grunted.

Amused, Hallenbeck shrugged.

"Who wants to be a hero with Jones?" Hallenbeck asked.

A chorus of boos rose from the crew.

Ortiz walked over to join me, of course.

Damarius said "Fuck it," grabbed his chainsaw, and dragged over Baby Einstein.

Nelson smiled.

"No chainsaws, won't need it. Shovels, axes and hoes only," he told us.

"Hoes? Y'all said the Malibu crews weren't here," Ortiz cracked.

Everyone laughed, and it somehow changed Vito's mind, because he came and joined us. Damarius and Baby Einstein swapped their chainsaws for shovels. It was uplifting to see guys stepping up to help, even though for me it was just a cover.

The rest of the crew stayed on their asses. Not so uplifting.

Hallenbeck looked us over.

"All right. You're with Lieutenant Nelson. Don't do anything stupid."

The air had been calm on the firebreak, but hiking into the wooded depression with Lt. Nelson, Ortiz, and the others, a strong breeze cooled the warm sweat on my face. Felt good, even though that breeze is what we were here to fight.

We walked out of a swath of pine and fir trees into the bottom of the depression, wading into high grass. The high grass and brush were scythed by an old dirt firebreak cut by a past hand crew. Last year, I guessed, because saplings, small bushes, and yellow grass now stuck out of the dirt everywhere. Without trees to break it up, the breeze was now a powerful wind.

It was the wind-tunnel effect the voice on the radio had described.

The fire was on the forested hill in front of us, 50 yards from the old firebreak, merrily floating embers down the wind tunnel. On a hill behind us stood a dozen houses. The mountain community we were supposed to protect. It was bordered by a dirt road.

"That's our escape route," Nelson told us. "If things go bad, call out a retreat to the next man in line and calmly and carefully hike up back there. I mean it on the carefully part. You could fall and sprain something, get stuck, or cut your face open with your tools."

"But then I'd get to ride in a helicopter, right?" I asked. I really wanted to ride in a helicopter. I was here to complete a mission, but that was one perk I'd allow myself.

"Funny," Nelson said. "But I'd rather the ships keep bucketing than stopping to medevac your ass. Shifting a resource like that can break a containment." He motioned an invisible line going through the depression. "Now, we're going to form a defensive line facing the fire, right behind the old firebreak. The job is simple. We want to make sure the fire stays behind that firebreak, so we're here to put out hot spots. The wind is throwing sparks and cinders into the green, so you're going to spread out in that line, keeping visual distance with the next man, and stamp out anything this old lady sends your way. Questions?"

"What if a hot spot becomes a whole fire? Like we can't stop it?" Ortiz asked.

"Good question. Shout out to the next man in line, who'll shout out to the next, until it gets back to me. Like the telephone game. I'll come to you, and if it calls for it, I'll radio a water drop. Same thing if the frequency of the hot spots goes up beyond what you can handle."

"You got it, boss," Ortiz said, then shot me a glance as Nelson turned his attention to the others.

"One last thing," Nelson said. "How many years you get if you run?"

"At least five," Damarius said.

"Good. Keep that in mind, yeah?"

I remembered the PowerPoint barked at us by a hard-ass C.O. in our training at SCC. The title of the presentation was "Don't Even Think About It", and the hard-ass had listed every fire crew escape ever. Every story had the same ending: Recaptured and a nickel added to their sentence. At least.

"Let's do it." Nelson motioned for us to spread out. "I'll be the last man on this north end. You all spread out south down the gully."

"We'll take the other end," I said quickly, gesturing to me and Ortiz. Nelson nodded and Vito raised an eyebrow.

We trudged off down the gully, parting the high grass, stepping over brush, twigs and dead logs crunching underfoot.

Fuel, I realized, and imagined a spark landing at my feet and catching instantly and blasting up a column of flames and turning me into a crispy con. *This is fucking dangerous.*

Baby Einstein took a place 40 yards down the gully, then Damarius about 40 yards down from him, then Vito, then me, and finally Ortiz took position at the farthest end.

A tiny spiral of smoke rose from a mess of twigs on the ground. Hacking at them with my axe, I exposed a glowing ember and stomped on it with my boot, extinguishing it. Excitement rippled through me as I scraped some dirt over it.

"Got one!" I shouted, energized by my feat. *Bye-bye, potential forest fire.* Smokey would be so proud. *Maybe these people aren't totally batshit*, I thought with a laugh.

My guts twisted, dousing the excitement faster than I had the ember. Caleb was dead, his murderer alive and well, and I was frolicking with fire. I was nauseous at my selfishness.

Remember why you're here, Mason.

I could see Ortiz on my left and Vito on my right, but the terrain was too uneven and the grass too high to see anyone else, or for anyone other than Vito to see me.

"It's time," I called out to Ortiz, loud enough for him but not for Vito.

Ortiz took out his phone and tapped it once – sending the text he had ready to go. A reply came back moments later, and he gave me a thumbs up.

"Ten minutes."

The flight time was only supposed to be five minutes, but that was from our original spot on the original firebreak. Twice as long from here, but at least the drone was on the way. We just had to wait.

"Oh shit," Ortiz said, and ran to put out a hot spot.

Over the next 10 minutes, I heard shouts from down the line as the others found and put out hot spots. Then, Ortiz waved me over, and I heard the whir of propellers.

I joined Ortiz in a ravine, out of Vito's sight, and the microwave-sized quadcopter hovered down to us, a taped-up brown paper bag attached to its undercarriage.

Vito's voice echoed down the gully, "Mace! Where you at?"

"Spot fire! I got it," I lied.

The drone came eye-level, its camera pointed right at us. Even though I knew it was a *Sureño* on the other end, it made me uneasy.

Ortiz held the drone steady while I took the package off. As soon as it was in my hands, the drone zoomed off.

It was Christmas morning, and I was opening a present. I ripped off the tape, tore apart the brown bag, and inspected my prize: the turnout gear of a professional firefighter. Yellow Nomex coat and pants, a shiny yellow helmet, plus a breathing mask. Not only would I pass for a CalFire professional, but with my beard gone and face covered by mask and goggles, Graham would never see me coming.

Ortiz read a text on his phone.

"Package two ready to load as soon as the drone gets back to him."

The glorious package in my hands was only one of two. The second would have a re-up of fentanyl, enough to last me a month.

My excitement must have been showing, because Ortiz gaped at me.

"Dude, are you hard right now?"

"Fuck off," I laughed. "Hurry up, let's pack it in."

We split up the uniform items, folding the thick Nomex and taping it on our chests, then stuffing the rest in our backpacks and coat pockets. It added to our already-considerable bulk, but it was hidden. I had the new helmet, and it barely fit in my backpack with everything else stuffed there.

Vito shouted at us from his place on the line, "Nelson is

headed over to check it out."

For a second, I forgot what 'it' was. Then I remembered my lie – the spot fire, which didn't exist.

Nelson could get over here in about a minute.

"I'm calling off the second flight," Ortiz said.

"Motherfucker."

"It's too risky."

"I know," I said. "Still. Fuck."

We had a more immediate problem. Lt. Nelson couldn't get here and not find a fire.

"Give me your lighter," I said.

Ortiz's eyes went wide and he shook his head.

"Hell no, we can't get caught starting a fire."

"We can't get caught *without* a fire. That leads to questions, and questions lead to inspections, and we're carrying five to 10 years of contraband."

I took Ortiz's lighter out of his pocket, flicked its flame to some dried pine needles, set them in some grass, then pried off the top of the lighter with my axe blade and emptied the fluid on the needles.

Fwoom!

A spiral of flame shot up, then settled to a crackling flicker and began eating up a stalk of grass. I took off my helmet and used it to fan the flames, spreading them to another stalk of tall grass, which was so dry it flamed up in two seconds. I pocketed the lighter and threw more twigs on the fire.

"Jesus," Ortiz said.

I heard approaching footsteps.

"Help me stamp it out," I said.

"This is nuts," Ortiz muttered.

We started chopping the grass and stomping on the fuel.

Lt. Nelson and Vito came in view and rushed over – the timing was perfect. We had reduced the 'spot fire' to some burning twigs, and they helped stamp out the rest.

Nelson knelt down by the ashes of the fire, sniffing. He paused.

He couldn't smell the lighter fluid, could he? *Shit.* He couldn't be that good.

Nelson stood up and shook his head, dismissing it.

"Good work," he said.

I remembered to breathe again.

Three hours later, ember patrol finished without incident. We killed dozens of hot spots and the winds in the depression had died. The sun was setting, pink and orange, wreathed by brown-gray smoke.

Our job was done, but Nelson told us that not only was the original fire uncontained, but *two more* fires had broken out on the opposite side, a quarter mile from the edge of this one. Likely spread by embers just like the ones we stamped out here, Nelson said.

Dry chaparral spread like a blanket around the blazes, pocked with mountain towns like Bell Canyon and running up against the West Hills neighborhood on the east, Calabasas and Malibu State Park on the south.

They'd set up a base camp for the area, so "You can expect to stay a while," Nelson told us. This was no longer just a small brush fire, but a serious complex.

"They're calling it the Patchwork," Nelson said.

I got my helicopter ride. It lifted off from Anchor Point Avalanche with the five of us and half a helitack crew. It was my first time in a helicopter and the view was incredible. I couldn't stop the smile that lifted my face as the weight of my limbs disappeared; I could float if I tried. The landscape the fire had not yet touched was lit instead by the sunset, warm and casting long shadows. The towering green pines and yellow grasses took on a pink hue, and we passed over an orange-blue river.

It reminded me of the opening scene in the O.G. *Lion King*, which had been Caleb's favorite when we were young. At the time, everything I liked was "gay," but even in the 5th grade, *that* fucker sang *'Naaa-savaynyaaa'* as the sun rose over Simba's kingdom. Watching it with him was one of the few things I could do that wouldn't lead to a fight.

An ache rippled through me.

Stolen. His entire life, just like that. And I was giddy over a trip in a chopper. *Fucking childish. Remember why you're here,* I told myself, clenching my axe to keep steady.

I could no longer enjoy the helicopter ride.

CHAPTER ELEVEN

The helitack crew got called back to the Patchwork, so the pilot dropped Lt. Nelson and us five inmates with an engine crew that was drip-torching grass along the 5. Prescribed burns. Nelson spoke to one of the fighters and we piled in the bed of a CalFire pickup that would take us to the base camp dedicated to the growing blaze.

The truck took the exit to Ash River and the town unrolled from the road ahead like a new carpet. Ventura County Fire Station 58, a vineyard, homes in neat rows in the chaparral, nicer homes above them in forested foothills. Backlit by the setting sun, the town lay in a valley dominated by those hills on one side, and a dusty ravine on the other that I guessed in wetter times was Ash River.

It smelled like pine and took its mountainy vibe seriously, with a High Mountain Market, a restaurant called the Falcon's Nest, and wood exteriors on most shops and homes. Rustic and ready to burn. But there were cars on the road and people at the tables of the Falcon's Nest – no evacuation yet. I was so far from the lines that I no longer saw any haze or smelled burning wood.

The air was clear as polished glass, crisp as a cold beer. It was like I was breathing for the first time.

A squat mesa streaked with lines of black rock rose on one side of the main road, which some creative genius had named *Ash River Road.* Hiking trails serpentined through woods surrounding it.

Great place to grow up. Not that my younger self would have appreciated it. I hated all two hikes I went on as a kid. Caleb would've gone running in these trails all the time, though. Two-a-days were never enough for him, always had to be the best on the field. Took him dying to get me on a trail and realize I *loved* it. A path through creeping wilderness, like being inside a Bob Ross painting. But my brother didn't lay down his life so I could go on hikes surrounded by happy little trees.

"Kinda nice," Ortiz said.

"Just wait. We haven't got to the base camp yet. 10 bucks says that won't be so nice."

"Not everything has to suck, Mace."

Ash River Road carried us beyond the picturesque town center to a flatter, dustier part of town, Ash River Mobile Estates. Silver Airstreams and no-frills single wides, holey outdoor sofas and rusty lawn chairs, yapping dogs and slinking cats.

Opposite the trailer park was pasture covered with trailers, tents, pallets of supplies, and firefighting vehicles. Base camp.

I turned to Ortiz.

"What'd I tell you. Right next to the trailer park."

The truck crunched onto the gravel road into base camp, but my eyes found their way back to the trailer park. I watched a granny in leopard print leggings share a smoke with a tank-topped mom hanging laundry on the line. An old man glared at a trio of teens in baggy pants walking by with over-the-top swagger. Baggy pants hadn't been in style for years, but they had to set themselves apart from the pre-frayed-skinny-jeans-wearing preppy twats *somehow*.

Except for the distant mountains and ever-orange sky, it was like looking back in time. I half-expected the spindly Kurt Prouty to come sneaking out the window of his double-wide with a shit-eating grin and a fistful of Roman candles.

My stomach twisted like someone wringing a wet towel. What if the fire I'd started with Ortiz's lighter flared up and came here?

Not possible. There was no fire. We'd stomped it out. There was no spark, no flames to catch the wind. Lt. Nelson had seen it and said, 'Good job.'

I knocked on the cabin window and got Nelson's attention. He turned in the passenger seat and slid the window open.

"How far away is the fire, sir?"

"Not sure the exact distance, but it'll be posted on the Fire Information board in the camp. Miles and miles. Ash River's only on precautionary alert."

Almost forgetting my honor-grad manners, I replied, "Thanks, sir."

Nelson nodded and slid the window shut.

Ash River Mobile Estates was safe.

Still, I got that light-headed, panicky feeling just at the thought of the blaze reaching this place.

With the sun disappearing, the lights of the trailers were coming on. Silhouettes crept across the window of a Fleetwood Eagle single-wide. One bed, one bath, 540 square feet. Just like the one Caleb had bought after Mom was evicted.

"I told him to stop selling to her. He didn't and now she's gone," Caleb had said.

It had been three months after Judge Lewis terminated Mom's parental rights, sent her away, and made Caleb my legal guardian. I was eating mac n' cheese when Caleb came in with a plan to take down her meth dealer.

Things had changed between us since I backed up Caleb during Patty's visit. Caleb would parade in, usually interrupting a late-night video game or my morning cereal and regale me about his latest job. But that night he came to me for help with one. His ballsy plan involved stealing from a cook and pinning it on the dealer.

"I'm done snitching," I told him. I was fifteen, but I knew the value of holding my mud. "Never again," I continued, "but this is different."

The money, the girls, the hustle itself – it *was* kinda badass. But it wasn't me.

Caleb seemed to read my mind.

"You don't approve of how I make my money. Fine. But Mom's brain is scrambled eggs because of him. This is the only way to make him pay," he growled.

The bag bitch's brain was scrambled because she was a bag

bitch. She chose glass over us. Caleb still had good memories of her, though, and I wasn't going to ruin that for him.

"*Good way to get shot, too,*" I had said, and shoved my face full of mac n' cheese.

T he Patchwork base camp was a small town of its own. Pallets and porta-potties, green tents, a canopied meal area, neat rows of vehicles, and air-conditioned white CalFire trailers for everything from laundry to medical care, and roadblocks covered with laminated print outs pointed to engine parking, showers, and food.

Me and Ortiz followed Vito down the main thoroughfare. A simple chain link fence surrounded and sectioned the camp. No barb wire, and I had yet to see a C.O. *Good.* I got Ortiz's attention and pointed out the fencing with a glance. He nodded, happy with the setup too.

Clean and well-organized, CalFire staff lined up to receive clean clothes from a CDCR prisoner. In fact, there were busybodies in orange scrubs everywhere – the inmates were running the asylum.

I compulsively tightened my breath mask to make sure it covered the lower half of my face. Vito noticed.

"The air quality is fine here, man."

"I'm sure it is, but my uncle died of lung cancer, so..." I lied.

Graham could be out on the fireline, he could be at La Cuenca Conservation Camp, or he could be right behind me. I was clean-shaven now and looked completely different than the thick-bearded LAC prisoner he'd stabbed and left to die, but I wasn't taking chances.

Vito '*mmm*'-ed with pleasure as we reached our destination, the canopied meal area, where a smattering of men and women sat eating and chatting. The fighters were easy to spot – weary, encrusted in soot and grime, and their plates wobbly with food. With the sky now dark, a few portable lamps lit the space, giving the canopy a buttery warm glow. We filled trays at a field kitchen manned by inmates – they had *steak*, and decent cuts at that.

Vito left to eat somewhere else, and I walked with my tray between the rows of tables, seemingly trying to find a good spot, but actually looking and listening for my brother's killer. Ortiz walked with me.

"You're gonna have to take that off to eat," Ortiz said about the breath mask.

"Making sure he's not here first," I whispered.

There was no sign of him.

We walked by a Sheriff's Deputy sitting across from a sooty CalFire bubba saying something about "… looking like arson. Found accelerants in the black of the – "

He stopped when he noticed Ortiz and I going by and started up again when we were out of earshot.

"Did you hear that?" I asked.

"Yeah I fucking heard it, you goddamn pyro," Ortiz snapped.

"Nothing to do with us. We put out that fire and Nelson checked it."

I took one last look around and put my tray down in the corner of the canopy area.

"I think we're good," I said, and pulled off my breath mask, plopping hard into my chair and releasing the tension bunched in every muscle.

"We got lucky," Ortiz said. "What if we hadn't, and we were the arsonists? Forget the years. Think about what these guys would do to us if we started one of these patches." He gestured at the weary responders.

My tensed muscles, somehow, had been keeping the pain at bay. Now that I'd finally relaxed, the stabbing sensation pulsed from my scarred hand. It came so sudden and so strong that I gagged on a piece of steak.

Coughing, I dipped my hand in the coldest thing available – my lemonade. It didn't help, and now my lemonade was cloudy with dirt.

"You okay?" Ortiz asked.

"I'm fine," I told him, but thought, *I need that goddamn fentanyl.*

I recited the plan in my head to distract myself from the pain.

Step One was already accomplished: *Get the Disguise.*

Next, we had *Step Two: Isolate and Trap Graham.*

Step Three: An 'Accident' Happens.

Step Four: Clean and Dump Disguise.

What was a little pain when I was one step closer to avenging Caleb?

Ortiz snored softly, murmuring nonsense. "Bogart my Bugles? My Bugles?" I stifled a laugh, shaking my head. In a previous life, I could've listened to this for hours, trying to imagine his dream world. He'd been asleep for an hour, but I couldn't even close my eyes. Not because of my stinging hand, but because I was finally ready.

The professional turnout gear was under my cot. Hundreds of people at this base camp. Only a handful knew inmate Jones. Most of them were off-shift, meaning those on-shift wouldn't know me from Adam. And with a helmet and breath mask on... I couldn't help smirking. My knee bounced, restless energy surging through me. Chirping crickets, Ortiz's breathing, and the low rumble of a distant generator – all sharp and unmistakable. I smelled sage and gasoline and every breath ballooned my lungs, stimulating my limbs. The drug was excitement. And a dash of nerves.

Start tonight, I decided with a thrill. This was why I was here. *Step Two starts tonight.*

To isolate and trap Graham, I had to scout him first. Was he at La Cuenca, out on the line, or at this camp? It reminded me of the first 'watch out situation' in the training manual. **'The fire has NOT been SCOUTED and SIZED-UP.'** Graham was the fire, and that's exactly what I'd remedy tonight.

I had no idea what Ortiz was dreaming about, but I had a damn good idea what he'd say about me suiting up tonight. '*Hold up, hold up, too soon, yo.*' So I wouldn't wake him. He needed the sleep anyway.

Watching his face, I quietly pulled the professional turnout gear out from under the cot and slid it into a pack. Stripping down to boxers and a t-shirt, I slipped out of the tent with the pack and a towel over my shoulders. Lingering outside, I listened for a change in Ortiz's breathing, but all that came was a mumbled "Never trust a Libra," followed by snoring.

The sun had been down for hours, but half the sky was still orange, painted by the so-called Patchwork on the horizon. The other half hid stars behind a curtain of gray. Still more stars than I ever saw growing up in Victorville. Hyper-aware, I walked through the fire-touched darkness. A C.O. sitting at the edge of the inmate tents glanced up at me, I pointed at the *showers* sign, and he nodded and went back to a game on his phone. Just a guy off to clean up.

I made sure the C.O. and no one else was looking and went past the showers to the last line of the porta-potties. Stood still for a full minute, listening, looking. No voices, no splashes, no boots against the plastic floors. No one in the porta-potties, no one around. I stepped in, locked the door behind me, and broke out the professional yellow turnout gear.

I'm Clark Kent in a phone booth. Which makes Pete McLean Superman. I couldn't fly and wasn't bulletproof, but I had one new superpower – the ability to move in and out of camp with no questions asked. I stepped out of the porta-potty as a professional firefighter, a hero.

An acid lump churned my stomach. *Heroes save lives. McLean's here to end one.*

I relived the moment when Caleb arrived in LAC to save me from the A.B.'s beatings. My breath had caught in my chest, gratitude that quickly became hot anger. "You shouldn't have come," I'd said. Caleb just flashed that devil-may-care grin of his and said, "At least it's not San Quentin."

My stomach settled, the memory erasing my qualms about posing as a hero to complete a murder mission. Graham hadn't left me any other choice.

I made my way to incident command. It was a single tent the size of a hangar, like something soldiers use overseas, with a line of CalFire dune buggies parked out front. This would be the first test of my disguise, and I paused in front of the entrance. Out on the line, I'd wear a breath mask to disguise my face, but it wouldn't make sense to wear it here. Incident command had its own staff, separate from the people who worked the fire. If anyone from the line was here, it'd be someone from a different shift than those who'd been out with me today. Most likely.

I'm Pete McLean, I belong here.

I strode in with the brisk, confident stride of a professional who was in the middle of something important. It was a large, open interior with four stations, hanging signs designating each one: *finance*, *logistics*, *operations*, and *planning*. Each station had an *incoming/outgoing* document basket, a hard-lined phone, and men and women at laptops. TVs on the wall displayed the news and a helicopter video feed, and laminated maps were strewn with pins and marker scribbles.

At the logistics station, I found the crew rosters. Black and white photos next to every inmate's name and CDCR number. A polo-shirted CalFire worker who was on the phone glanced at me, then returned his attention to his call, writing down notes.

"Second time the Governor's office has called for updates and we owe NPS a report," he said, hanging up the phone and turning to his female counterpart. NPS… probably the National Park Service, I guessed. "Still no ETA on the liaison officer?"

"I don't even know who it's supposed to be," she said.

A few pages into the dusty roster I froze, my pulse drumming in my ears. The pale, freckled bastard was smiling at me from the page. Grayson Graham, La Cuenca Crew Four. Smiling like he didn't have a care in the world.

That's gonna change. The roster shaking in my hands, I set it down on the desk and leaned over it as if studying it closely. Something I actually needed to do. Crew foreman: Capt. Thompson. I'd need to know that name. I scanned the rest of the inmate photos, skipping the names and committing as many faces as I could to memory. I looked at the butcher's smiling face again, and this time I stifled a laugh. *I know your crew number.*

So where was Crew Four tonight?

I went to the operations station, the busiest of them all, with several more tables than the others and double the staff milling around it. I nodded at a dispatcher on the radio and found a shift chart under her elbow. She noticed me looking and politely pushed it over to me. *It's good to be Pete McLean.*

'Anchor Point Bravo: Kern County Engine 7, LC Hand Crew 4.'

La Cuenca Hand Crew Four. Anchor Point Bronco.

I found the spot scrawled out in marker on a topographic map. They were a little over five miles away. It took everything to keep from bouncing off the walls, the restless energy threatening to burst now.

I know where you are, you son of a bitch.

I had 12 hours of off-shift. I could hoof it.

Then again, it was the middle of the night. **'YOU are in country YOU HAVE NOT SEEN IN DAYLIGHT'.** It was one of the first watch out situations in the manual.

All those buggies outside were just begging to be used.

Near the entrance was a compartment with keys hanging from pegs. I swiped a set helpfully labeled *IC BUGGY #3* and marched out of the tent.

CHAPTER TWELVE

There was no sky. Just an amber haze above a crackling orange horizon. The furnace on the hills ahead was growing – its edges like smoldering fingers grasping the landscape, spitting as it hit the brush, whooshing as it hit the trees.

I watched the blaze from behind Anchor Point Bronco, a rocky ridge facing the burning hills. The back of the anchor point was fenced in by a backburn, and there in the darkness next to it was a bulldozer and an inmate crew. Adjusting my breath mask, I made sure my face was well-covered. Now that I was here, I couldn't believe I was this damn close.

I took a deep breath and made my approach. The dozer sat in a little depression on the side of the ridge opposite the fire front, right next to the backburn. The inmate crew was using it to smoke sausages. Their orders were to wait for the blaze to hit the ravine and suppress it from the vantage on the ridge, holding that anchor point against whatever onslaught dawn would bring.

With them was a firefighter in yellow Nomex with a narrow face and a permanent frown. He had to be their foreman. I didn't see any C.O.s – guess they kept 'em at base camp to keep assholes like me from slipping away.

I nodded at my 'fellow firefighter' and offered my hand. "Pete McLean, CalFire liaison officer." I'd thought of it on the drive over. The logistics people at incident command had been waiting on a liaison officer, didn't know who it was, and it seemed like the kind of position that required linking up with various crews.

"Thompson," the foreman said with a grimace. He shook my hand quickly, like he wanted to get it over with. Did direct responders look down on support guys?

"This your crew?"

Thompson nodded, and that energizing cocktail of nervousness and excitement surged in my veins. The roster had listed Captain Thompson as the foreman of La Cuenca Inmate Crew Four. I was on the money.

I studied the dirty, tired inmates gathered around the sizzling sausages.

I didn't see Graham. I looked over them again. Nothing weird about a liaison officer inspecting a crew on the line, so I took my time. I recognized faces from the roster, but the numbers were off. There were only 11 eleven inmates. Graham and two others were missing.

"This everyone?" I asked, straining to sound casual.

"Three guys on an expendable run," Thompson said.

I hid my disappointment. So goddamn close.

I just had to wait.

"Jumped the Stoke Canyon fireline. We lost the Stoke Canyon fireline," said a voice on Thompson's radio. He shook his head.

I recalled the map displays at incident command. The Stoke Canyon line had been opposite Anchor Point Bronco on the southern edge of the fire. Eight or so inches on the map, and though I hadn't checked the scale, it probably translated to thousands of acres away in reality. From all the chatter and the pins and the markings, I knew almost all the birds and bodies were there, trying to stop the blaze from spreading into the Malibu-Pepperdine area.

I watched *our* edge of the monster grow a new limb. Ever closer. And there on the ridge, silhouetted by the fire, was a fire engine and water wagon. Someone was up there. Maybe Graham, dropping off whatever he got on his supply run.

The winds were fast. And getting faster.

"I'm going to take a closer look," I told Thompson.

"'Kay," he said.

I skirted around La Cuenca Crew Four's backburn and hiked up the ridge.

The fire engine and water wagon parked on Anchor Point Bronco were apocalyptic with soot and the reflection of the fire. From here, I could see the entire northern fire front, and acres of the monster's molten body before it disappeared in the orange horizon. There were broken-topped trees spurting cinders like sparklers, fireball bushes decapitated from their roots and rolling down hills, propelled by the wind. The heat getting closer, the ashes thicker.

I looked around the ridgetop and bit back a curse. No sign of an inmate crew member. Instead, a lone firefighter stood near the engine, her back to us, speaking into a radio.

"Strike, this is Martin," she said. "Have eyes on the northern boundary and advise an indirect attack ahead of the control line. Permission to mobe a suppression detail."

"Martin, Strike." The strike team leader's response squawked back on her radio. "Remain on your anchor point and maintain the control line."

"Riskier to wait, Strike. If you could see what I'm –"

"We wait, Martin. Hold position."

"Son of a bitch," she said. I'm guessing not over the hook. She turned to my approach, and her mood turned a 180. Clearly excited to have company. "Morning!"

Cinched inside the bulky hood, beneath a scratched-to-hell helmet, supple lips parted to reveal a stunning smile. I'd noticed how bright everyone's teeth looked inside their ash and dust-smudged faces, but damn. This was something else. She had dark skin beneath the ash.

"Kamilah," she said, offering her hand. I don't know how long I stared. I'd like to think it was seconds, but it could have been an eternity. The blaze reflected as pinpoint embers in her almond-shaped eyes.

Finally, I said: "Uh, Pete."

"That's a pretty risky move you had in mind, Martin," Thompson butted in, trudging up to join us. I detected a condescending tone and was pissed off on her behalf.

"I don't know, check it out," I cut in, and pointed at the fire front. "It's blowing more southerly now. Think it's speeding up. She might be onto something with this indirect attack."

'Never agree with a woman right off the bat. Makes you look weak,' Caleb would say.

Kamilah smiled, and there was a flutter in my chest. I didn't care what Caleb would say.

Thompson sneered.

Yup, it was for sure. Thompson definitely did not respect Pete McLean, Liaison Officer. As inmate Mason Jones, I had an even shittier understanding of fire behavior. This was my first time on the line.

They'd taught the fundamentals at SCC, and I knew enough to know I was smack dab in the middle of a watch out situation: **'YOU are in an area where you are unfamiliar with local factors influencing FIRE BEHAVIOR!'** Forget Caleb's chauvinism. I shouldn't have agreed with Kamilah because I had no clue what I was talking about.

What are you doing, Mason? I asked myself.

I looked back toward the dozer and the inmates around the backburn. Squinting, I counted the same number as before.

Graham had not returned. I could stay up here a little longer.

"Orders are to hold position." Thompson said, like that was the end of it.

"Can't wait for it to get here," she insisted. She pointed to the jagged ravine below us, just ahead of the front. "It'll jump the ravine and then race up this hill. There's all kinds of ground fuel below us here, and then it'll be on this ridge."

Thompson looked at the fire engine, water wagon, and the dozer and crew below, then back at her. Without speaking, his reply was clear. *'And what the hell are we gonna do with just this?'*

"What do you think?" Kamilah looked at me.

She wants my opinion, I thought with a thrill.

I gauged the fire. About two hundred yards from the ravine. How long would it take to get here? Hour? Half hour? A real firefighter would know. I needed her to think I was smart. If I kept her talking, eventually I'd have a chance to impress her.

"Who'd go in?" I asked, struggling with sudden-onset cotton mouth.

"Two firefighters, four inmates," she said, and motioned at the inmates below. "Two of us, two Sawyers, and two Pulaskis."

Kamilah and Thompson studied the fire. I tried to look like I wasn't completely lost. Apparently, it didn't work, because Kamilah tugged me to edge of the ridge. Might as well be a cliff, the downslope was so sheer.

"Sun up brings God knows what. We gotta beat the sun," she said, then pointed at the trees on both sides of the ravine below. "We take out these trees, this ravine has a better chance of breaking the fire."

I tried to see what she saw. Visibility was shit. It was night, the fire cast shape-shifting shadows, and swirling smoke and ash shrouded substantial streaks of terrain.

"Take out enough, I think we actually can stop this advance. Right here, before daybreak," she finished.

Thompson tapped the radio strapped to her Nomex. "You heard the man," he said.

Kamilah snorted. "He isn't here."

I snorted too, unable to stop myself. No respect for authority.

My kind of girl.

"You don't know what kind of flash fuels are down there," Thompson said. "With this wind, a flare up down there would be a death sentence. I'm not risking my men getting trapped down there in a burnover."

Kamilah nodded at Thompson; she could accept that. But she wasn't done.

"Belay me, Pete," Kamilah said, and tossed me a rope. Before I realized what she was doing, she had already clipped into a harness.

Belay? I knew it had to do with climbing, but they hadn't taught it at SCC. She took my axe and started climbing down the ravine.

This is a woman.

I looped the rope around me and anchored myself, probably looking like an idiot.

Thompson sighed and took up his radio. "ICS, Thompson. Request priority air support to knock down the northern edge. We have a fighter going in close."

"Thompson, ICS. Stand by."

Stand by? Not a good sign.

Two tugs in quick succession came on the rope. I guessed that meant she reached the bottom.

Not sure what I was doing, I tied the rope to the engine and started down it myself. A complete fucking idiot.

Breath hot in my mask, I clung to the rope, then let it zip through my gloves as I scrabbled down and landed next to Kamilah. Turns out she wasn't at the bottom, but on a lip halfway down. The gravelly surface grated beneath our boots. Stunned, she swatted my arm.

I smirked. "What's a girl like you doing in a place like –"

A pendulum swooped through my insides and everything turned upside down.

Crack! Stars exploded across my vision and I was lying on my back at the bottom of the ravine, gasping for breath, the wind knocked out of me. I watched orange sparks drift in the haze.

I fell? I must've fallen. Nomex scraped and rocks skittered, and she was next to me. Mask off, her cheek brushed against mine. Warm. Checking my breath. Was I breathing? Glove off, fingers pressed against my wrist. Pulse.

"You're okay," she said. "You're okay. Foothold gave way."

Finally, I caught my breath. She put her gear back on. Helped me with mine. She held out two fingers. "How many?"

"Fucking embarrassing." I lurched to my feet. "Two."

She radioed in a report, and I realized that whatever cred I'd earned coming down with her was shot.

A blast of hot wind brought sparks and burning ash against our faces. I looked at the fire. Snarling, popping, throbbing, roaring, a yellow and orange wall moving right at us.

CHAPTER THIRTEEN

The wall of fire was only 20 yards from us in the ravine. It had been so much farther when we'd started the climb down.

"Was I out? Did I lose time?"

"No," she said, aghast at the blaze, "Flare up. Thompson was right."

I scrambled to the ridge-side. The rope end was halfway up, where I'd fallen.

"No time," she said. "We'll roast before we can climb that. Move down the ravine, we'll try to get to the flank of it."

The snarled rock of the ravine was interwoven with vegetation, shrubs, and dead wood. Fuel city. I looked up at the top of the ridge, now shrouded in haze. Couldn't even see the engine. Thompson had called it, and I was mostly pissed at myself.

La Cuenca Inmate Crew Four – Graham's crew – was on the other side of this ridge. The butcher himself was on an errand, probably due back any minute. Instead of keeping my head on straight and waiting a few minutes to finally get eyes on my brother's killer, I'd chased some pussy off a cliff. And now I was gonna burn alive for it.

"Goddammit."

"I'm sorry," her eyes were genuine. She looked away, "I can be…"

"Fucking crazy?"

She smiled ruefully. Even then, that smile was bonkers. She avoided my eyes and radioed in a report.

I started moving down the ravine, parallel to the fire front, and I heard her scrabbling behind me.

"My captain says I have a problem acting without thinking."

Nice fucking excuse.

But I couldn't stop the laugh that broke out of me, and I found myself wanting to teasingly jab her arm. It suddenly struck me why: it reminded me of Caleb.

"My brother was like that," I said, finally. She caught up to me and looked over. "He played football in high school and tried to get me to take after him. He always said, 'don't think, just move. Snap, charge. Snap, charge.'" Of course, that mentality is what led to his first stint in prison.

"So you won't hold it against me?" Kamilah asked.

"Only if we die."

There was a spark in her eyes, and she looked at me with interest.

"What engine are you with?"

I hesitated. I didn't want to lie to her.

I pointed at the blaze, avoiding the question. "We need to move."

There was no flank to this fire. All front, as far as either of us could see. Nowhere to cut around and get away from its roaring advance. It was a body's length from the ravine now. Ahead, a boulder pile made a bridge into the fire, baking in the heat. The wall of flames seemed thinner there. I could see black, burnt-up landscape beyond the yellow-orange whirlwind. Looked calm.

Kamilah got on the radio: "Overwatch, Martin. South flank, half a click along the ravine below Anchor Point Bronco. Danger close. Looking to get clear. Please advise."

"We need to go into the black," I said. The area that had already burned. In training, we'd learned that it can be safer because all the fuel has been consumed. But here in this ravine it was a radical choice, because we'd have to go through fire to *get to* the black.

Kamilah shot me wide eyes. Even for her, that was a crazy idea. I was hoping to the devil that commanded these flames I was wrong.

The answer came over the radio. It was Thompson: "Martin, McLean, move into the black." *Shit.*

"Snap, charge," I said, and taking my axe from her, I dashed down the baking boulders like stepping stones, attacked flaming branches with the axe, and bull-rushed through a tiny gap in the 40-foot flames. I smacked the baked earth on the other side, tumbling through ash and embers. But not flames. I was through.

Coughing, I looked back at Kamilah. She stood on the

boulders, tensed herself, and charged. Throwing her gloved hands over her face, she leapt through, clipped a burning stump with a boot, and hit the ground beside me, tucking and rolling.

She laid in a fetal crouch. A vice squashing my lungs, I helped her to her feet. Kamilah nodded; she was okay, "Just catching my breath." The vice loosened.

"Jesus," she said.

We trudged uphill, further into the black. A 40-yard dead zone encircled by burning forest. Probably a meadow once. Now it was a hellscape. Cracked spire-stumps like stalagmites protruded from a swath of still-hot ash. The warmth seeped through my boots, boots that exposed glowing embers in the charcoal ground. I struck a stump-spire with my axe, knocking crumbly char off and revealing brown wood deep inside. Not completely consumed. Kamilah and I exchanged looks. The black wasn't as black as we'd hoped. And this tiny scorched patch was surrounded by the blaze on all sides.

"Overwatch, Martin. We're in the black."

"Copy." There was a staticky pause as Thompson continued transmitting without speaking. That pause scared me more than anything. "Be advised. The sun is coming up."

The hazy dome over us was getting lighter, grayer – backlit by a sun we couldn't see. A sharp wind whistled over the scorched hill, so strong I used my axe to brace myself.

Another helpful voice came over the radio: "Wind speeds are increasing."

No shit.

A burning timber fell into the black 10 yards away. Cinders rolled and exploded at our feet. The monster was carrying fuel with it. The flaming noose got tighter, snarling and blasting us with heat. Our 40-yard dead zone became 30.

The safety instructor at SCC had said that almost half of wildfire deaths were a result of a burnover. That's what they call it when there's no escape route and the fire roasts you alive. He'd loved to tell us these fun facts.

"How about some air support?"

Kamilah nodded in agreement and put in the request.

"All available birds are working the south and western fronts," a harried voice from incident command told us.

Fuckin' Malibu, I thought.

The black got smaller still. 30 yards became 20. The dawn winds toppled burning trees and elongated the flames.

"Martin, what's your status?" Thompson radioed.

Kamilah's face was pale. "We're going to deploy shelters." she replied.

This was the absolute last resort in wildfire survival. Calm, she unzipped a blue carrying case, pulled out a shiny block, and shook it, making the block pop open into an aluminum shell the size and shape of a sleeping bag. It reminded me of a giant Chipotle burrito.

"Let's go, shake it out," she said.

I checked my utility belt, patted down all my pockets, and checked again.

"I don't have one." Everyone's kit, pro or inmate, had an emergency shelter. The one that came with my inmate gear was back in the tent, and I hadn't got one with my illicit pro kit.

She spun me around, checked my kit, looked at the area around my feet.

"What the hell, Pete?"

We both looked at her shelter. These things were meant for only one person.

The ring of fire around us constricted, the flames so high on each side it seemed like they were touching. I was dizzy.

I'm gonna die I'm gonna die I'm gonna die...

"You're not gonna die," Kamilah barked.

I hadn't realized I'd been saying it out loud.

Kamilah grabbed me by my helmet and looked into my eyes.

"You're not cooking on my watch."

She started kicking away ash and charred stumps. I stood there stunned.

"Drop your extra shit, get rid of any potential fuel. Weren't you trained on shelter deployment?"

I *was*. 200 shelter drills, and I was panicking like a child.

I helped, kicking and tossing away everything in the spot. I threw my pack across the clearing, Kamilah followed suit, and it was clear.

Then, Kamilah picked up the shelter and put one of my arms through the strap on the inside layer. Muscle memory kicked in, and I put my other arm though and the drill sequence flooded in.

Next, I would lie face down on the ground, keeping my arms down and using the lip of my helmet to hold it in place. Remembering not to panic or move before the fire has burned over. Because that's what gets you killed.

I looked for the best position on the ground. Then it hit me.

"What about you?"

"I got you into this," Kamilah said. "It's only fair you get the shelter."

"No. Hell no."

I couldn't die while Graham still lived. But I wasn't going to take her shelter. I took my arms out of the straps.

"What if I wear it like a turtle shell …" I thought out loud. "Climb on my back. You can be between me and the inside of the shell. We can plug any gaps from the ground with our Nomex."

200 drills were more than enough to know that my idea was probably suicidal. The shell could tear. It might not cover us completely, leaving us exposed to the blaze.

Kamilah hesitated. I met her eyes, pleading with my own.

"Worth a shot," she said. "Keep yours on, you're gonna be against the ground."

She tore off her Nomex fire jacket and I knelt down, tucking my axe in my arm. It'd help hold the edge of the shelter down. Kamilah put the radio in her waistband. We cinched our helmet straps and pulled our breath masks tight. She climbed on my shoulders and slipped the shelter straps over my hands, tugged them down my arms.

"Ready?" I grunted. She straddled my lower back, put her arms around my shoulders, and urged me down. Slipping in the ash, I scrambled down and laid straight. Struggling with the awkward position of her weight, I yanked the shelter over us.

"Is it good?"

"Good. Lean right, I'm plugging left," she shouted over the approaching blaze, and spread out the Nomex on my left side like a lining, trying to close us off. Seconds later we were encased in silver darkness. "Set. Don't move."

My heart was pounding, and I could feel Kamilah's pounding against my back.

I heard the crackling of the fire. Only feet away now. Her sweat mingled with mine, pooling in the small of back and cascading into our charcoal bed.

She began to tremble.

"I'm a little claustrophobic," she said.

Without moving the strap and shelter, I twisted my forearm, reaching my fingers up. She found them with hers.

"We're gonna make it."

Then the roar of the fire drowned out any words we could say to each other and the flames hit our little shell.

The shelter was stretched beyond its design – heat surged from the edges beneath us. Our world was silver and red. I pushed down with both hands, Kamilah pushed down on the interior and her makeshift Nomex heat-dam. It wasn't enough. It was an oven in a hurricane.

The sweat soaking our bodies disappeared. Searing white-hot wind buffeted the shelter and baked my skin. It was like being blasted by a giant torch, and I fought to keep us pinned down. Fiery debris smacked the exterior and Kamilah knocked it away from inside, but the wind and fire stayed on us. A heat cocoon driving me insane. We were roasting alive.

She writhed and wormed on top of me. Trying to get out. Panicking. But the fire was still on us.

"Stay inside! Stay inside!" I frantically fought to keep the shelter pinned down.

She screamed, "I can't! I can't!" I jabbed her with my elbows

– I couldn't do anything else. But she stopped thrashing, wrapped her arms around me and clung to me like I clung to the straps. For a beautiful moment, the gusts died down, the roar became a throb.

Then a fresh blast broke our seal with the ground, sending a surge of heat and smoke into our shell, there was a swirling vortex of agony, and then the monster ripped the air from our lungs.

I could hear her sickening, useless heaving behind my ear – we both gasped for oxygen that wouldn't come. A clamp squeezed my brain and electric cobwebs overtook my vision.

Then, with a sucking, coughing wheeze, air filled my chest. The cobwebs retreated, and the clamp opened. The red glow on the aluminum interior dimmed. I could hear the fire dying around us, the heat ebbing.

But I couldn't feel her heartbeat against my back anymore. I didn't hear her breathing.

"Kamilah."

I tore off the straps, rolled out from under her, and yanked the shelter away. The ground around was black and glowing with embers, but no fire. I cleared a spot and laid her out. Her eyes were closed, her face was pale, and her mouth hung slack. Her breath mask askew.

"Kamilah!"

Terrified, I threw the breath mask aside and smacked her chest.

She coughed, took in a massive breath, and coughed some more, hacking spittle on my face. Relief swept through me.

"You're okay," I said. Kamilah caught her breath and looked up at me.

"Sorry. Spit on your face." She wiped my cheek and a thrill

swooped through my chest as her skin touched mine.

"We're *alive*."

Electricity coursed through me, a surge of energy and warmth almost transcendent. We were *alive*.

I grinned. She grinned back. She felt it, too. Without the flames reflecting in her eyes, I could see them in full detail. Russet brown with flecks of green.

CHAPTER FOURTEEN

The fire moved on, blown away from us by the wind. We sat on ground that was still warm and caught our breath.

Our meadow of ash was surrounded by what was left of the forest. A few black trunks, even fewer branches, and scattered, smoking embers. The strength of the wind seemed to corral the smoke and haze above the advancing blaze, like a storm cloud, and we could see a vast burn scar up against green hills that had somehow been spared.

For now, I thought.

Kamilah's hands whispered against the fabric of her pants, shaking. Mine were shaking, too, I realized. Jittery from adrenaline.

We were quiet for a long time. The wind sighed through the hills, the fire crackled in the distance, and Kamilah's breaths wheezed. Long breath in, long hold, long breath out. Slowing her breathing from the heaving and gulping revival to measured beats. She obviously knew what she was doing, but I could still hear a rasp when she inhaled.

Smoke must have come into the shelter and risen to the top, trapping right where she'd been. All because I didn't bring a damn fire shelter, because this uniform was contraband, because I wasn't Pete McLean, because I wasn't supposed to be here.

Shit.

I looked at her, and it must have been written on my face.

"Hey, we're alive," Kamilah said.

She squeezed my hand, then pulled back. Clearing her throat, she busied herself wiping dirt and ashes off her clothes.

Suddenly self-conscious, I looked around at what was left of our equipment. We still had our Nomex tops and bottoms, helmets, masks, and my axe. Everything else had been flung clear of our shelter zone and sat in a smoldering pile. Contorted filaments of plastic were all that was left of our backpacks and gear belts, and the outer layer of the shelter was charred and peeling.

I pulled Kamilah's radio out from the steaming shelter. The plastic was hot to the touch and its LED screen was blank. I clicked the power knob back and forth a few times, but nothing came on screen, and nothing came out of the speaker.

"Well that's fried," she said.

"Then we should sit tight … right?"

"Yeah. Duh." Kamilah shot me a smart-alecky look, and I chortled while my ears burned.

It was standard protocol to stay put if you weren't in imminent danger, making it easier for rescuers to find us. And we weren't exactly in the best shape to make the trek back to the fireline.

"Stupid question."

"Our brains are probably a little fried, too," she said, and winked at me.

My pulse thrummed up a few notches. I couldn't remember the last time someone winked at me. Who even winks, anyways? I might've winked at someone once, years ago. Trying to flirt with a girl at a bar. *Is she flirting with me?* Or maybe she was just trying to make me feel better. I had to know.

Rapport check. A trick I learned conning a trust fund douche from Huntington Beach. If a mark matches your body language, you've earned rapport and things are going well. The same applied to women.

I stretched my arms and laid my hands in my lap. Kamilah did the same, and I struggled mightily to suppress a smile.

"You must do this often, since you're clearly crazy," I teased.

"I prefer 'highly motivated,'" Kamilah said, smiling.

Driven, she could take a joke… what other fascinating qualities waited behind those eyes? "And actually, it's my first time almost dying. How about you?" she asked.

This was my second time, I realized.

My mouth tasted like pennies from blood that wasn't there. The alarm shrieked, and Graham ripped open Caleb's back with a shiv. My blood got as hot as the shelter had been. I forced a smile for Kamilah.

"First time too," I said.

Kamilah sighed and laid back. I tried not to notice the shape of her body against her undershirt and failed miserably.

I glanced away, but when I looked back at her face, she wore a sly smile. I think she caught me. I wasn't some wussy schoolboy, so I met her eyes with confidence.

She looked away now, suddenly shy, making my cheeks and ears hot.

Heat that flash-froze into an icy knot in my stomach.

You're not here for this, I told myself. To remind myself why I was here, I clenched my right fist and looked at the scar-warped tattoo on it. The stabbing pain returned – the adrenaline had worn off. Soreness and exhaustion crept into my body, but it was tempered by the nervous excitement that spiked every time our eyes met.

"I could really go for a cold one right now," Kamilah said.

"Shit, me too."

"When we get back, we'll do a toast, then. To being alive."

I imagined Kamilah sitting across a table from me, in jeans and a t-shirt, a frosted beer glass upraised, her supple lips parted as she said, '*To being alive!*' The energizing fantasy played in my mind, and it took me way too many moments to realize she was asking me out. I had no idea how to respond.

As Pete McLean, it couldn't hurt to gain the trust of a professional firefighter. When the time came to take Graham with me on a special job, she could back me up. She clearly didn't have issues with risky undertakings. But the thought of dragging her into the mission, into my world – even without her knowing… I couldn't do that to her.

If I shut her down, what then? We'd get rescued and I'd never see her again? If I stalled, she might be insulted or think she'd crossed a line. Or she might think I'm playing hard to get, making her want me even more. Which didn't sound terrible.

I'm overthinking this.

"I'm glad I met you," I said. Stupid. We'd just nut-punched Death. *Glad I met you?* Stupid. Kamilah looked right at me.

"Me too."

Goddammit, Mason.

Seconds or hours later, I heard the thumping of rotors.

T he helicopter that whisked us away had four EMTs, and they attended to us in pairs. They told us they were taking us to the hospital. Alarm bells went off in my head, but before I could come up with a lie, Kamilah ripped off the oxygen mask they'd put on her face and told them to land at base camp. She demanded a doctor see her there so she could be released ASAP back to duty. They must've been impressed with her *cajones*, because they did.

These people are batshit.

Upon landing, they quickly whisked us into medical trailers, keeping firefighters and camp staff away. Thank God.

W hat the hell happened to you?" She was blond, petite, and doe-eyed, but this EMT did not mince words. Alone with her, I sat shirtless on a folding chair. Instead of finding fresh wounds, the EMT eyed the scars left by Graham.

At least the ones she could see. Two puckered stab scars on my stomach and a thin pink line across my chest.

"Gardening accident," I said.

The EMT laughed. She eyed my throbbing right hand, seeing the fingers resting in their unnatural curl. Before I could stop her, she picked it up and extended two fingers, making me gasp in pain.

She raised her eyebrows and carefully set my hand down on my lap, and on their own, the fingers went back to the claw position.

"If you don't take care of it, it'll stick like that forever."

I laughed, picturing a kindergarten teacher scolding the kid who won't stop making goofy faces.

"I'm serious," she said. "Make sure the doctor looks at that, okay?"

"Okay," I said.

"What was the tattoo there? Before the injury?"

On the back of my hand, the unfinished night sky was broken and twisted by whitening scar tissue. It was an ugly mess. The EMT wasn't grossed out, though, just curious. I would've told Kamilah, even Ortiz. The mutilated tattoo was entangled with bloody memories and an interrupted future, and I couldn't tell this woman.

"It doesn't matter now," I murmured.

"All right," she shrugged and cleared her throat. "Other than the internal issues with that hand, you're looking good. But you need a full physical by a doctor. I'll go check the ETA on that. Keep hydrating and wait here."

The EMT went to the trailer door, writing on a clipboard.

"Have him check out Kamilah first."

"He or she will, we already triaged you two," she said,

then looked up from her clipboard and cocked her head at me. Recognizing that I was worried, that I wanted to be sure Kamilah got taken care of.

"That's very considerate. She's going to be fine," the EMT told me, stepped out, and the door banged closed behind her.

A whole minute later, it occurred to me that delaying the doctor with Kamilah's exam would also give me more time to slip away. My first thought hadn't even been keeping Pete McLean from being compromised.

This girl had really done a number on me.

It was time to go, so I suited back up and peered out the window. No one else in sight.

I slipped out and found myself lingering next to Kamilah's medical trailer. No voices came from within, so she was likely alone. I almost walked right in but stopped. She might not be decent.

All the more reason to barge in, I thought. But I decided to be a gentleman and knocked on the door.

"Come in," she called out, and I entered.

In a T-shirt and shorts, Kamilah sat next to a card table full of medical supplies. Her face was fresh and clean. She looked healthy, thank God.

My stomach did a backflip. It was stupid to be here, but totally worth it.

Kamilah spared me a glance, then went back to staring at her crumpled pile of gear on the floor. Her shoulders sagged.

"How are you feeling?" I asked.

"I'll be fine, thanks. You?"

"I'm great," I said, hiding my claw-struck right hand behind me.

"So, what's up?"

"Oh. Yeah." I cleared my throat. "How about we get that beer soon?"

"I think our adrenaline got the best of us," she said, her mouth in a thin downward line.

My stomach lurched. What happened to the girl who had been next to me this morning?

Kamilah spared me another glance, reading my dismay. "I messed up bad," she said. "I almost got us killed."

"But you didn't."

Kamilah was quiet for a while, massaging her neck and avoiding my eyes.

"I'm never going to make captain now," she muttered.

"I won't say anything against you."

I wasn't going to say anything to anyone, because Pete McLean's name didn't need to be on an incident report. "All you have to do is grab a drink with me," I flashed what I hoped was my most charming grin.

"Look, Pete. It is Pete, right?"

She damn well knew it was. That was just cold-blooded. What was this act she was putting on? Or had everything *before* been an act? It couldn't have been.

"When you type up your report…" Kamilah continued, "tell the truth. That it was my fault. Because that's what I'm going to do."

"Integrity move. That's one way to go."

"It's not a move," she said, voice rising. "Forget it. You should go back to your trailer and wait for the doctor."

Kamilah turned away. I vented an angry breath and left, a sinking sensation in my chest.

I messed up too, I thought. I'd chased pussy into a wildfire, almost died, exposed Pete McLean, and I had nothing to show for it.

No. Fuck that.

I turned around, stormed back into her trailer, and said, "So today shouldn't have happened. But it did. And it wasn't just adrenaline for me."

I grabbed a sharpie and a strip of gauze from the table and scribbled down my number. With Kamilah staring at me in surprise, I left again.

Walking back through the camp, I suddenly became aware of my feet. Like lead, attached to wobbly legs that had turned to rubber. I was exhausted.

I wasn't thinking with my dick. Pete McLean would need connections, allies in the legitimate world.

I looked at the deformed tattoo on the back of my hand and told myself nothing had changed. My chest tightened as I thought of Kamilah's russet, green-flecked eyes, and I knew that was a lie.

CHAPTER FIFTEEN

By the time I stumbled back into the tent I shared with Ortiz, the events of the morning had caught up with me. I collapsed into my cot, barely able to keep my eyes open.

It took me a whole minute to notice he was nursing a goat with a baby bottle.

"What the fuck?"

"Nope. You don't get to ask me questions right now," Ortiz said, and glared at me while stroking the goat. Apparently, he'd become a Bond villain while I was gone.

"Are you okay?" he asked finally.

Am I? My throat was sandpaper, my vision was blurry, and I already missed her.

"Yeah," I said.

Ortiz put down the goat. It was a baby, the size of a Chihuahua, and covered in burns.

I waited for him to bitch at me for slipping out without consulting him, or to ask where I'd been and what I'd been doing.

"So, what'd we get out of it?" he asked, way too calm. Even more annoying, really.

I met Kamilah, I thought. I'd lived an entire lifetime in the time I'd been gone.

"I found the anchor point his crew is assigned to," I said.

"Seems like a shit ROI for almost dying."

"ROI? And who says I almost died?"

"Return on investment. Read a damn book. I was in the chow line and heard about the shit that went down with two firefighters named Martin and McLean. You fucking asshole."

"Did you say chow line?" I was starving, I realized.

I opened a canteen and splashed water on my face, desperate to stay awake long enough to get food in my belly. I almost didn't remember to change back into inmate orange, but I did. With my head hammering and my body one big ache, I reverted to Inmate Jones.

"You do shit like this, you go from being an asset to a liability," Ortiz said.

"Ooh, look at you, Mr. Macroeconomics." I didn't have enough energy to argue, but I had just enough to be childish.

"That's microeconomics, bro," Ortiz said.

"Thanks, Professor. I forgot, which way is the chow line?"

"Find it yourself," he snapped.

I walked out of the tent, almost tripping on the fucking goat, and followed the smell of bacon and eggs. Sweet Jesus, it smelled glorious.

Eventually, my nose brought me to a line of inmates and firefighters into the field kitchen, where aproned staff cooked over fryers and griddles and supplied a buffet line of steaming food. There were only a handful of people in front of me, but it seemed to take an eternity to get to the food.

I walked away from the kitchen, a paper plate loaded with waffles, bacon, sausage, and eggs. It was so enticing that I almost didn't see that freckled face, the reddish-brown hair in a high-and-tight, bulging arms, tree trunk legs, the barrel chest on a 6-foot-6 frame.

Graham.

A cold sweat tingled over me as it hit. The world went out of focus, the air went thin, and my heartbeat boomed fast and heavy in my eardrums. *It's happening again.* I forced myself to breathe.

Graham walked between tents with two inmates, all three of them carrying rations. One of them was a short, skinny, beady-eyed white trash type, and the other was a brute, even bigger than Graham, at 6-foot-8. They crossed my path within spitting distance, and then were gone behind a row of tents.

The world returned. My food lay scattered on the ground, next to my knees. *Why the hell am I on my knees?* A nearby inmate was staring at me. "Dirt don't hurt," I announced, and scooped as much of the food as I could back onto the plate, burning with shame.

He didn't see me.

I was here to kill that virus, and I was cringing like a fish on his first day in the yard. Shame became rage, muscles tensing as I imagined dragging him over to one of the sizzling griddles and slamming his face onto it.

If I didn't break down like a little bitch.

He didn't see me, didn't recognize me. I'd gone baby-faced and shaggy up top just for this reason. But that was supposed to be in tandem with a firefighter uniform and mask. In deception, context makes all the difference in the world.

I went back to the tent. Ortiz was asleep. The goat, lying down, looked up at me.

Fucking goat.

I was no longer hungry, but I forced myself to eat. I was exhausted but couldn't sleep now. I needed to stand guard. With all the tools locked up, my only weapon was my helmet. I sat next to the tent flap, ready to pounce.

I could be wrong, and Graham *had* recognized me. He could come and finish what he started, using the same freedom I'd used to track his crew down.

My eyelids were made of lead, and I slapped myself to keep them up. I checked my watch.

8:42 am.

Yawning, I promised myself that I'd wake Ortiz if I felt myself nodding off.

I woke up to a slap in the face. Ortiz stood over me, suited up for the fireline.

"We gotta go. Shift starts in five."

"Fuck," I said, standing up and wobbling from cobwebs that radiated over my vision. I pulled on my gear, the fog of sleep lifting to reveal everything that had happened yesterday.

Checked my watch. 9:25 am. Not even yesterday. Today.

"Drink some water," Ortiz ordered.

"Protecting your investment?" I asked.

"Damn straight," he said.

Guzzling down a water bottle, I realized I'd have to tell him that I'd seen Graham. Now didn't seem like a good time, though.

I didn't know which was worse, that I'd fallen asleep when I'd meant to stay on guard, or that I had got less than an hour of sleep.

The lack of sleep was definitely worse. Chopping and digging with my Pulaski axe, the rest of Hallenbeck's motley convicts seemed to move at light speed around me. A hotshot crew worked above on the hillside, prepping it for a prescribed burn. If the inmate crew was moving at light speed, the hotshots were at double-ultra light speed.

The thunk of axes in wood, the scrape of tools against dirt, the revvs of chainsaw firing up and then the grind as they bit into tree trunks – the sounds of work had become a lullaby, and I kept drifting off into a trance. I had been caught just standing still twice already, once by Ortiz and once by Hallenbeck.

"She's coming down!" A voice shouted, and I heard a tree crack and crash on the hillside above.

"Hookline, break!" Hallenbeck barked. "We'll get going again once the hotshots are done," he motioned at the trees coming down on the hill.

Everyone dispersed, looking for shade in the nearby trees.

I moved toward a leafy oak, then stopped dead in my tracks at a wave of warmth. A vertical seam of burning wood, pink-orange coal throbbing around white char, drew me over. I could walk right into the seam and be swallowed – it was as wide as me and a foot taller.

I didn't understand how this could be – this burning cave *inside* a living tree. I looked away from the fire cave just long enough to see that it was in a massive pine with a trunk wide enough to hold three people, with bristles reaching up to the sky.

My eyes went right back to the burning mouth. There were no flames, it was all shimmering charcoal. I heard a rumble, someone shouting, but it was distant and I ignored it. Consumed by what was in front of me.

It was like a giant, red-hot scoop had been taken out of the tree trunk, leaving the inside to torch itself while the outside stayed green and whole.

I was mesmerized and I didn't know why.

I heard creaking and rustling, but it was in the distance. And I couldn't look away.

"MOVE!"

A booming voice brought me back to reality, and I rubbernecked to see Hallenbeck shouting at me, running down the hill.

He was pointing at a tree timber of hellacious size rolling down the hillside on course to crush me like a gnat. I sprang like a runner off a starting block –

Crunch.

I fell forward, filleting my hands on rough bark as my lower body wrenched to an agonizing stop. I tried to jump to my feet, but only one foot had grip. My left leg was buried up to mid-thigh inside a rotten log covered with moss, and I was stuck in the path of the timber rolling down the hill. Its approach vibrated through me. A few seconds away.

I pushed on the log I was stuck in, but my hands slipped on slick moss.

Crack! Something splintered the log around my leg and flung me backwards – I was falling – the sky above blue with a haze of smoke. The timber whirled over, the wash of its drag whisking my face.

I crashed backwards on something that grunted, and the timber crashed to a stop a few yards past where I had been.

Belatedly, I noticed two arms locked under my own. They relaxed, and the man they belonged to muttered a string of angry Spanish and rolled out from under me.

Ortiz. He laid there face up, catching his breath. I tried to catch his eye, but he wouldn't look at me.

I looked over – the rotten log had been smashed to bits by the timber, and a broken Pulaski axe laid amidst the wreckage. Ortiz's, I realized. In less than seconds, he'd laid into that log with the axe, dumped it, ripped me out, and pulled us both clear.

I laid out next to him.

Ortiz saved my life.

I reached out and gripped his shoulder. My throat was suddenly swollen and tight, and I was relieved as Hallenbeck reached us.

"Goddamn, son," he said, shaking his head at me. He eyed the smashed log and broken axe. "Goddamn," he said again.

I finally got to my feet. Ortiz held out his hand, and I helped him up. I gasped and stooped over from the agony pulsing from my bad hand.

"You all right?" Hallenbeck asked.

"I'm good, sir," I lied.

He took off his helmet and looked us over, "You've got yourself a guardian angel."

"Just trying to get a reduced sentence," Ortiz joked.

Hallenbeck chuckled, then focused on me, "It's your second shift, honor grad. You sure you're cut out for this?"

"I got this. Put me back to work," I said.

Hallenbeck took my hands, turning my palms up. Fresh pain pulsed from the strafing cuts across my palms. "No. Not with these cuts. And on top of a previous injury, too," he said, looking with interest at the scars on my right hand. "Maybe next time keep your gloves on."

Hallenbeck reached into my pack – I flinched, then remembered I had hidden my pro gear under the floor of our tent. He gave me some side eye, then pulled out my first aid kit. First, he emptied his canteen on my hands, lightly brushed the cuts with gauze to remove dirt and debris, then wrapped it in cloth.

Just covering his ass, probably. Yet there was genuine warmth in his eyes. *Maybe he actually gives a shit.* I didn't mind this old fart.

"What's your name, Rescue Ranger?" he asked Ortiz.

"Ortiz, boss."

"Take him back to camp to get medical attention. Do you know where the aid station is?"

"I think so," I said, knowing exactly where it was. Jesus, I'd just been there.

"Hop to it, then, honor grad." Asshole. I minded him a bit now. "And get your first aid supplies replaced while you're there –

always keep your FAK stocked, copy?"

"Yes sir. Copy."

Walking away, Ortiz and I took the path of flattened grass we'd made hiking here this morning. Jeering shouts from the crew followed us. "Take your sweet time, we'll just be here working!" "Yeah, go get your boo-boos kissed, honor fag!"

It had taken less than 24 hours to go from honor grad to a laughingstock. Awesome.

"When we get to the aid station, go in first and make sure there's not a petite blonde EMT around. She saw me as Pete McLean. Oh, and uh, a sexy black chick. She saw me as McLean, too."

"I hate you." Ortiz said. "You burning-the-candle-at-both-ends motherfucker."

"Yeah…"

He knew I'd been in an incident with a firefighter named Martin, but right now he didn't need to know more than that. My guts twisted and I avoided his eyes. He'd just saved my life. I hadn't told him about Graham yet, either.

"Don't know if you noticed what the man was implying, about you not being able to do your job?" Ortiz asked.

"I noticed."

Now was not the time to tell him about Graham.

"'Kay. So, you noticed *that*, but not the tree headed for your daydreamin' ass? What were you thinking?"

"What were *you* thinking?" I asked. He could've died trying to save me.

"Trust, if I had time to think, you think I would've saved your ass?"

"Gotta protect your investment, right?"

"Not everything's business, man," Ortiz said, walking ahead of me.

Before taking me into the aid station, Ortiz made sure the doe-eyed blonde and 'sexy black chick' weren't around. All clear for inmate Jones. A medic treated my hands – a scrub, no stitches, antibiotic ointment, and fresh bandages – then sent us back to our tent. Me to rest, and Ortiz to monitor me.

"Free nap, man," I told him, trying to get him to smile.

Ortiz grunted and turned away from me to feed his goat. I still had no idea where the hell this goat came from.

"Ortiz."

"Mace." He did not turn to face me.

I got a water bottle off the floor, filled the lenses of my goggles, and presented it to the goat. It lapped it up thirstily, *wagging its tail.*

"Holy shit. Do all goats wag their tails?" I scoffed.

"You think just because I'm Mexican I know about goats? That's racist."

Ortiz still avoided my eyes. I looked closely – he had the tiniest smirk. Barely detectable. I couldn't help but laugh. His smirk broadened. It was now or never.

"Thank you," I said.

"Yeah, man," he said, accepting. We both kept our eyes on the goat.

I patted the goat and went to my cot, falling asleep immediately.

CHAPTER SIXTEEN

I woke up to Guerrero barging in our tent. One of the inmates who came with us from SCC. Why can't people just let me sleep?

"Pack your things."

Minutes later, Me and Ortiz stumbled out into early morning. The sun hadn't risen and the sky was a blue-gray canvas. We joined the other inmate graduates gathering on the path between the tents.

Hallenbeck waited for a straggler, then spoke.

"ICS says there's enough coverage here. Time for you all to go to your home camp and get in-processed."

Across the road, the mobile homes lumped in the dim, hazy light.

"Is the fire contained enough?" I asked.

"I'd prefer we stay, too," Hallenbeck replied. "But they brought some crews down from up north."

He left it at that and waved us toward a row of CalFire transport trucks parked on the edge of camp. A C.O. with a clipboard stood at the door of each one, calling out their destination.

The seven of us lined up to the C.O. shouting "Mountain Home!"

With the illicit pro turnout gear carefully hid in our packs and clothes, and the goat in Ortiz's arms, we joined the other five inmates from the truck that had been bound for Mountain Home Conservation Camp. That seemed like a lifetime ago.

"Inmate Ortiz!" A C.O. called out, approaching with two women, one middle-aged and one in her twenties. They wore hoodies that said '*animal rescue*.'

Ortiz frowned and went over to them with the goat.

"Hi there. We're with the Ventura Humane Society. Heard you've been taking care of this little guy," the younger one said.

"Got a little crispy, but he's doing better now," Ortiz said.

"Well, hand him over," the C.O. barked, impatient.

Drooping, Ortiz stroked the goat and handed him to the 20-something woman.

"Are you a kill shelter?" he asked.

"His owner is probably an evacuee. Don't worry, we'll find his home."

"You better."

The 20-something's eyes went wide, paling at the heavily tatted inmate's rough remark. But the middle-aged woman smiled, seeing it for the affection that it was.

"Thank you," she said.

The goat bleated as they carried it away from Ortiz, and my chest tightened.

Stupid goat, making me feel things.

"Tim Puglisi, Mason Jones!" Hallenbeck approached, calling out to me and one of the other inmates who came with us from SCC. "You've been reassigned," Hallenbeck said. He pointed to a different truck.

"Sir?" My breath caught in my throat.

Hallenbeck snatched the clipboard from the C.O. and showed it to us. There were our names, right under the bold text: La Cuenca Conservation Camp. *Where Graham's stationed.* With about a hundred inmates per camp and shared spaces like gyms and cafeterias, I'd have God-knows-how-many chances to run into him every day. Wouldn't matter that I got my pro turnout gear, because the only time I could slip into the disguise was during the 24-on, 24-off fireline shifts.

Ortiz glanced at me, mouth hanging open. I shook my head, at a loss. We'd be separated. No *'Rescue Ranger'* to watch my back. In one bureaucratic swoop the plan was falling apart.

And what if I never saw Kamilah again? The thought compressed my lungs. *'Bigger fish to fry, Mason,'* I told myself, but couldn't shake the glum possibility from my mind.

Hallenbeck was talking to me, I realized. "… Mason Jones, Tim Puglisi. That's you two, right?" Hallenbeck asked without waiting for an answer. "Get in."

He opened the back door of a CalFire transport truck – sweat crackled across my scalp – no Graham. Damarius and the rest of Hallenbeck's inmate crew, plus three inmates I'd never met, but no

Graham.

"Let's go, honor grad," Hallenbeck barked.

I remembered to breathe, and climbed in. There had to be a way out of this. *Think!*

Ortiz raised his eyebrows at me – *was I panicking?*

"Hey boss," Ortiz called out.

"Let me guess, you wanna go with your buddy," Hallenbeck sighed, looking at his watch.

"I'm his sober sponsor. You separate us, and he'll fall off the wagon." Ortiz put on the most patronizing face I'd ever seen, brows furrowed and mouth scrunched.

It was genius. The prison system was riddled with addicts and alcoholics, and I doubted the inmate fire crews were an exception. The instructors had made a point of mentioning the AA and NA programs available at the camps.

Hallenbeck scratched his mustache, giving Ortiz his full attention. I was just a prop at this point. "First the goat, now you wanna save this guy?"

"Keeps me busy. Trust. Idle hands are what got me locked up."

Smart. Not overselling it. Concerned but humble.

"I'll see what I can do," Hallenbeck said, his voice gruff, his eyes twinkling. He marched off to ICS.

Would Ortiz's charm and Hallenbeck's pull be enough to get us both on the bus to Mountain Home Conservation Camp?

Not quite.

An hour later, Hallenbeck ushered Ortiz over to join me – on the truck to *La Cuenca*.

"Keep him on the wagon," the fire captain said, and closed the truck door.

I sagged against the seat, able to breathe easier. It wasn't the separate camp we planned, but at least I wasn't alone. Ortiz and I bumped fists.

"There's something you need to know," I said.

A coincidence or a trap? Neither of us knew what the camp reassignment was. The inmates in the truck had nodded off and I'd told Ortiz about crossing paths with Graham. I was sure he hadn't seen me. 60 to 70% sure.

Had he heard about Ulrich and guessed I was behind it? Or maybe it had nothing to do with Graham. It reminded me of one of the watch out situations. **'YOU notice that the wind begins to blow, increase, or CHANGE DIRECTION!'** I had no idea which way the wind was blowing.

I knew what I had to do until I found out, though.

"If it's a trap, it's probably just for me," I whispered to Ortiz. "If he figured out I'm coming for him, there no reason to think he knows about you." He raised his eyebrows at that. It *was* a big maybe, but if it turned out to be the case, we had to keep it that way. "The only way to use an ace in the hole is to keep it in the hole until you need it."

"That's cool, but I don't swing that way," Ortiz said.

"Funny." I almost laughed, but the gnawing anxiety wouldn't let me.

Ortiz chewed his nails, not thrilled by the situation, but he agreed to do what I asked. When we got to La Cuenca, we'd bunk separately and avoid being seen together. Keep an eye on each other from a distance, at least until we got the lay of the land.

Not wanting him to feel abandoned, I tapped his shoulder and gave him a grim smile before I moved seats. It was just an act, but my chest hollowed as I turned my back on the only person in the world who had mine.

CHAPTER SEVENTEEN

Yellow hills rose from the left side of the road, and on the right, La Cuenca Conservation Camp sat in a scrubland bowl, its far-most edge running up against another circle of hills. La Cuenca was made of up low, ranch-style buildings painted a calm mint green. I half-expected to see a cowboy lassoing cattle, but instead a CDCR guard checked the driver over and waved us through the gate. The fence was three strands of barb wire on spline posts and there weren't even any guard towers.

Yeehaw.

We passed a sandlot and parked in front of a pristine headquarters building with the American and California flags clinking out front. I watched a handful of C.O.s in tan, CalFire bubbas in black and khaki, and all the inmates in orange, milling about freely.

"All right fellas, off the bus!"

I stepped out, shadowing the veteran inmate crewman Damarius. Ortiz and I exchanged a split-second glance and then kept our sightlines and personal orbits apart. There was a basketball court, a Muscle Beach-style outdoor gym, and a neatly cultivated vegetable garden. A visitation area with picnic tables and a guard shack baked in the sun. Serene scrubland encased the hills beyond the fence.

The air was so crisp, so clear. It all seemed so… tranquil.

"Not bad, right?" Damarius asked, noticing me.

I didn't want him to think I was soft.

"Depends on how they have us living."

Still, I almost felt free.

Then a pot-bellied C.O. stepped up, hands on hips.

"This is Cuenca. I'm Sergeant Fredrickson. Count in."

We counted in, and Frederickson pointed to a guard shack in the center of camp.

"You'll check in there every four hours during the day. Don't ask me about gate passes, that'll be your assigned officer. If you see a coyote in the camp, don't bug a C.O., let someone from CalFire know. And this is really important – don't feed the deer."

Me and the other new inmates laughed.

Hallenbeck's gruff bark alerted us to his presence:

"Not a joke. It's becoming a real problem," he said, striding over. "You break the rules, say goodbye to the fresh air and sunshine, 'cause we'll ship you back to prison. Questions?"

Bambi better fuck off, I ain't going back to the big house. Still taking it all in, I kept my mouth shut, and the other inmates had the same idea.

"This is fire camp," Hallenbeck continued. "Prison is behind you. Act like a firefighter, and we'll treat you like a firefighter."

Hallenbeck showed us to our cabin. It was an open dorm with single-bed bays – and windows. "Starting now, you're all a part of La Cuenca Crew Nine, and you'll bunk together, eat together, and sweat together. Listen to me. Learn from your senior crewmembers like Damarius." Damarius tucked his thumbs in his belt and gave us all a regal gaze. Baby Einstein, Vito, and Skeevy Steve started unpacking by their lived-in bunk areas. The eight other inmates in the cabin, fish like me and Ortiz, surveyed the remaining bunks. Hallenbeck continued, "Take a look out the window. See the tallest hill outside of camp? We're hiking it today, one hour from now. Full turnout gear, so be sure to hydrate." He checked his watch. "See you all at the gate at 2 pm on the dot." And with that, he left.

Looked like Hallenbeck was making sure we knew who was in charge. *Wish I'd gotten better sleep, but what else is new?* Vito and Skeevy Steve shared a knowing smile, and I looked to Damarius for explanation. The huge man shook his head, unreadable as he unpacked his things. *Was this hike some kind of initiation?*

I took the empty bunk next to Damarius and out of the corner of my eye, watched Ortiz take a bunk across the cabin. Separate but in sight. *This'll work.*

"Are these cabins in crew order?" I asked Damarius. "Case I get lost…"

"Yup."

I looked out the window. Less than a hundred yards away, a number four was painted over a cabin door. Graham's cabin. If he *hadn't* noticed me at the base camp, it was crucial he *didn't* before we were ready.

It didn't change the plan: *Isolate and Trap Him, an Accident Happens, Dump Disguise*. It was just going to be much, much harder.

An hour and some change later, I started on the trailhead with the 13 other members of Crew 9. The hill was steep but not extreme, the sun was bright but not baking, and before long I was enjoying the hike. We hadn't tooled out, leaving my right hand loose and pain-free. The rhythm of my steps and the open landscape uncluttered my mind, and I drifted to the time I found a plastic bag of Mom's crystal and Caleb flushed it down the toilet with his devil-may-care grin, flowed to the moment Kamilah snapped at me for calling her decision an *'integrity move.'* A hawk winged its way to mountains on the horizon, and a breeze brought the scents of wildflowers to our dusty column.

The summit was flat and rocky, and a grill and two coolers sat in the middle of it next to a pickup truck. This was an initiation I could get behind. Hallenbeck started the grill and waited for everyone to gather around, then swept his hand over La Cuenca below.

"Some people say this is exploitation," he began, pacing, then stopping and looking skyward. For the right words? This wasn't a canned speech, at least. "I don't know much about politics, don't know all that much about the justice system."

'Don't know much biology,' I thought, the song springing to life in my head. I wanted to share the joke with Ortiz, but we had to maintain our separation. Vito was beside me, and I sang the next line to him in a whisper, *"Don't know much about a science book..."*

The balding Italian smirked and whispered back, *"Don't know much about that French I took."* We shared a laugh and I tuned Hallenbeck back in.

"Maybe you think this is mindless grunt work," he said, holding up a fire helmet.

Can he read my mind? The sentiment had popped in my head dozens of times while axing away next to the Patchwork.

"But you're here now, and I suggest you make the most of it," Hallenbeck continued. Not a mind reader. Just experienced and practical. "I'm not here to help you turn your life around. I'm here to keep you safe and make sure the job gets done."

Almost the opposite of what Warden Hearst had said when we got to SCC, and I couldn't help but smile. Sure, Hallenbeck was trying to bond the group with this hike and barbecue business, but he clearly wasn't a bullshitter. He'd sent me to the aid station instead of keeping me on the line – even when I'd insisted I could stay.

"Be safe and take care of each other. That's what's important," he finished.

Take care of each other – Hearst *had* said that, but it was completely different coming from Hallenbeck. Hallenbeck wasn't a pig or a C.O., he was a fire captain who stood on the line with us.

"All right, mandatory fun time," Hallenbeck barked, "I'm getting burgers and hot dogs on the grill – yeah, I got your Impossibles, Damarius – and there are cold drinks in the cooler. No alcohol, though," he said, glancing in my direction. "You all socialize while I get this going."

Careful not to meet Ortiz's gaze, I studied the rest of the

group. Vito sidled up to the other Crew 9 veterans, and the rest of us grew roots. Inmates didn't really socialize outside their cars and gangs, unless you count gathering around a good fight. This wasn't prison, though.

"C'mon, this isn't prison," Hallenbeck barked.

Seriously, is he a mind reader?

I waited for someone else to start. Not that I was shy. Pete McLean needed every fire professional connection he could get, but Mason Jones had to be cautious and find out which inmates were prey, which were predators, and which steered clear of the food chain completely. Vito didn't seem bad – he'd gotten my song reference, which was a plus – but that didn't mean I was going to tell him my life story.

"Fuck it." Ortiz piped up, loud enough for everyone to hear. He pointed at Damarius. "Craziest fire crew story. Go."

"I try to avoid crazy," the huge man replied, and everyone seemed to agree to leave it at that.

Skeevy Steve cleared his throat, "I got one," he announced, taking center stage. "So, we were taking a break by a river, and it was getting dark. I see this beaver chewing on a tree – did you know their front teeth are orange? – and I try to sneak up on it. It spins around and sees me, staring at me with its beady little eyes. And I talk sweet to it, 'cause I don't wanna kill it. Just hang out, have a wildlife moment, you know? And the little bastard *charges* me, orange teeth snapping, *screaming*." Damarius shook his head, and an inmate in the back called '*bullllllshiiiit*' in a sing-song tone. "True story!" Steve insisted. "Sounded like an old man who broke his hip! I reach for my axe, but all the tools were locked up in the truck! Next thing I know, I'm running like hell through the woods, a screaming beaver coming after me. I'm telling you, that thing was rabid…"

The new members of Crew 9 exchanged looks and skeptical mutterings

"I knew a girl with a rabid beaver," Ortiz said. "Almost snapped my dong in half. Never hooking up with an ab model again, I tell you that much."

The inmates guffawed and chortled, and even Hallenbeck snorted. Conversations sparked across the group as everyone relaxed. I couldn't help but smile. No denying Ortiz knew how to break the ice.

I went to the cooler and grabbed all the Gatorades I could carry, handing them to Ortiz and the crewmembers orbiting him. I listened to the voices and the sizzle of meat on the grill as the sun dried the sweat on my scalp.

We didn't have to make friends. But we could be friendly.

A week after arriving, I took stock. Everything I'd encountered told me that my reassignment to La Cuenca was a coincidence. It seemed Graham hadn't recognized me outside the field kitchen. *Makes sense.* It'd been a split-second in passing, and he was probably too busy pretending to be a rehabilitated golden boy to work out I was after him.

Outside of physical training, work projects, and check-ins, our time was our own. The flexible schedule had two advantages: I could make sure to hit the cafeteria, kitchen, and other common areas at different times than Graham, and it gave Ortiz the free time to surveil the bastard. Much as I wanted to have eyes on the shitbag myself, it was too risky. If he caught me, there was a damn good chance he'd recognize me. Neither of us thought I'd get lucky a second time around.

I'd met with Ortiz once, at the urinals after lights out. The stocky go-getter'd gone sneaking and got some solid intel. Graham had a routine that he rarely strayed from. He wasn't looking over his shoulder, and no murderous messengers visited me in the night. He *did* have the protection of a two-man entourage everywhere he went, though.

The same two dudes I'd seen with him at the Ash River base camp. They called the short, skinny one with beady rat-eyes Roach, and the 6-foot-8 gargantuan Sasquatch. Probably the most fitting nicknames I'd ever heard.

"Committed to rehabilitation my ass," I said. "An inmate trying to make good doesn't keep bodyguards."

"Hi, my name is Mason, and I'm an addict," I told the men seated in the circle around me. The shadow of a crucifix covered the carpet between us. Ortiz was three chairs down, and Damarius was across from me, a 'Trusted Servant' leading the meeting. I stifled a sigh. This was a real chore. At least the chapel's AC was working, and I tuned into its hum, tuning out the addicts as introductions continued around the circle.

To make Ortiz's lie true, we'd both signed up for Narcotics Anonymous the first night at La Cuenca. We just needed to have both of our names on the roster in case Hallenbeck followed up on the 'sober sponsor' ruse. In the group itself, nobody needed to know Ortiz and I were linked. The convict grapevine was too chatty.

After what seemed like hours, but was only fifty minutes, the meeting was finally over. The addicts spilled from the chapel into harsh sun. Ortiz went left toward the outdoor gym, so I went right toward the basketball court and watched a three-on-three game in progress.

"Inmate Jones?" A man wearing a CalFire shirt and tactical pants approached. He was clean-cut and wiry. A firefighter or heavy equipment operator, probably.

"Yes sir?" I stopped and pasted on my helpful 'honor grad' smile.

"Saw you got arrested for grand theft auto."

Jesus. Something car-related got stolen or lost so he's rounding up the usual suspects. And what I got arrested for was boosting a container truck with four dealer-bound Benzes and replacing the VINs in transit. 'Grand theft auto' made it sound like I was some teenager who jacked a Civic. What's a CalFire dude doing looking at my records anyway? "I just got here. If something's missing, I don't know anything about it."

"No, no," the man laughed, and ran his hands through his hair. "Asking because our mechanic is on leave and I don't want to have to call a tow if I don't have to. You know anything about cars?"

On the one hand, the more CalFire dudes who knew Inmate Jones, the more I had a chance of getting recognized when I was posing as Pete McLean. On the other hand, the more brownie points I earned as Inmate Jones, the less scrutiny I'd be under.

Giving me more chances to slip away and become Pete McLean. "I know a bit, sir," I said.

"It's Sean. Come with me."

I followed Sean to a two-bay, stand-alone garage reflecting harsh sun from its aluminum roof. He opened a bay with a clicker and led me to a wildland fire engine, a white F-450 glinting under a row of fluorescence. The walls were lined with tool cabinets and in the other bay a tanker sat in the dark. Good place for a trap.

Paranoid much? Plus, I had about two inches on this guy and there was a lug wrench near my feet. I could take him if I had to. The smell of the garage filled my nostrils, calming me. La Cuenca's fresh, scrubland air was something, but the incense of oil, metal, and rubber was like going home. Reminded me of when I was replacing the pistons on my Indian.

"Won't start. Full tank, battery's only 6 months old," Sean said, popping the hood. He put his hands on his hips, then ran his hands through his hair again. Noticing me studying him, he tapped his watch rapidly. *In a hurry.*

I turned my focus to the car. Super Duty 6.8-liter V8. *Nice.* I lifted the engine cover, all the spark plugs were intact and in place. No loose wires or fuel injectors.

"You check the ignition switch?"

"I don't know much about cars. That's why you're here." He fidgeted. So impatient.

I told him I'd see what I could do, and he smiled with relief, practically racing to the door before he stopped.

"Oh." Sean came back over and put the keys on a table. "I have to close the bay door to keep you from driving off," he said with an awkward, forced laugh. He pointed out a normal, person-sized door across the garage. "Regular door over there if you need to take a break."

I nodded, but still walked around the truck, checking all the angles of the room, the nooks and crannies next to and behind the cabinets, looking in the cabins of the truck and tanker and even the ground clearance beneath both. The bloodstorm in the LAC kitchen had taught me a hard lesson. But no was one here but me and Sean.

"And when you're done," Sean continued, "I have to inspect you and the car, because, well, you know…"

"I'm a convict. I got it."

His preoccupation with the regulations was reassuring. Less likely that this was a trap.

"How will I find you when I'm done?" I asked.

Sean cocked his head. He obviously hadn't thought of that. He eyed the walls and pointed out a hardline phone. "That phone dials out. The extensions are on there, just ask for me."

"Sean," I repeated his name, doubt edging in my voice. Something was off.

"That's right. Okay. Good luck," he said, and stepped out, hitting the clicker.

The bay door clanked down about an inch per second, eclipsing the sunlight. At the halfway mark a claustrophobic cloud lowered over me.

"Sean, you mind leaving it a foot or two open? Be good to have some fresh air, still won't be able to drive through."

The bay door kept lowering, the bottom lip at shin-level. Had he heard me?

"Sean! Hey, please leave it open a bit!" I shouted over the mechanical chain, then pounded on the door, making the metal reverberate.

Thunk. Its rubber lip settled to a stop against the concrete and Sean didn't answer. The cough of footsteps in gravel grew quieter until they were gone.

What the hell?

You're being paranoid, I told myself, and picked up the phone. No dial tone. Cord from receiver to base? *Check.* Cord from base to wall phone jack? *Nonexistent.*

Stop freaking out, Mason. Forcing calm, measured strides, I made my way across the bay to a regular door. It'd have to be able to be opened from the inside. Garage safety 101.

Squeaking rubber on concrete – I whirled around – Sasquatch and Roach rushed out of the water compartment of the tanker, holding a furniture blanket between them.

Quashing my arms askew against my sides, they wrapped me up like a bug in a Kleenex. I kicked out, but beefy arms bear-hugged me and lifted me off the ground, while some tape or cord cinched the blanket around my feet, and then again around my arms at the middle, and again around my shoulders. I could barely move and fought to breathe. Smothered light showed their shadows through the fabric.

Sasquatch slid me onto the floor – *gently* – and Roach stood over me. I heard Sasquatch's thudding steps, the truck door opening, and the engine starting. Revving. Sasquatch pushing the pedal to the floor, pushing the RPMs to the max.

To fill the garage with exhaust.

Throwing my weight, I rolled across the floor. I looked for a blade or edge through the open top of the rolled blanket.

"Where you rolling, runaway burrito?" Roach said, his voice a slow twang, and kicked me in the back. A sharp pang rippled from my kidney, making me gasp.

"Easy," Sasquatch said with a soft, melodic voice that only made him scarier. "Can't leave bruises."

I rolled the opposite direction, rattling a tool cabinet. My arms were stuck, but if I could get a tool to fall out, maybe… Roach's feet shuffled toward me.

"Let him tire himself out. Nothing he can do," Sasquatch said, and Roach stopped. Sasquatch pushed the gas pedal down for at least a full minute, then clomped out of the truck. Their footsteps walked away, and the door I'd been running to opened and closed.

Craning my neck, I looked out of the top of the burrito. A sliver of light between that door and the floor interrupted by four shadows. Their feet. Standing outside in the fresh air, waiting for me to suffocate on the exhaust.

'*Can't leave bruises,*' Sasquatch had said. When I was dead, they'd unwrap my corpse and do what they needed to cover their tracks. Cause of death would be carbon monoxide poisoning. Without bruises, no sign of foul play. *It'll look like a suicide.*

I coughed, my throat grating with every breath.

Count-in every four hours. Last count had been before NA, the meeting had been an hour, how long had I been here? Minutes. Three hours until next count. Ortiz? Separate ways. I'd told the only guy who had my back to steer clear of me. Stupid. I'd be long dead before anyone noticed I was missing. How long did it take to choke to death on car exhaust?

Longer than it would take to block the tailpipe. I rolled toward the thrumming engine and growing noxious haze. If I could sit up against the pipe – where the poisonous fumes were most concentrated – and block it with my mummified body, it'd stop the engine in… between 5 and 15 minutes. I wasn't a potato, but I'd do.

The engine heat radiated through the blanket. Reaching the truck, I wiggled, bumping tires and a hitch to feel my way to the tailpipe. Fumes ravaged my lungs. Coughing non-stop now.

Stop the engine and they'll hear. Come back in here and murder me some other way, and how could I stop them? Wouldn't be the 'suicide' they wanted, but that didn't mean shit to me. I'd be dead.

The heat. Exhaust makes tailpipes hot, hot enough to burn through this blanket. As spots swam across my vision, I inch-wormed myself against the tailgate and slid into position, jamming the circular ember of the tailpipe against the small of my back. My left hand pinned behind me inches from that spot. The spot of fabric warmed, burning my skin but not *through* the fabric. Not hot enough?

I'm a baby in swaddling clothes. Mom stood over me, smiling, taking a toke and blowing meth smoke in my face.

A sizzle and then scalding pain – the edge of the exhaust pipe seared through the fabric and some of my skin. Collapsing to the concrete, I wormed my hand out of the still-burning hole and ripped it wider. Kept rolling.

"No babies in the castle," seven-year-old Caleb yelled, pushing me

away from the blanket fort built against the back wall of the trailer. I'll get him. Steal those stupid Hot Wheels he's hiding in there.

Could reach my whole arm out. It was twine cinched around me at the top and bottom. Missed a few times before I tore them off, clumsy and slow. Fingers not quite connected to my body.

I spilled out of the blanket and fell trying to stand. Room spinning. Not enough clean air left? Turn off the truck, it'll stop. For a few seconds. They'll hear it's stopped and run in here and finish me off.

Kamilah, grimy and pale after the burnover, but radiant with that sly smile as she caught me checking her out.

Stumbling to the tanker, I pawed at the cabin door. Unlocked! I opened it and gulped in the compartment's glorious pocket of clean air. Slammed the door shut. Wouldn't last forever, but I could think. *Think.*

Sasquatch and Roach stood outside the regular door. Go out that one, get dragged back in and killed. That bitch-ass 'Sean' had the fob clicker for the bay door.

He had *a* fob. I was sitting in another vehicle belonging to this garage. Popping the visor down, my hunch materialized. Another fob clipped right above my head. Taking a deep breath of the clean air, I snatched the fob and climbed out of the tanker into the mind-bending fumes.

When I clicked the fob, I wasn't in starting blocks by the bay door. Instead I stood next to the regular door, inches away from the bastards trying to kill me.

The bay door clanked open, spilling hazy clouds into the blinding outside light. Sasquatch and Roach shouted and ran toward the opening bay. I slammed open the abandoned door and sprinted into the light, heaving in precious, revitalizing air.

Sasquatch and Roach turned and made to come after me, but I was already at the basketball court. A full five-on-five game going now, with a dozen inmates and two C.O.s watching. Stifling coughs and slowing to a walk, I put the court between me and my wannabe assassins. Glaring at me, swearing at each other, they stopped.

Safe, for now.

I met Ortiz at the urinals an hour after lights out, when the cabin was quiet and dark, and told him what'd happened.

"Graham knows," he summarized, the whites of his eyes practically glowing in the dark. He ran a hand through his hair and sighed.

My throat was a gravel road and my head was the whirling storm clouds over it, splintered by blinding lighting and earsplitting thunder. I'd been flinching at birds and shadows all afternoon. All those months ago in the kitchen at LAC, I hadn't died like I was supposed to. Graham deciding to wipe me off his plate was always a possibility. Now it was a reality.

"So he knows," I said with a shrug.

"Ain't no coincidence brought you here," Ortiz said. "He brought you here so his boys could kill you. That don't worry you?"

If Hallenbeck had the pull to get Ortiz assigned to this camp, then 'Sean,' who led me into the garage, probably had the pull to get me switched from Mountain Home to here. Behind it all, Graham was pulling the strings. He was more formidable than I thought.

My shirt clung to me, damp from a persistent sweat. I slurped water from the faucet and paper-toweled my face and pits, but it was a finger in the crack of a dam. It's not like the mission wasn't serious before, but now we were under the gun. Literally, for all I knew.

"Guess it changes our sleep schedule," I said, forcing a light tone.

"Night watch," Ortiz guessed.

"Exactly," I said, and broke it down. During the night, we'd keep an eye on each other from across the cabin. It was a simple breakdown. Two of us, two shifts. Four hours each.

"Jesus. Cuts our sleep time in half. You're right, but it sucks," Ortiz groaned.

"I'd be dead if not for you. Let's say six hour watch for me, two for you." It was the least I could do, and he was no good to me irritable and sleep deprived.

"You don't have to do that, man. I mean, that's losing a lot of sleep."

"For now."

We stood in the dark, sharing a pensive silence.

Ortiz 'hmm'-ed, then gave me some very cautious side eye. "What if we didn't have to do it?"

"What do you mean?" I had a damn good idea what he meant, but I needed to hear it. Now was *not* the time to puss out. We'd gotten the butcher's apprentice arrested as a sex offender, I reminded myself, lungs expanding, head cooling. We had the *disguise*. We had *each other*.

"This camp life ain't bad, is all. Do we gotta protect ourselves from Graham? Trust. But maybe there's another way to handle it, you know?"

"No, I *don't* know. You mean snitch? Or what?"

Ortiz shrugged.

It also wasn't the time to pick a fight. He was probably just scared, and I couldn't blame him for that.

What would Caleb do? He'd never show fear, that's for sure. He'd just strike back. Hard. That clarified things. Was I scared? Sure. It just got way more dangerous. But the basics of the plan remained. *Right?*

Isolate and Trap Graham, an Accident Happens, Dump Disguise. My enemy would be on guard, so we'd have to work faster and quieter.

"*I* was the one attacked. Mason Jones," I told Ortiz. "But not you, and Graham's not one to let a threat go unchecked. That's confirmation he doesn't know about you. And he doesn't know about Pete McLean. It's kill or be killed now. We keep going."

Ortiz nodded, grim, and we tapped fists.

CHAPTER EIGHTEEN

To isolate Graham, we had to get rid of Sasquatch and Roach. La Cuenca's biggest export, besides us, was well-crafted wooden signs. They came from a workshop and lumber-mill that filled its corner of the camp with the buzzing of saws and the scent of freshly cut wood. For a few inmates, the woodshop was their full-time job, and they made signs, chairs, and name plates for camps and prisons all over the state. For others, like Graham, Roach, and Sasquatch, it was a trade class.

Thanks to Ortiz's surveillance, we had the bastards' schedule down to the minute. The workshop class was Tuesdays and Thursdays at 10 am. Before every class, a gaggle of inmates gathered in a designated smoking area 100 feet away. Concrete trash receptacles with metal lids on a patch of gravel and concrete, plus numerous signs: '*place cigarettes, butts, and ashes in receptacles.*' CalFire would be pretty embarrassed if their camp caught on fire.

A mammoth crane used by the Forest Management Task Force loomed over the woodshop and smoking area like a skyscraper over a slum. While the nicotine hounds got their puffs in before class, Graham, Sasquatch, and Roach went behind the crane and relaxed against its shoulder-height tank-style tracks. Each time, Roach slipped a grizzled old-timer a carton of Marlboro Reds. The old-timer smoked the Reds and kept an eye out as Sasquatch and Roach smoked meth. Before every workshop class, very routine.

This time, I risked joining Ortiz walking along the fence line, to catch a glimpse of Graham and his two-man entourage sitting against the crane tracks. And then I couldn't glimpse anything else, bile scorching up my throat, my pulse thumping in my ears, that metallic taste on my tongue. Phantom blood.

"Yo," Ortiz nudged me. "You're grinding your teeth. Making *my* teeth hurt."

I touched my face – *I'm here* – my jaw sore, my skin hot. Took deep breaths to make the blinders fall away, to take in all of the camp around me, not just my three targets.

Sasquatch and Roach shared a pipe, but Graham wasn't interested. He was tapping out texts on a cell phone. For Graham, these smoke sessions were office hours, and he probably paid for Sasquatch and Roach's meth habit in exchange for protection. "Guess this is when he's calling shots," Ortiz said. What kind of shots was he calling out here? Contraband ring? Extorting a fresh vic? It didn't matter. *His new hustle will end with him.*

We had to figure out a way to get rid of his muscle.

"Graham never takes a hit?" I asked.

"Nope. Respect."

I glared at Ortiz, who shrugged in reply.

"He's a piece of shit, but he's a disciplined piece of shit."

He was right, but I didn't want to give Graham credit for anything.

We walked out of the trio's eye-line, keeping our distance from the smokers, too. No need to be seen together.

"That Roach dude looks like he's been doing meth a *while,*" I said.

"Seriously. And I wouldn't fuck with Sasquatch when he's riding the high."

Sasquatch had already got the better of me once, and though I'd been wrapped up he'd seemed sober. Ortiz was right. I'd hate to see the giant powered by crystal. A physical throwdown was out of the question.

"If we tip off the C.O.s, Graham could get caught up in it," Ortiz said, thinking out loud.

"So he gets sent back to prison when I just got here? No thanks."

"Exactly."

"Let's find the supplier and taint that shit," I said.

Ortiz raised his eyebrows and nodded toward the cabins.

In the privacy of our cabin, I continued: "Sasquatch and Roach are the targets. We lace their supply with something that fucks them up. They get *themselves* caught."

"Might be on to something," Ortiz said. "Meth's an upper – can actually help with work and whatnot. Probably why it hasn't been a problem at the workshop. If anything, mighta helped. We put in a downer, or something to make them crash sooner, people are gonna notice. Then it's a safety issue. Trashed inmates in a room of saws? The peoples here are all about safety."

"Holy shit, did we just agree?" I asked.

Ortiz laughed.

"I'll follow 'em to find their supply situation, you stick to keeping your distance."

Telling me what to do again. *This is my mission, dude.* I decided to let him have this one, because we were on the same page for once.

"So… what's the worst possible thing to mix with meth?" I wondered aloud.

"Rat poison?"

"I don't wanna kill them," I said. Sure, they'd tried to kill me, but they were symptoms, not the disease. "Graham's the only one who has to die."

"Suit yourself."

For the *Sureños*, having more of Graham's associates out of the picture couldn't hurt.

"Maybe I'll Google it," I joked, and we both laughed.

"Ambien," Ortiz declared.

"Ambien?"

"Ambien," Ortiz grinned.

Their supplier was Sgt Fredrickson, the pot-bellied asshole who'd laid down the law when we first arrived. They made the exchange during the weekly inspection, when all the inmates lined up outside the mint green cabins for scrutiny by sluggish C.O.s. Frederickson slipped a packet of yellow powder in Roach's hand while patting him down. It was pretty slick.

"Powdered, not crystal. Easier to hide," Ortiz said.

We knew Roach was the carrier – he doled out Sasquatch's portion at each smoke session. Trying to make a deal with a corrupt C.O. was out of the question, so we'd have to lace the meth ourselves.

Ortiz traded places with the Hispanic inmate who cleaned Crew 4's cabin – for the cameras – and 'spilled' the mop bucket in Roach's bed bay. While cleaning up, Ortiz did a quick check – Roach wasn't hiding the meth there. It was damn unlikely he kept it on him at all times. After following him three more days, Ortiz still couldn't find out where Roach's secret stash was.

That meant we'd have to cut the meth during one of the two times we knew he had it – right after a re-up, or right before a smoke session.

A straight switch was out of the question. We needed the meth – not just Ambien – in their systems when they got rolled up. They'd be kicked off the line for good over that, unless they had the best lawyer of all time. We needed to add powdered Ambien to the powdered meth.

It was a slip, not a switch.

"A roofie colada for the ages," Ortiz said.

Behind the door of a shitter stall, I dripped yellow food coloring on the crushed white powder of an Ambien. It clumped and crystallized. It was supposed to match the yellow meth powder, but it was a lumpy mass the color of a carrot. I passed it under the divider to Ortiz in the next stall over.

"They're gonna notice that," Ortiz said, stating the obvious.

"Yeah, and a little too orange for my taste."

"We keep it white, then. Just gotta mix it well and do the slip right before they smoke it, give 'em less time to notice any difference," Ortiz said.

"Or it'll be so different that they can't *not* notice. We do the slip after the re-up and they'll think that's how the batch looks."

"Maybe… it could go either way," Ortiz muttered.

"This is your area of expertise. Your call," I said.

Ortiz grunted.

"Dude, are you shitting?"

"Why not? I'm already here," he said.

I heard a wet plop.

"Jesus. I'm out."

I put the unused Ambien powder in a sandwich bag and tucked it in my sock.

"Right before they light up," Ortiz said, voice straining, "That's my call."

"Fine," I said. I had my doubts, but he was the one who had to make it happen.

T he day came, and that fact was the forefront of Ortiz's mind. He was nervous as hell.

"Your sleight of hand game is strong," I told him. "That's how we know each other, remember?"

"Uh, you *saw* it. So it's not that strong," Ortiz pointed out.

It was a Thursday, 9:56 am, four minutes before the class, and we were going through the motions at the Muscle Beach-style outdoor gym. The cluster of rusty equipment and ragged vinyl stood across a gravel path from the workshop, smoking area, and looming crane. Ortiz was breaking a sweat on the bench press, and I was crossing the area doing weighted lunges. Seemingly separate inmates doing separate workouts, but every time I lunged past, we exchanged whispers.

"You can do this," I said.

"I have to do this, because we can't risk Graham seeing you." Ortiz heaved the bar up and down, hissing breaths in and out, face red.

"Also true," I grunted, lunging away.

"Fuck," he sighed and clanked the bar on the rests, standing to stretch.

"Just stop thinking about it," I dropped the weights on my next pass. "Remember the tree? You weren't thinking then. Saved my life."

"Regret that every day." Then he shrugged, "Aight, here goes."

I pulled a baseball cap low over my face and sat on an incline bench to watch.

Graham, Sasquatch, and Roach pushed through the smokers. Ortiz intercepted them before they got to the old timer.

First stop.

Ortiz was grinning, and though I couldn't hear him, I know he was begging for a cigarette. Something like:

'Yo, I seen you handing out them Reds, them's my favorite. Hook it up!'

Graham kept walking – this was for his underlings to deal with – but Sasquatch stayed. Ortiz acted intimidated, shadowboxing around the gargantuan as a joke. At that, Sasquatch shook his head and moved on.

Ortiz showed Roach some cash.

My foot was bouncing and I stamped it down, but it didn't stop the flow of twitchy energy through my muscles. I thought Roach would tell him to fuck off, and Ortiz would have to wrangle a handshake to mask the take. Instead, Roach brought out the carton, took the cash, and they exchanged a homie handshake.

Ortiz's *other hand* slipped in and out of Roach's pocket, lightning fast.

Roach took Ortiz to the old timer, and as they walked over, Ortiz had his hand in his own pocket, adding the Ambien powder to the meth. Roach grabbed a pack of Reds out of the carton, but instead handed *both* to the old timer, smirking.

What an asshole.

I clearly saw the word 'spic' come from the old timer's lips, and he and Roach squared their shoulders and stared down Ortiz.

Real buyer beware shit. Didn't matter, though. Ortiz needed to make the *second stop.*

Ortiz acted mad and pawed at Roach. '*Gimme my money back,*' he was obviously saying, and – God I fucking hope – that's when he made the return slip.

The racist old timer pushed him away. Seemingly cowering, Ortiz beat his retreat, weaving his way through the smokers and to a weight rack behind me.

"Fucking assholes. Should've gone with rat poison."

"So you did it?" I glanced back at him.

Ortiz shook his head, face red.

"They had _crystal_ this time, not powder. Slipped it back as-is."

"Shit. Shit, shit, shit." We couldn't add powder to a packet of glass-like shards and expect the addicts not to notice.

Now, all three men were behind the crane tracks. I checked the time – 9:59. The workshop class started any second now. My stomach sank. We'd lost our shot. Ortiz couldn't approach the racist old timer again, not after getting screwed over the first time. They'd know something was up. And me? Sasquatch would toss me like a beanbag.

I kicked the weight bench pillar. Maddening pain shot from my big toe. These were tennis shoes, not work boots. I muttered a string of Yosemite Sam curses and hissed breaths in and out, trying to dampen the agony and exasperation, "If we'd done it after the exchange like I wanted to, we could've done something about it."

"Not helping, bro."

He was right. _Fix it, Mason._ There was a way to fix this. Maybe. I pulled the visor of my cap even lower and walked briskly through the smokers, whispering, "Surprise inspection, heads up. Surprise inspection coming, hide your contraband…"

In moments, a third of them were dispersing, looking for places to stash contraband.

The old timer whistled, alerting Graham, Sasquatch, and Roach. Keeping my head down, I walked along the fence-line and watched Sasquatch and Roach stow the drugs and pipe in a roller of the crane track. Graham winced, hand down the back of his pants as he shoved his cell phone in his prison wallet. Must be some important shit on that phone.

The inspection never came, of course, and the bell for the

workshop rang. Lateness meant points, and guys like that couldn't afford points. Graham and his bodyguards went into class.

They could assume their stuff would be safe until after class. The Forest Management Task Force's next outing wasn't for a few days.

I wish I had thought of this before. Necessity, the bitch mother of invention.

In awe, Ortiz came over and handed me the Ambien powder.

I moseyed over to their hiding spot.

Crammed in the cylindrical track roller, many of the meth crystals had broken down into smaller bits, the smallest ones becoming powder.

Perfect.

Sasquatch and Roach didn't smoke before class and show up faded on a meth-Ambien blend like we planned. They did smoke after class, though, and they did fall into a ditch escorting Graham to the visitation area.

I heard Sasquatch was shuffling along the path, then just toppled like a professionally-cut tree, taking poor little Roach with him. Supposedly, it took four C.O.s to fish the pair out of the suction-like mud coating the ditch.

The exact details of how it went down didn't matter. What mattered is that the camp commander had them tested for substance abuse and boy did they pop.

Graham's bodyguards were gone the next morning.

"We fucking did it!" Ortiz whooped when we got back to our

cabin that night.

I brought out two cups of Gatorade and opened a baggie with leftover Ambien, ready to make two very relaxing cocktails. I emptied half of the crushed sedative into one cup, but Ortiz put a hand over the other.

"Naw, man. I don't touch the stuff."

I blinked hard, and Ortiz smiled.

"Don't be so surprised. Drug free, brotha. I'll sell the shit all day, but partake, never. Only thing I need is a good reposado."

Fair enough. I could respect that, even admire it a bit. Not in Graham, but in Ortiz? Definitely. I emptied all the Ambien into my cup and swirled it with my pinky,

We raised our cups and toasted our success. I took a long drink. I was going to sleep well tonight. "An excellent vintage," I noted, pinky out.

Ortiz chortled.

Halfway through another gulp, Hallenbeck barged in the cabin.

"Toilet wine, gents?" he guessed, narrowing his eyes.

"Gatorade, sir," I said.

"Sure it is," he grunted, and shook his head. "Don't go too hard, we're leaving for the Patchwork base camp at 2 am."

Ortiz raised his eyebrows.

"How many crews, boss?" he asked, quick-thinking enough to ask the important question.

"All of us."

"It's that bad?" I asked.

"Doesn't get much worse. Be ready," Hallenbeck said, and left.

First, I pictured Ash River Mobile Estates – the chain-smoking granny, the old men in lawn chairs, the baggy-pantsed, chip-shouldered teens – my people. Then I imagined Graham alone on a precipice over roaring flames, and me kicking him in. I wasn't sure which was more motivating, but I dumped the rest of my cocktail in the toilet. I needed to be sharp tomorrow.

CHAPTER NINETEEN

Choked with haze from two Patchwork fronts in the surrounding mountains, Ash River was officially under threat. In the mobile park, some trailers had trucks hooked up. In the nicer part of town, some homes were covered in pink fire retardant. Everywhere, cars were still in the driveway.

ICS had announced volunteer evacuation status only for the area, and no one wanted to leave.

We arrived at 3:30 am. Me and Ortiz got the band back together, claiming a tent at base camp and hiding the pro yellow turnout gear beneath it. We needed to bunk together out here so we could scheme, and soon, enact that scheme. Hallenbeck raced us through a meal and jammed us into an engine.

Echoing from the sheer walls of the mesa, I heard wind chimes clanging out a breathless tempo, tangled and tuneless from high winds. It was that wind and the cinders it drove that had Hallenbeck pushing us so fast. The engine cut through town and across a bridge over the dusty Ash River ravine. The guardrail was plastered with handmade signs that I couldn't see in the dark, until the headlights caught one.

'Thank you, firefighters, for protecting our community!'

Of course, they only meant the yellow-suiters, not us inmates. Our asses were on the line, too. Our sweat keeping the homes from burning down. Not that me and Ortiz were here in good faith. But still.

A fifteen-minute drive and ten-minute hike later, we arrived at the ground level of a strip mine. Four terraces in the shape of a giant C, carved into what used to be hills, carpeted with equal parts vegetation and duff. Fences blocked off the crumbling joints of the C shape, where crevices cracked open into pitch-black pits.

'Tapo Mine Reclamation Area'

With the lights of Ash River in the distance, I had a good idea why we were here. And as I looked at the nooks and crannies of the former strip mine, I had some other ideas.

We unloaded and tooled out. I whispered to Ortiz, "good place for an accident."

The Reclamation Reversal Task Force. It sounded like a military special operations unit, which Ortiz thought was awesome. I was less psyched.

Muscles aching, soaked with sweat, I stood with him, Damarius, and the rest of La Cuenca Crew 9 on the bottom terrace as the sun reached the top of the sky. Noon. Our 'day' was almost over. We had started the shift with a CalFire crew, an NPS Ranger, an EPA rep, and the drone-flying researchers who directed us to this spot. It was 110 degrees out at a bone dry 16-percent relative humidity, and only us and the CalFire crew remained.

A crane lifted the last timber from our zone into the cargo truck bed, and Hallenbeck whistled.

"Nice work, gents. That's a wrap. Now let's bag every last bit of duff and clear out."

We weren't a special ops unit. We were peasants doing manual labor.

We'd scraped a 200-square-yard area of grass, bushes, rotting trunks and dead needles down to bare rock. Revealing granite streaked with limestone – the scar that surrounding towns had spent years vegetating. A fast-moving arm of the Patchwork was a few miles in front of the scar, and behind it was Ash River – I could see the orange thimble of the mesa on the horizon. The town *seemed* far, but I now knew how fast these fires could run. Returning the scar to its ugly origins would create a massive fuel break if the Patchwork came this way. When we were finished, this would be Ash River's shield.

That *was* pretty cool. I thought of the flare up that had trapped me and Kamilah and stood taller.

Hallenbeck led us down to the flat ground level of the former mine.

A middle-aged woman stood next to the open flatbed of a civilian truck. She had milk crates full of apples, oranges, and a ten-gallon Gatorade cooler waiting in the bed. The woman smiled and waved at the crews. The CalFire team reached her first.

"Thank you for your service," she said to them, handing out cups of lemonade and telling them to help themselves to the fruit.

"You too!" the woman said, opening her arms to all of us in orange.

Huh.

I looked her and her truck up and down. Expensive Patagonia boots, muddy and worn. Newer Ford, dusty and dented. I couldn't tell if she was well-off or a regular Jane.

Guess it doesn't matter. Her smile was warm and her eyes soft.

"Thanks," I said, taking a lemonade.

"Thank *you*, sweetie," she replied, and squeezed my arm.

Sweetie. Weird. I was obviously an inmate – it said so on my pants – and here she was treating me like a human being. I suddenly had a lump in my throat, and all I could do was smile back.

I sipped the lemonade. Tart and sweet and the most goddamn refreshing thing that had ever hit my lips. Until I bit into an apple – *holy shit* – and wolfed down the whole thing in five bites. I downed the rest of the lemonade in one gulp.

I was so busy savoring the sweetness I hadn't noticed Ortiz step away. Returning, he sidled up to me and whispered, "Graham's crew is on a new Patchwork line. Most crews are. Fire complex keeps sprouting new patches outside the containment lines."

The flavors in my mouth soured.

You're not here to play hero and eat num-nums, I reminded myself.

"We gotta find a way to get him off that assignment and over here, before he gets backup," I said.

W e got time, bro," Ortiz argued on the ride back. The timber next to us in the truck bed shifted, making the straps securing it go taut. "It's gonna be a minute before he can get backup again, if he can at all."

He was right. Graham had connections, but loyal enforcers couldn't exactly be Amazon Primed onto an inmate crew.

Our truck pulled into Ash River from a side road, taking us through a rustic neighborhood of wood cabins and yawning pines. Ortiz hung over the lip of the truck, taking in the sights and smells, loving it. To me, the neighborhood was a pile of life-size Lincoln Logs ready to be lit on fire. The Patchwork's smoke haze was inescapable, setting the entire sky ablaze in a day-long sunset.

"I was a city kid. Never got to do this kind of stuff," he said.

"This isn't, like, a retreat. We're the governor's grunts," I pointed out.

"Doesn't mean we can't enjoy it. Stop and smell the roses, bro."

A vibration from my inside pocket – my phone. Only Ortiz and his people had this number. And one other person.

Back at base camp, I let Ortiz get chow alone so I could check my phone in privacy. I had a text:

'I need to see you. – Kamilah'

My pulse quickened. Had she finally come around? Gave into what we felt after the burnover?

I typed four different messages until I decided on:

'Okay. Today? Working near Ash River.'

'Let's meet at a water tower near Moorpark. About halfway between us. 3 pm?'

It was a two-hour drive. Our next count was in six hours. It'd be damn close, but I texted yes. I needed to see her, too.

Filled with restless, buoyant energy, I went to look at the shift schedule.

There was an opportunity. CalFire Lt. Suzuki, who had worked with us this morning, was on the same shift schedule. He rested when we rested, and from eavesdropping I knew he didn't have a wife or girlfriend, so no one to go visiting during his off time. What Suzuki did have was a CalFire pickup truck parked outside his cabin.

I raced to the field kitchen, hoping to catch Suzuki loading up on food. I still had some Ambien on hand, and I needed to be sure he stayed in his cabin.

Suzuki was clearing his tray when I reached him, finished. I say him eye the hot beverage dispensers, and moseyed over there first, filling up on coffee. He walked up next to me, filled a cup with hot water, and put a decaf teabag in it.

"Sir? Can I ask your advice?" I stopped him before he could leave.

"Call me Jon. What's up?" he asked.

"Does someone like me have a shot doing this when my sentence is up? Professionally?"

Suzuki frowned and set down his drink.

Perfect.

"Every case is different, I think. Every person. It's a tough road even for people who…"

"Haven't done time?" I provided.

"Yeah. I did two years volunteer firefighting before I could get in with CalFire. So."

I channeled Ortiz and gestured up at the mountains, now dazzling in the morning light.

"It's just… I mean, look. A job where you get to be surrounded by this?"

Suzuki smiled and took in the Ash River backdrop. I slipped a crushed Ambien in his tea and gave it a stir with my finger before his gaze returned down.

"It's not impossible, I'll tell you that," Suzuki said. "Just keep your head down and take things a day at a time."

"Thanks, sir. I mean, Jon," I said, projecting humble gratitude.

"Sure thing," he said, taking his tea.

As he walked away, he took a sip, frowned, and sipped again. He shook his head and kept drinking.

Back in our tent-cabin, Ortiz was falling asleep. He grunted and glanced up at my entrance before slumping back against the pillow.

I needed a change of clothes. I put on jeans and a t-shirt for my rendezvous with Kamilah, then the pro turnout gear over it so I could move freely in and out of camp.

Groggy, Ortiz sat up.

"What are you doing?"

"If anyone asks, I'm taking a shit," I said.

"*Are* you taking a shit?"

"I'll be back before our next count. Just cover for me." It was 1 pm, and count was at 7. I needed to be back by sunset, 6 pm, to be safe.

"Motherfucker, you gotta sleep sometime," Ortiz muttered.

You're the one who said to stop and smell the roses.

S neaking out of the fenced-in inmate area was the easy part. Breaking into Suzuki's trailer was the hard part. He was passed out from the Ambien, but I had to pick the lock in broad daylight without attracting attention. Then it took forever to find his keys.

But I did, and now I was burning down the highway, minutes away from seeing Kamilah.

The lie to Suzuki about career advice had knocked something loose.

I saw myself at a professional tattoo parlor, inking a Maltese cross on Kamilah's shoulder as she watched with fascination. After a long day on the line, she smelled like the woods and was still wearing her fire pants. She was tough and didn't flinch as I tattooed her, her russet, green-flecked eyes flicking between me and the buzzing gun. '*Gotta keep the canvas steady,*' I told her, and held her hand. I cracked jokes and she laughed.

What am I, a lovestruck schoolgirl? I couldn't remember the last time I fantasized like this. Caleb had warned me not to get hung up on the first woman I met when my sentence was up. This wasn't like that. Not because I was still serving my sentence, but because I'd encountered plenty of women since he died. The sweet and surprisingly strong Filipino nurse. She was cute. And there were all the other female nurses from my recovery, and a handful of Joe's physical therapy assistants had been hot girls. There was the demanding Dr. Chu. The pretty EMT who'd examined me after the burnover. But none of them had made my insides do backflips.

Kamilah had set her mind to telling her bosses that getting trapped by the fire was her fault – she was honest. I wasn't used to that, but I respected it. Respected her for standing her ground. She was tough and driven. In ways that reminded me of Caleb – *and yeah, that's weird.*

Weirder still, this was the first time I had thought about anything that might happen after the mission since the day I took it up.

If I could be with Kamilah…

How would that even work?

I could confess to being an inmate. I could explain it all – selectively. Nothing about Graham or Caleb. I'd say that I'd let her believe I was Pete McLean because I liked her. That much was true. Why had I been wearing the pro yellow uniform in the first place? Because my inmate orange was compromised by the flare-up of a prescribed burn. That was plausible.

I could beg her for forgiveness, and maybe she could give it. If women fall in love with serial killers on death row, why couldn't she fall for me? I was a far cry from that breed.

The navigation app blinked the destination pinpoint but had given up providing directions miles back. I turned onto a dirt road toward the pinpoint and accelerated up a steep hill, pine trees looming on both sides of me. The brown-gray haze of smoke rising from the Patchwork was thick in the rearview mirror. The higher up I got, the more the view of the fire widened out behind me.

The road took me to the top of the hill, where a modern-looking water tower stood over an open-water tank that looked a lot like an above ground pool. This was something new – a filling station for water bombers. The tank was lit by a ring of lights, making it look like a UFO.

At the foot of it, Kamilah stood waiting next to a Yamaha sport bike. She'd suped it up with an aftermarket exhaust system and installed a racing-style velocity stack with a clean chrome ring that glinted in the sun. On the back fender, she'd mounted a studded black leather bib with a bright red Maltese cross patch stitched in the center. *She rides* and *she tinkers.* I imagined the two of us burning rubber, popping wheelies, weaving between cars stuck in traffic, neck and neck on the open road.

I parked and approached, trying to read the poker face she was projecting. My mouth was a desert and my mind flailed for something charming to say.

Start with not being an idiot, Mason.

It was a pretty damn remote meeting spot, and I made a show

of looking around. "You bring me here to kill me?" I joked.

She didn't smile.

The text – *I need to see you* – could be read good or bad, but on the drive over, I'd really got attached to the good way.

"Why didn't you make an incident report, and why can't I find a record of Pete McLean?" Kamilah asked.

She brought me here to call me out? I was so surprised that I had a delayed reaction to her classic interrogation blunder – asking two questions at once.

"You must not be looking hard enough."

"My brother is a cop. If there was a record, he'd find it," she said.

Shit. Was that a bluff about the brother? I doubted it. She was honest.

No way I was going to tell her I was an inmate now. I racked my brain for a lie to cover the lack of a report and records and stalled by venting my genuine anger.

"And here I thought we were gonna hang out. What's it to you?"

"Three segments of the Patchwork were deliberately set."

"You think I'm a fucking arsonist? I almost died trying to help you. You stopped breathing and I revived you. Would an arsonist do any of that?"

Kamilah's nose wrinkled, and she looked down. That had reached her. Kamilah shook her head almost imperceptibly.

I wanted to keep yelling, make her understand how shitty of an assumption that was. She couldn't be serious. *Arson?!*

I needed to keep cool. The best thing to do in these situations was to avoid lying and let the mark supply you with your own cover story. I knew now why she'd wanted to meet me here. The view of the fire – the arsonist's creation.

"I don't know what to think," Kamilah said, biting her lip.

That was a start. Doubt was the wedge, and time and her imagination would hammer her certainty apart. I acted very wounded and waited.

She was supposed to backpedal. Start questioning herself. Come up with stories that explained my behavior, so I wouldn't have to. But she didn't. Had her pig brother trained her?

Kamilah's jaw tightened and her poker face was back on. She stared at me, waiting for an explanation.

Fuck this. Being wounded was no longer an act.

"I'm done with this," I said, and now I *had to* leave her with a lie. Always best to keep it simple. "I submitted my report yesterday, so maybe it hasn't hit the system. And I don't know why you can't find a record of me. Honestly. Blame the bureaucracy, but don't blame me."

I got into my truck and drove away.

CHAPTER TWENTY

Instead of a booty call, I'd got an inquisition. Was I a complete dumb fuck, or had she led me on? I gunned it past some grannie and looked at the text.

'I need to see you'

Not 'want', no 'hey' with extra y's, no use of my – Pete's – name. And no emojis. The kind of stuff you see when a girl's into you. *Why was I making excuses for her?* She knew I liked her and she dragged me to a water tower in the middle of nowhere. Talk about entrapment.

She fucking led me on.

BEEP!

A rusty pickup, headed straight for me – I was in the wrong

lane.

I swerved back into my lane, slamming on the brakes, jerking to a stop mid-doughnut. On the other side, two rednecks in wife-beaters jumped out of their pickup, which had done a full 180 and spilled shingles and a toolbox out onto the shoulder.

The shorter of the two grabbed a shotgun from his truck.

"You stupid motherfucker!" he shouted, coming over.

"Easy…" I said, putting my hands up.

His eyes landed on the side of my truck, and he stopped. Put the shotty back in his truck.

Like an idiot, I looked at the side of my truck. The *CalFire* logo.

Oh yeah. I was a fireman.

"Just be fucking careful, okay?" he said, and nodded at his buddy. They tossed the shingles and toolbox back in the truck bed and got back on the road.

"You *are* a stupid motherfucker," I told myself, getting back in the truck.

The pinpoint of Ash River Mobile Estates glowed on my phone's navigation – I had routed myself on backroads through hills and valleys of yellow grass, withered trees, and indifferent chaparral. Flash fuel.

Running down the fire environment helped keep my amped nerves steady, not to mention the shit with Kamilah. I could see why firefighters did it.

After an hour and a half of rage-driving, I was 10 minutes from base camp. It was only 4:45 pm. Plenty of time to return Suzuki's truck and sneak back to the inmate tents before the 6 pm sunset and 7 pm count.

"Channel, Dispatch," the radio was going off. "Brush fire reported at Eagle View campsite. Any crew in the area, please respond."

Fuck that. I had to get back to my own camp and crew.

"Channel, that is Eagle View campground in Oak Canyon Park."

Oak Canyon Park. That had shown up on the navigation app on the drive here. It was only a few miles away.

"Engine 30 has been dispatched but is over 40 minutes away," the radio said.

"Son of a bitch." I said.

I'm not who I told her I was. But I am not a fucking arsonist.

I set the phone destination to Oak Canyon Park and put the pedal to the floor.

Minutes later, I was barreling past an empty park entrance station as a frantic young couple in a dusty SUV shot out of the park.

I looked to the sky and followed the wispy gray-white smoke to the campsite. That was a good sign. The fire was still young.

The campsite was a bushy, boulder-strewn area surrounded by conifers. It sat close to the foot of a castle-like rock formation rising from the forest and had a brick bathroom. It'd be picturesque if not for the end-zone-sized patch of bushes and trees burning next to a smoldering fire pit.

Two cars, three people. A pink-haired woman, a woman with thick-rimmed glasses, a man-child in skinny jeans with a handlebar mustache. Hipster types. Glasses Chick was trying to get a signal on her phone, Skinny Jeans was wide-eyed and useless, and Pink Hair was frantic, pacing. They were all a safe distance away.

"This everyone?" I asked.

"No! My son's out there," Pink Hair said, "My husband went after him."

Not good.

"Okay," I said, "anyone else?"

"That's everyone here," Glasses Chick said, "There was a couple that just drove off. I think it was their fault."

I'd seen them. Nothing to be done about that right now. And nothing I could do for the dad and kid out in the woods. My priority was the fire.

'Know what your fire is doing at all times!' The words from training burned in my head like a marquee sign. The fire burned roughly parallel to the road, its heel at the campsite, its head crackling into the green of the forest. The forest spilled out over the ridges and hills I'd just driven through, becoming scrubby chaparral. Light fuel that burned quick.

If the fire wasn't contained, I knew exactly where it would go. It would tear across that dry yellow grass and hit Ash River trailer park. Not rich assholes in mountaintop mansions. My people.

And I was the only one here.

"Troy! Jace!" Mama Pink Hair yelled, but there was no reply from her son or husband.

"What do we do?" Skinny Jeans asked.

Damn good question, I thought.

Dig a line. Contain the flanks. Use natural firebreaks. The rest of my training began kicking in. I went to the truck and suited up in my disguise – yellow fire pants and jacket, boots, helmet, and gloves. The only other gear Suzuki had in there was a dirty hose, an oxygen mask, and a single shovel. I grabbed the shovel and got to work.

"Stay clear, be ready to get out of here," I said, finally answering them. They should probably all get out of here.

"Troy! Jace!" Mama Pink Hair shouted, moving into the forest.

"Stay out of the green, lady!" I snapped.

She turned to me, her face streaked with tears, and I hated myself for shouting at her.

"It's gonna be okay. I'm sure they're fine," I said. "But you can't go further in. Just trust me."

I stopped myself from explaining why. No escape route in case of a flare up.

Yeah, they *should* get out of here, but Pink Hair couldn't be dragged away, and for the moment, they were safe.

Shunk. I started scooping out duff and scraping the beginnings of a line on the left flank of the fire.

Skinny Jeans snapped off a cooler lid and started scraping the forest floor next to me.

"What are you doing?"

"Helping?"

I nodded and pointed to the road, which was along the right flank of the fire.

"The road's one firebreak. We're making one on this side of the fire, try to keep it spreading into the forest. Chop and dig. We're gonna make a line clear of anything that burns."

"Got it," Skinny Jeans said.

Maybe not a man-child after all.

Glasses Chick grabbed a cookware pot and joined us.

"Spread out a bit," I told them, "If you find a hot spot, smother it."

It wouldn't be enough, I knew. The fire was burning faster than we could work. We needed the fire engine and its crew to attack the head, but they were at least 30 minutes out.

Someone else was closer.

"Fuck."

I took out my phone, opened it to that fucking thread, and tapped speech-to-text.

"Brush fire. Eagle View campsite. Need you."

I hadn't meant to throw that phrase back at her. I dropped a pin for our location and got back to shoveling.

Eight long minutes later, she jumped off her Yamaha and came running.

"Shit. I don't have my scanner on the bike," Kamilah explained.

I gave the bike a once over. None of her fire gear either. I tore off my fire jacket and threw it to her.

"Doesn't matter. What do we do?" I asked, voice low.

"You're off to a good start. But it's not enough," she said.

"No shit. Ideas?"

Kamilah looked around.

Before she could answer, a bearded man dirty with soot came crashing out of the forest. He was coughing and wore singed yoga pants – I could smell the melted polyester.

"Where's Troy?!" Mama Pink Hair screamed. "Where's our son?"

The bearded man was alone.

"I don't know! I don't know! I couldn't find him!"

The parents looked at me and Kamilah, and we looked at each other.

I went to the truck, found an oxygen mask behind the front seat.

"No," Kamilah said, following me. "There's –"

"No escape route if it flares up. I know." I had fire pants and boots and training – only two weeks of it – but I was here. As firefighter Pete McLean, not as inmate Mason Jones. And the mom and dad were looking at me – and so was Kamilah. *Pete McLean lives for this shit. Pete McLean is a hero.*

"How will you even find him?" Kamilah demanded.

"By getting on those rocks."

"I tried that," the Bearded Dad said. "Fire's in the way, almost burned off my legs trying to get up there."

"I'm not wearing yoga pants," I said, focusing on Kamilah. I gave her the oxygen mask and motioned at the fire, "You're better at this. And after what happened, you need to protect your airway. There, covered everything."

"Fine," Kamilah said, and snatched the shovel from me.

"It's Troy, right?" I asked the parents.

"Yeah! Please find him!" Mama Pink Hair said.

I went off into the thicket, glancing back. Kamilah marched to the campsite bathroom.

"It's not working. There's no running water," Glasses said.

"Let me look," I heard Kamilah say, then lost their voices to the sound of my feet crunching vegetation, and the rising throb of flames.

Quickly reaching the castle-rocks, I came to a skirt of waist-high flames encircling the base, a moat of fire.

"Troy!"

No answer.

The rock formation was two-stories high in places and covered an area the size of a football field. Plus, the fire. A lot more intimidating than it looked from the campsite. Maybe climbing up there to spot the kid really was a bad idea, but I didn't have any others.

I ran around the rocks, wincing at the cracks of dry and dead vegetation underfoot – so ready to burn. The fire moat was unbroken.

That's what fire pants are for, right?

I ran through the moat, flames snapping my elbows and toasting my bare arms. I threw myself on the rock face, the baking heat seeping through the gloves. Slipped and slid – damn hard rock climbing with work gloves on, but it was that or burn my hands off.

On the lip of the cliff, my right hand spasmed.

But I held on, hissing, jammed my legs into a crevice, and pushed myself atop the rock. It was one of many, and from here it didn't look like a castle, but like a game of dice left behind by giants.

"Troy!" I shouted. No reply, but I heard Mama Pink Hair call out from the campground, desperate for good news. I kept moving, hopping from rock to rock. My right hand was numb and wouldn't unclench.

Deal with it later.

"Troy!" I shouted again.

"Dad?" I heard a voice croak and scrambled to it.

"Your dad sent me, buddy," I told him.

The boy sat in a five-foot deep crevice, hugging his knees, tear tracks on his face. The crevice was the result of two house-sized rocks mashed against each other, like massive cleavage, but instead of a bra, the open side was hemmed in by the tops of burning pines. Like flaming teeth. The walls of the crevice were sheer and gravelly to the touch. Troy was stuck. If I went down to him there was no guarantee I'd be able to climb out again.

I remembered falling into the ravine next to Kamilah. *Poor kid.* He looked about seven, and he was in shock.

The burning pines at the opening dropped cinders and ash into the crevice, which was lined with pine needles and bird shit. At the edge, the lining was already smoking. Even if it didn't flame up, soon enough the smoke would get him.

No time to wait for Search and Rescue.

I got on my belly and reached down – Jesus Christ, it hurt. I could extend my right arm, but the fingers were stuck clenched. *Jesus Christ.*

"Can you reach me?"

Troy stood and reached up, hands shaking – all his fingertips were bleeding, as if from road rash. He'd tried to climb out and slid down the rock face, skinning them. *Damn.*

With my fully working left arm, the best I could do was brush his blood-slick fingertips.

"Okay, easy on the hands," I said, ready to try something else, "use your legs to run up the wall. Can you do that? I'll grab you."

Troy shook his head, too scared to try. It was climbing with a different name.

Two injured-ass motherfuckers stuck in rocks surrounded by fire.

I need rope.

I didn't have it, so I took off my shirt and twisted it into a loop.

"Turn around, arms through the loop…" he did… "now over, elbows out, there you go."

And I pulled –

Must've been the pain, because I blanked out the entire moment and the next thing I knew I was gasping on my back, the boy next to me atop the rock.

Troy clung to the t-shirt, still afraid.

"Here." I tore it in two and wrapped his fingers. It seemed to help.

"Let's go."

I went to the edge of the rock formation and spotted an area at the base that had burned out. Fuel that lights quick burns out quick. But the rock face to it was steep, with a gap at the bottom.

I went first, pointing out the hand and footholds as I went. I jumped to the ground at the last bit. Troy paused at the edge, and I held out my arms, ready to catch him.

"I got you," I said.

"I can do it," Troy said, and he did.

"Awesome."

He took my hand – my right – as we walked back to the campground. I put up with the pain. He needed something to hold onto.

Mama Pink Hair and the Bearded Dad sprinted over when we came in sight, almost tackling Troy with a double hug. The mom burst into happy tears.

"Sweetie!"

"Are you okay?!"

"His fingers are scraped, need to get cleaned up," I said.

"It hurts, but I'm okay," Troy said.

"You're a champ," I said.

"Thank you!" Mama Pink Hair looked up at me, never letting go of her son. The father stood up, eyes red and watery, extending his hand.

"I can't thank you enough," he said.

I shook his hand, at a loss for words. It wasn't that *I* brought Troy back, it was that *the kid was back*, and the family was, once again, whole. And seeing them, in that happy wholeness, together… The reunion of a few strangers, flipping me upside down like a rogue wave. *Am I going soft?*

"Sure, sure," I eventually croaked, my throat thick.

The parents went back to embracing their son. Mama Pink Hair knelt at his side, checked his fingers, Beardo stroked his son's hair.

I backed away to give them space, with a fullness in my chest that made my eyes watery. It was unlike anything I'd ever felt before, uplifting, but humbling. Like I was a witness to something essential.

Sirens echoed, making me flinch and return to reality.

I reminded myself that I was one of the good guys – for the moment – and that was salvation coming. A fire engine, not far away.

I sat down hard, heaving. Focusing on my breathing to stave off the insanity of pain at the gates. Scoped out the fire. That would help.

The hose from my truck now snaked from the campground bathroom, through freshly shattered pieces of a toilet, delving down through the floor.

Kamilah held the other end, methodically knocking down the flames. They were low and *contained*. Under her supervision, the hipsters had completed the flank line, stopping it on the far side, while she doused the front.

She was incredible.

The fire engine pulled up and Kamilah directed the arriving crew.

A paramedic came to Troy and his parents, ushered him to the truck to take care of his fingers. Troy followed, then stopped.

He ran back and hugged me. "Thanks."

My heart swelled.

I remembered the moat of flames around the rocks, and with a lurch of my stomach, pictured Ash River Mobile Estates. This wasn't done yet.

I needed a distraction from the pain anyway. "Around the rocks, too. Bushes, pines," I told a crew member, and he followed me to the fire crackling around the rocks. The sun set behind the rock formation, and pink-orange beams burst through its crags, catching on the steam and haze of the campground.

I started shoveling, making a new line, and found a rhythm that kept the pain at bay.

A hand on my shoulder – skin on skin. I knew it was her.

"Hey," Kamilah said, pulling the oxygen mask from her face. "You need a break."

I turned carefully, slow, not wanting her to pull her hand away. She didn't.

Kamilah's fingers traced my scars.

Her touch… a soothing tingle that made everything else fade away.

"These aren't from fighting fires," she said, tilting her head. Her eyes enveloped me, bright and unblinking.

"No. They're not."

I remembered I was mad at her. It was hard to be, her eyes on me like that.

"I'm sorry," Kamilah said, "I've been going a little crazy."

"Almost dying can really do a number on you," I teased, hoping to make her smile. "And as I recall, you prefer 'highly motivated.'"

"You remember." Her lips twitched, an almost-smile. She put on a show of cross-examining me, her forehead creasing, but I knew it was a show because her voice lowered, soft and husky as she said, "Seems like you're 'highly motivated' too. Most liaison officers wouldn't repel down a cliff to scout a fire. Or come here to do this."

She likes a man of action. The warmth and energy surged through me again, same as it had when our eyes met after the burnover. Unblinking, Kamilah brushed her hair back. I think she felt it, too. *And now that she doesn't think I'm an arsonist, maybe I have a chance.*

"Can you forgive me?" she asked.

Her hair was wild and perfect, highlighted by the sunset, framing those mesmerizing russet eyes with flecks of green.

"God, you're beautiful."

"It's the lighting," Kamilah said, that shy smile making an incredible return.

Throwing caution to the wind, I kissed her.

Caught off guard, her lips held firm for a second. Then she melted against me. I fell headfirst into the electrifying sensations and lost all concept of time.

CHAPTER TWENTY-ONE

When our lips parted, Kamilah took a hit of the oxygen. "So that kiss was either really good or really bad," I surmised.

"It was good," she laughed, "and thanks for letting me use this. It's a bigger gesture than you know."

"Oh yeah?"

We drifted away from the commotion of the campsite.

"Yeah. They sidelined me. Smoke inhalation from the burnover and all. Meds and rest, can't be on the fireline for a month."

"And you still came here?"

Kamilah shrugged.

I'd agonized over coming here, but I bet she hadn't given it a second thought, even with the risk to her lungs. *Snap, charge.* Just like Caleb.

"I didn't leave grad school to sit on the sidelines," she said, shaking her head. "I used to be an *academic*. I was at the Fire Weather Research Lab at SJSU."

She said it like I should know the place and be duly impressed. Instead, I channeled Caleb and took the opportunity to tease her. "Okay, nerd."

"Oh yeah. Big nerd," Kamilah chuckled. "Don't get me wrong, the work was important. We can't do anything that matters without facts. But I got sick of studying wildfire dynamics while people's homes burned down." She kicked a pinecone farther into the forest. "Anyway, that's why I've been going crazy," she explained with a sigh. "If I can't fight the fire, I'm going to catch the guy starting them."

"So *that's* your deal." As we drifted deeper into the woods, the steam drifted with us. It caught rays of fading daylight and wreathed the trees in a rosy glow.

"Yup. And you? What's your deal?" she asked.

The way Kamilah's eyes pierced me, I knew she wanted me to open up. To tell her what made me tick. What if she could understand? *I'm not an arsonist, I'm a man avenging his brother.* She had a brother, too, and she was a snap-charger who didn't stay on the sidelines. Wouldn't she do the same?

"What do you mean?" I replied, playing dumb.

Maybe she wouldn't. That brother of hers was a cop, and she was honest. She might not be a big fan of revenge.

"I know you're a good kisser, and probably not an arsonist. Other than that, not much," Kamilah said. Her forehead creased, cross-examining me again, and this time it wasn't a show.

My chest ached. I wished I could let her see me for who I was, but it was too risky. "Think I'll keep it that way," I said, pasting on what I hoped was a roguish smile. "Women love mysterious men, right?"

"Not this woman," she smirked right back at me.

"So needy."

"Ass!" Kamilah jabbed me playfully, her elbow leaving a burst of white on the pink scar under my ribcage. "Sorry!"

I waved off her apology, and while her gaze lingered on my scars, she said nothing. She wanted to know how they got there, what *'my deal'* was, but she respected me enough to let it be. It'd be shitty to leave her hanging. She'd told me why *she* was going crazy. *I can't tell her why I'm really on the fireline, but I'm not going to lie to her.*

"After the burnover… when I said that was my first time almost dying? That wasn't true. I was stabbed… and I almost didn't make it." The ache in my chest eased; it was liberating to share even this small piece. "I'm sorry I lied."

"You don't owe me an apology. We'd just met, and… that's major trauma. I'm sorry you went through that." Kamilah squeezed my hand.

She was quite a woman. "Thanks," I said. "It's the reason I'm doing this." It was the truth, or at least the shadow of it.

Kamilah nodded in understanding, and muscles I hadn't noticed tensing relaxed. *I shouldn't have told her any of that.* And yet her simple nod sent a wave of comfort washing over me.

"Nice work everyone, ninety percent containment," the engine's captain shouted, his voice muffled by distance. One of his crew was patrolling for embers almost a hundred yards away. Kamilah noticed it, too, raising her eyebrows. We'd wandered damn far away.

I checked the time: 6:13 pm. A jolt of panic zipped into my gut. Count was in less than an hour.

"I should get going. Need to get some sleep before my next shift," I said.

"I'll handle this," Kamilah said, pointing to the fire engine and crew, "because if you're the reporting officer the paperwork won't be seen for weeks."

"Thanks."

Kamilah smiled and said, "This was…"

"Yeah. It was," I laughed. "Should I call you or something?"

"You should definitely give it a shot."

I couldn't contain the electricity coursing through me. Weightless, I floated to the truck, and the road embraced me as I sped back to camp.

My phone buzzed with a text from Kamilah.

'Drive safe. I dig your scars, but I think you have enough. ;)'

I crowed in triumph, warmth spreading from my core.

P ale blue twilight on one horizon, the Patchwork's yellow-orange glow silhouetting black ranges on the other. Ash River, and our base camp beside it, was caught between two worlds. A guard waved me through the rear entrance to camp, and I stopped the truck in the gravel a stone's throw from Suzuki's trailer.

He stood outside it, wobbly and confused, flanked by a C.O. and a Sherriff's deputy. They were investigating why his truck was gone.

I checked the time – **6:57.**

The weightlessness I'd felt on the drive back disappeared. Instead, the twilight sky wrapped around me like a python, trying to squeeze me into nothingness.

'Delay the count' I texted Ortiz.

'You motherfucker' he texted back.

'Just need 5 minutes.'

I pulled off onto the porta-potty path and parked behind a row of them. I wiped down the wheel, signals, dash – everything my hands had touched, including the keys, which I threw into the bushes. Hopefully no one at the campground fire had taken note of the license plate.

I made my way back to the inmate section of camp in Pete Mclean's uniform. I had to get over a fence into the CDCR section to get my inmate orange without being seen, and I had to hope Ortiz had delayed the count.

It was 7:04.

A C.O. patrolled behind the fence. I hit the deck before he could see my yellow helmet and jacket. Taking off the jacket, I turned it inside out and hid the helmet beneath the blue lining.

Keeping my eyes on the C.O., I army-crawled to the fence. His patrol took him within five yards of me, and then he turned around. He was a damn slow walker.

C'mon…

Finally, he was about 100 yards down the fence, and I vaulted over it, sending a maddening jolt of agony from my right hand. Then I walked calmly back to my tent. *Nothing to see here.*

7:09.

Dozens of inmates milled around the gathering area outside the tents, not lined up. That meant they were waiting for count, because if it had already happened, they'd be in their tents or at the field kitchen.

I ducked into my tent, where Ortiz waited with a glare.

"We've got maybe five minutes," he said. "Hid the count C.O.'s roster. Once he finds where he 'misplaced' the clipboard, he'll give a whistle and we'll do the count."

"Nice, dude. Thanks." I said.

"What the hell are you up to?" he asked, tucking my inmate uniform under his arm.

A fair question. What the hell was *I doing?*

"You want someone to walk in here with me like this? Gimme my stuff."

"Not until you tell me what you've been doing," Ortiz said.

"Covering Pete McLean's tracks from the Patchwork."

Ortiz knew I'd got trapped in a burnover with a female firefighter, but that was it. It wasn't just that going to see her was stupid, it was that I wanted to keep me and Kamilah's thing, whatever it was, safe.

"Good," Ortiz said, and gave me my stuff.

He'd hit the roof if he knew I'd given her the number to my

contraband phone.

My stomach churned at lying to him again. I wasn't supposed to give a shit.

He's just a pawn, I told myself.

But that was just another lie.

CHAPTER TWENTY-TWO

I woke up but couldn't shake the sensations of a dream-turned-nightmare. Kamilah caressing my arm, her skin so soft. Caleb's corpse standing over me, dotted with a dozen bloodless wounds, his cold hands scrabbling at my face. Graham, grinning with a bloody shiv.

Where am I? My thoughts were a smudge.

I was on a sweat-soaked cot. In a tent with Ortiz. Patchwork Fire. Reality arrived like a muddy river, dumping layers of sludge in my mind.

My crew was deployed to the Patchwork Fire base camp outside Ash River, and we had completed our work on the Reclamation Reversal Task Force, scraping the mine scar bare. We had just finished a 24-hour shift.

"Time to work," Ortiz said, dragging out the syllables.

And, apparently, I burned through our 24-hour *off* shift. *How long was I asleep?*

"Sorry," I said, sliding out of the cot, slopping a puddle of sweat onto the tent floor.

Ortiz snatched my fire jacket before I could put it on, handing me a towel and a bottled water instead.

"You're soaked. Dry yourself off and drink."

I did what he said, mumbling thanks.

The kid, the kiss, sneaking back into camp – that had been three days ago. Seemed like months.

I shuffled out of the tent for some fresh air, but there was none. The ever-present haze and its burnt scent greeted me. It was early, no sun yet, but far from dark and quiet. Just outside the fence, firefighters drip-torched lines around the camp to create fuel breaks. Red and blue police lights flashed on every surface of the camp, and uniformed personnel were scrambling everywhere.

My gut twisted in paranoia, but a split-second later my still-booting brain processed what was happening. Across the road outside of camp, the people of Ash River Mobile Estates emptied their trailers and crammed in cars. CalFire vehicles were driving through, urging people to leave. Down the road, the same was happening in the nicer part of town.

Ash River was no longer safe.

This is what we're up against," Hallenbeck said. He gestured at the digital fire map on the screen. It showed four separate patches splattered between and around the urban areas of Santa Clarita, Simi Valley, and the San Fernando Valley. TVs, whiteboards, and maps filled the briefing tent. We sat around folding tables on bales of hay. The logistics people had run out of chairs.

The Patchwork spanned three counties – Ventura, Kern, and LA. The governor and the President had both declared states of emergency. The satellite perspective didn't capture the monstrosity of it all.

Sitting in the back, I didn't see the freckles and red-brown hair of the monster I was after.

"Where is Graham?" I whispered to Ortiz.

"In his tent, off-shift," he whispered back. "We have a four hour overlap between our 24-on and his."

My insides twisted in knots. First, I was relieved that I had 20 hours without the risk of a run-in, then furious with myself for being relieved.

Nut up, buttercup.

"We're on the southern line of the central patch today," Hallenbeck continued, "We'll get transpo to an anchor point and hike to the area where we'll be digging a new line. Remember your watch-out situations. Know what your fire is doing at all times. It could explode beyond the line at any moment."

"You mean someone could set off a new spot outside the line anytime," an NPS firefighter barked.

ICS had not publicly announced it, but it was all but certain that some of the new patches were the result of arson. If not all.

"I'm not ruling out anything. Everyone keep your eyes open," Hallenbeck said. "Communicate. If there's a hazard, speak up. Even if you're wearing orange. Last week, a CalFire H.E. operator and an inmate firefighter died in the northeast patch."

That's when they ramped up personnel commitments, only for a brand-new patch to open up 10 miles west from the center patch.

The natural bark in Hallenbeck's voice softened.

"Last night, 11 civilians in Tapo Canyon. Firestorm." He looked down and shuffled his charts.

Jesus. That couldn't be far from the Tapo Mine scar we'd turned into a fuel break. I hoped it did its job and shielded Ash River. Hallenbeck didn't mention how many "structures" – homes, more often than not – had been destroyed. Had to be up in the thousands by now.

Hallenbeck straightened and continued, "We gotta bust ass out there. The entire state is stretched thin and every minute counts. So far, we've kept it out major populace areas. That's the goal. It's smack up against Simi Valley and Santa Clarita and not far from the Valley. Hundreds of thousands of people in its path. Let's get out there."

We cut a new line 500 yards from the sweltering head of the central patch. God knows how many hours into the new line we were digging, Hallenbeck gave me permission to go off into the woods to take a whiz. The only thing I had going for me was that I was well hydrated. My right hand was a claw, I was exhausted, and I could barely see two feet in front of me because of the smoke.

I wove through the trees, found a wooded ravine, and let loose over the edge. The 20-yard yellow stream barraging the bushes below was the highlight of my morning.

Months of maneuvering and I had Graham isolated and I had access – my firefighter turnout gear. His crew was assigned to the same central patch, with a shift overlapping mine by four hours.

'Hundreds of thousands of people in its path.'

What had the people of California done for me? I didn't owe them shit. Caleb had bought a single-wide when Mom got us evicted, a block from school to keep me from dropping out. I owed him everything. I owed *him* Graham's head on a platter.

But what if taking down Graham hurt the fight against the Patchwork? His absence? Whatever else the snake was up to, he was a part of a crew, and at the campground Kamilah had shown me the difference once person could make. She kept a troubling blaze from becoming an unchecked inferno.

'What if we didn't have to do it?' Ortiz had wondered, a lifetime ago. The same spineless question sprang to mind now. *What if I don't have to do it?*

A slap in Caleb's face. A betrayal. I'd be dead if he hadn't used his last moments to pull the alarm. But to be Pete McLean, a hero that gets angry rednecks to put down guns, a guy that can kiss Kamilah…

I had to see her. It was an insane thought, but maybe she could help. She was a generous, fierce, and formidable woman. *I need to give Caleb the payback he deserves.* I could start over as Pete McLean. *Keep dreaming, dipshit.* I didn't have the resources to create those kind of bona fides. Could I let a man who ripped my brother to pieces just walk away? Unscathed, 'rehabilitated,' Graham was due back in the world before year's end.

I zipped up, shouldered my Pulaski axe, and began walking as slow as possible back to the line. I had to do it. *Right?*

That kiss, though. *Holy shit.* Kissing had always felt like work. A means to an end. But that… a merging of lips and a current of intoxicating electricity that took me to another place.

A shadow flitted over me and something tightened on my neck, smacking me to the ground, pulling me down the ravine, through bushes, against a tree – *ow* – and I crashed to a stop in a dirt pit lined by logs.

Head spinning, I found a noose around my neck. On the other end of the rope, outside the pit, stood the man who'd led me into Sasquatch and Roach's trap. 'Sean.' In full turnout gear this time. A firefighter. I got pulled down a 20-yard embankment into a pit by a professional firefighter.

I tried to push myself up and my right arm collapsed beneath me.

"Surprised he gave you a do-over," I said, spitting dirt. He tugged on the noose in reply, but I managed to pull it off, blistering my face with rope-burn. I tottered to my feet as the firefighter swung a stick.

Crack! Knocked me straight back on my ass with a face full of splinters.

A burlap sack thumped on the ground next to me.

Shzzz… something sliding against the burlap, *fwip-fwip…* tiny forked tongues flicking… tan scales and blocky brown spots… yellow eyes with black vertical slits … a hollow rattle.

Three rattlesnakes slithered out of the sack. Between me and Sean and the way out of the pit. The one shaking his rattler wound towards me, head reared up. *Pissed.*

I was empty-handed. Dropped my axe on the way down.

The pit was all dirt and pebbles, no rocks.

I rolled – *snap* – the snake's teeth clamped into the ground where my shoulder had been.

The other two coiled, heads back, rattling a warning.

Sean prodded them with the stick. One turned toward him, but the other was flung right at me. I scrambled back, kicking as its fangs flashed –

Into my boot.

Panicking, I kicked against a log while its fangs were still buried in the boot, cracking its head.

The snake that struck first looped itself in a defensive coil, rattling.

I grabbed the dead snake by the tail – it twisted in my hands! – still alive. I fell back in shock, trying to shake it off my boot. It flopped. Not alive. Some kind of reflex.

This time I grabbed its head – disgusting – pried it out and took off the boot.

I threw the dead snake at the live one, tangling and confusing it, then slammed my boot on the scaly bastards, hammering down until nothing moved.

The firefighter's eyes were big as dinner plates looking at me, and there was still a snake between the both of us. In its defensive coil, it faced and rattled at him.

He dropped the stick and ran.

Oh hell no.

Checked my foot. No bite. The thick, fire-resistant boot had saved me. I put it back on and dashed out of the pit. Jumping over the snake, I snatched the stick and ran into the woods after the firefighter.

The dude could move.

Injured, exhausted, I'd never be able to catch him. Should've picked up the rope instead so I could lasso his ass.

I heaved the stick, going for the back of his knees – it raked his feet, sending him to the ground. Panting, I straddled and pinned him down.

"Please," he whined.

"Please, motherfucker?" I pounded him with my claw hand, thankful for the numbness.

Sean didn't resist, showing me open palms.

"You tried to kill me with rattlesnakes!" I shouted.

I picked up a nice, cabbage-sized rock.

"I had to. He forced me," the firefighter said. *Graham.*

I was a Roman candle, heat and gunpowder ready to explode, and I wanted nothing more than to end this pathetic hitman.

Nobody has to die except Graham.

No. I wasn't going to kill him. But he didn't need to know that.

"What's your real name, '*Sean*'?" I flourished the rock threateningly.

"That's my real name."

I feinted with the rock.

"Sean Wolfe," he said.

"You a real firefighter?"

"Yeah! Please…" Wolfe whined again.

I didn't have time to interrogate the snake-tossing bitch. Had to get back on the line before anyone noticed I was missing.

I slammed the rock on a kneecap and there was a wet crack.

Wolfe shouted in pain, eyes watering.

I knew the feeling. He had some surgery and physical therapy ahead of him for sure. The injury took him out of this fight.

I flipped him over and patted him down, just like the arresting officer had done to me so long ago. Leatherman multi tool, smokes, and a cell phone. Yanking his arm, I put his thumb against the phone, unlocking it. Wolfe didn't resist.

I took the phone and the Leatherman, leaving him the smokes.

"Enjoy your hike back," I said, and made my way up the hill back to the line.

CHAPTER TWENTY-THREE

Y ou careless motherfucker," Hallenbeck said, while a bald medic removed the splinters from my face. "Can't go one fire without medical attention."

Ortiz stood nearby, waiting, and the rest of the crew was still working the line.

"Guess I just have bad luck, Cap," I said. "Didn't lose any gear, though."

I held up my axe, which I'd retrieved from the embankment, and forced a cheery grin. Hoping boyish charm would prevent suspicion.

"Well, don't let it infect the rest of the crew. You can be our bad luck lightning rod," Hallenbeck said.

Inside, I was an inferno. Graham sent that bastard to pull me down a goddamn ravine and kill me with rattlesnakes. Too much of a coward to do it himself.

Rattlesnakes. Wish I'd thought of that.

Hallenbeck slapped me on the shoulder and went back to the line.

The medic furrowed his brows at me.

"Tripped and fell, huh?" he asked skeptically.

"That's right," I said.

"Because the splinters are horizontal-ish on your face. You somehow fall sideways and turn your face toward the ground?"

"You a medic or a forensic scientist? How about you just stitch me up."

I didn't have any boyish charm left.

The medic studied me, his eyes more suspicious than clinical. Like he knew I was hiding something.

I should probably be less of a dick.

"If you fell, I should check you for other injuries, internal and external."

"Just the face. I'm fine," I told him.

That would mean stripping down, and I didn't want to give this nosy shit a chance to find the Leatherman or contraband phone – now *phones,* plural – hidden in my layers of clothing.

The firefighter hadn't lied. The accounts on the phone ID-ed its owner as Sean Wolfe and the pictures on his *wolfe_it_down* Instagram account matched the man I'd left in the forest. Who'd tried to kill me twice for Graham. Sean Wolfe. Dammit if that name didn't sound familiar.

"Okay," the medic said. "If you experience any headaches, stroke symptoms, or bloody stools, tell someone. Could be internal bleeding."

He scrubbed my face roughly with astringent.

"No stitches. Neosporin," he ordered, giving me a small tube of the antibiotic and hopping into a white and red dune buggy.

"Thanks, sir," I said, remembering to act like an honor grad.

The medic *pffed* and drove away. Ortiz walked over, his face full of questions.

T he 10-foot minimum between hookline members gave me and Ortiz a chance to talk as we chopped bushes to pieces. Ortiz sighed too many times when I explained what had happened.

"Graham is on the ropes." I told him, bursting with fiery energy. *No more doubts and dilly-dallying.* "His backup on the fire crew are gone. He's so desperate he sent a civilian to kill me. Sean Wolfe won't say shit. He thinks his life depends on it." It wasn't exactly true, but I added, "Nobody's asking questions about Pete McLean."

Ortiz shook his head, and we axed branches in a silence that stretched for minutes.

"You're not the only one who's lost a brother, you know." Ortiz said. "I been in the game since I was thirteen. So have a lot of the dudes I grew up with. But not all of 'em got to actually, you know... grow up. Two of the dudes I got jumped in with, they got mercked. They were my brothers. Not in blood. But in every other way."

"I'm sorry, man."

"Yeah. It's shitty. I know how shitty it can be. And I'm sorry, too. For, for… your loss." Then he shrugged. "That's the game."

"You're saying Caleb deserved it." My face heated.

"Hold up, *no*. I'm saying maybe this isn't about your brother. It's about you."

"I'm alive because of him."

"Yeah, but weren't you in danger because of him, too?" He read my face and held up his hands defensively. "Hold up, hold up, I ain't shitting on the man. And you survived that, what happened at LAC, and everything since – you're welcome for that shit with the tree, by the way. Maybe don't push your luck."

My anger dipped, his doubts reminding me of my own. *Not doubts*. Distractions. Sean Wolfe's attack was a wake-up call. I'd been an idiot, distracting myself with Kamilah and Ash River. None of that mattered. Graham wouldn't let it go, and neither could I.

"You losing your nerve, buddy?" I teased. "We're supposed to psych each other *up* for the job, partner."

"This isn't your business partner talking. Just me. I'm *saying*, maybe Graham ain't worth it," Ortiz said gently.

Damn right he's worth it, I thought.

"Maybe," I said to Ortiz, hoping to convince him I wasn't as far gone as he thought. "Or maybe I keep surviving because I have to finish this. When I was in the hospital, I was about to call it quits. Until I decided to pay Graham back for what he did. That's what's kept me alive through all this. The mission."

Ortiz threw a stack of branches onto a pile and said nothing.

"We've come so damn far. I need you with me on this," I said, pleading.

"As long as this stays between us cons, I will be," Ortiz finally replied.

"C'mon man, chin up and shit. The end game starts tomorrow."
It wasn't just between us cons, though, and telling him '*Nobody's asking about Pete McLean*' was a lie. Kamilah had asked. I'd met up with her as Pete McLean and kept it from him. He wouldn't approve, rightly so. She was a distraction.

Forget her until this is done.

Ortiz chopped a branch and whisked it past my head. "You've got first watch tonight," Ortiz said, and pulled his breath mask up. The conversation was over.

I was a real piece of shit these days. *I'd rather be the man who saves the kid and feels that fullness in his chest.* Instead I was lying to Ortiz, conning Kamilah, fueled by rage. But I *had to* be this liar, con man, a weapon powered by rage.

This is who I have to be to give Caleb the vengeance he deserves.

CHAPTER TWENTY-FOUR

The Tapo Mine scar was ugly. I couldn't think of a better place for Graham to die.

Our task force had scraped off every bit of vegetation, returning the mine to its original eyesore condition. The angular terraces got lighter the farther down they went, from black and brown at the top to the dirty-white limestone at the bottom. Jaundice-yellow prefab buildings that looked to be from the 70s dotted the scar like mold, some connected to even older wooden mining sheds that looked to be from the days of the Wild West.

I, *Pete McLean*, stood on the top terrace, the only person around for miles. Ortiz and I had ID-ed this spot during our task force assignment. As soon as our shift ended tonight, I'd changed over to my yellow turnout gear and made my way here.

I shoveled away the dirt support of a guardrail post, leaving it loose in the ground. I'd already dug out the foundation around the post next to it, and I pushed on the horizontal plastic panel of the guardrail. It gave, pitching back toward the dark pit it guarded. With the weight of a man against it, the guardrail panel would give way completely, and Graham would drop 50 feet through a fissure in the terraces to a mess of sharp rocks below surface level.

Kick up the dirt around the posts and it would look like erosion. An inmate crashing through a poorly maintained safety barrier and falling to his death. That was step two, and all it took was a push from me.

Step one relied on deception, a greater challenge. I sawed through a chained-off fence with Wolfe's Leatherman and then through a combo lock to get into an ancient wood shack practically falling apart from rot. Inside was a generator and gas. I ripped the cord to get it started and went next door to a yellow aluminum prefab. I'd seen the drone researchers keeping cool inside it while we worked the scar.

I picked the lock, found the power cord, and dragged it to the generator. When I connected them, the lights of the prefab kicked on, casting the dusty interior in harsh fluorescence. It housed card tables and chairs, an empty fridge, and a raspy AC unit.

There was also a rubber-headed sledgehammer on the floor. I put it out of sight in the fridge. I taped a tent stake I'd borrowed from camp under a chair. Hidden weapons to give me an edge – it wouldn't be easy to take down the butcher.

Stepping outside the prefab, I took it all in. The light shone through a single window, the AC and motor of the generator combined into a sputtering throb. From outside, it looked occupied.

That's what I'd need Graham to believe.

I wore work gloves to keep my prints off it all, and I'd do the same when Graham joined me. After it was done, the gas can for the generator would tip over and meet a spark, a spark that would burn the shack and prefab to the ground, torching any forensic evidence that could connect me to it.

Step one. As Pete McLean, I'd get Graham to come to the Tapo Mine for a working party – additional cleanup at the scar. The lights and sounds here would give the lure of legitimacy, like people were at work in the prefab. I'd get the jump on him, tie him up, knock him out.

Step two. Untie him, push him through the guardrail into the fissure pit. It'd seem like he fell, and he wouldn't even be conscious when he hit bottom.

A merciful death. Far less painful than what he'd subjected Caleb to. I'd be lying to myself if I said I wasn't tempted to drench him with the gas and burn him alive. The thought of the pain was… satisfying.

But I'm not the monster.

Step three. Use that gas to burn this spot down. The scar was bare rock and there was no threat of it spreading.

If anybody even found Graham's body, the cops could waste years uncovering and then investigating Graham's shady background, missing the real story. Pete McLean would never be seen again.

I killed the generator and closed up. Ready.

Something brushed against my leg.

Startled, I bent down. It was a sickly juniper sapling in the shadow of the decrepit shack. Juniper needles smoked and sparked, so I uprooted it, chopped it up, and threw it into the pit.

I didn't want the juniper shooting off its cinders into the wind.

Crazy. I was going to kill a man here, but damned if I was going to be irresponsible about the fire that would cover it up.

"Mason Jones," a man's voice called out behind me.

I turned to see Kamilah and a black man with one hand resting on a hip-holstered pistol. Windbreaker, work boots, tall with a quiet confidence. Probably a cop. Kamilah glared daggers at me.

Mason Jones. They knew my real name. My pulse pounded in my ears.

Eyeing the piece, I put my hands up.

"Kamilah, please, can we talk? Alone?" I could fix this. I had to fix this.

"No. He's with me. It's all I can I do not to kick you in that pit right now."

As fucked as everything was, I was damn curious to know what she meant by *with.*

"Kamilah. Let me explain." Just not here. Not like this. I suppressed the urge to run to her. Or maybe it was his hand on the gun that did.

"I'd love to hear an explanation," the man said.

"I'm not talking to you," I muttered.

"Maybe you should," the man said, and showed me a badge. "Richard Martin, LA County Sheriff's Department."

The brother.

"Tell us what's going on," Kamilah demanded, nostrils flaring.

What did they know? What *could* they know?

They caught me posing as a professional firefighter and they knew my real name. Only two things for certain. In my previous life, this is where I'd say '*lawyer*' and keep my trap shut. But now, that would mean getting hauled in, and that would be the end of the mission. I needed a lie to keep me out of handcuffs long enough to finish this. What lie could possibly do that?

'*I'm an undercover FBI agent.*' '*I'm with the CIA.*' '*I can't say because it's a matter of national security.*' There was literally no plausible lie to keep me out of cuffs, not when they knew I was actually an inmate. I had to throw them some chum.

Keyser Söze this shit.

"It's a contraband hustle. I just do pickups, that's what the uniform is for," I sighed.

Implying there were bigger perps in this fake hustle and catching those perps could give them a reason to keep me in play. I just needed one day. 24 damn hours.

Richard looked skeptical.

"Anybody helping you out?"

Ortiz was in the tent miles away. No reason to think they knew about him.

"I'm the only boots on the ground. I don't trust *anybody*," I said. *Used to be true,* I thought. Ortiz had grown on me, the bastard. "Maybe you're more interested in who I'm working for," I added.

"You mean Grayson Graham?" Richard asked.

My mouth dried out instantly. Where the hell did that come from? Why did they think Graham was my boss in this fake hustle? I had to keep him out of this – Graham was mine.

"Who?" I asked, acting like I'd never heard of him.

"We know Grayson Graham ran the contraband hustle at LAC," Richard said.

Sasquatch and Roach, I realized. Must've snitched to reduce their charges.

"Pretty big coincidence," Richard continued, "You and Graham both at LAC and now both out here together."

"Life is full of surprises," I said.

"Don't fuck with me, Mace," Richard said quietly.

"You don't get to call me that. It's Mason," I said. Still, as royally fucked as I was, I appreciated him cutting to the chase.

"Hey asshole, you lied to me and called yourself Pete McLean. I think he can call you whatever he wants," Kamilah snapped, gesturing violently.

She's pissed. Her flinty eyes wrung my guts like a wet dishrag.

I couldn't tell her the whole truth. I was in a corner, not down for the count. *Gotta keep dodging,* I resolved, a vice tightening around my chest. "I'm confused. Who's good cop and who's bad cop here?" I asked, stalling.

"She makes a good point. You've been telling a lot of lies, Mace. Are you really going to pretend you don't know anything about Grayson Graham, an inmate who's from La Cuenca just like you?"

"There's like 80 inmates there, man. You think I know every one of them?"

"Enough bullshit!" Kamilah snapped. "You said you wanted to explain this to me. Start explaining. You owe me that much."

I couldn't look at her.

"That was before your pig brother was involved. No offense."

There was no other way out now.

"I'm not saying anything without a lawyer," I said.

"We have a lot to work with, Mason. Multiple counts of felony escape, obstruction of justice, and first-degree criminal impersonation. But you're not under arrest," Richard said.

That's interesting, I thought.

"Graham is a person of interest in the arson investigation," Richard said. "If you tell us what's going on, we can help each other. If not, then I *will* put you under arrest. Looking at 20 years, ballpark."

Graham, the arsonist? *Holy shit.*

If I said nothing, I'd get arrested and lose my shot at Graham. But what could I say that wouldn't endanger the mission? Or Ortiz? I was so goddamn close.

"The death toll from the Patchwork is at 23 now," Kamilah said, "and if Grayson Graham is responsible for it, that makes him a murderer." She crossed, then uncrossed her arms. "From what you did at the campground... I – I don't think you're that kind of a man."

"I'm not big on coincidences," Richard said. "You and your brother were at LAC the same time as Graham, and now here are you and Graham, together again. Only two possibilities as I see it. Either you're working with him, or you got beef."

I stewed. Furious that he could think I was working for Graham and racking my brain for a lie to get me out of this.

"Nothing to say, just like at LAC. That been working out for you? Your brother's killer still at large, isn't he?"

"Richard..." Kamilah said.

"Either you're working with him, or you got beef," Richard repeated.

"I'm not fucking working with him, that's for damn sure!" I roared.

"Why was your brother killed?" Kamilah asked. Her eyes X-rayed me, and I could almost see the cogs turning in her mind.

Fuck me. Of course *she* was the one connecting the dots, not her dumbass brother. I couldn't let them connect the dots all the way – that he was the killer, my target. They were after Graham for arson.

"Real talk," I said. "If you had evidence that Graham was the arsonist, you'd have moved on him already. He's as snug as a bug back at camp."

"You do know him. What a surprise."

"And if you arrest me, you'll lose your best shot at him. So, let's talk about how we can help each other."

I was in a corner. And so damn close. For the first time in my life, I'd have to snitch. Betray the only scruple I had left, the one Caleb and I'd shared since I was 15 and Patty the social worker came to visit. I was adrift, no waves or wind or paddles. A con without a code. Like Graham. *Maybe it takes one to kill one.* And maybe Richard and Kamilah could give me the opportunity.

"Put a wire on me. I'll get him to talk," I told them.

"How?"

"All I'll say is… we have a history."

Richard and Kamilah dropped me off on a hill with Ash River spilling below on one side and fire-eaten mountain ranges rising up on the other. Even at 11 pm, the view was striking. Liquid orange splashes of the Patchwork spread over the dark lumps of hills and ridges, in many places bleeding to the horizon. The sky was two-thirds haze, one third stars. It was horrible and beautiful at the same time.

Richard stayed in his police truck, but Kamilah walked a ways with me until we were out of earshot.

She handed me an envelope.

"They spent a week trying to track you down, then came to me. You should read it."

To: Mr. Peter McLeen
From: Troy Cooper

The boy from the campground. I put it in my jacket without looking at it. If I read it, I might think about his grateful hug, his parents sobbing with relief, and how it'd made my chest swell.

I couldn't stand the way Kamilah looked at me. The spark I'd seen after the burnover and campground was gone from her eyes. Replaced by pure disappointment, and it twisted my stomach into a sinking knot.

"I'm sorry," I said, and she knew I wasn't talking about the inconvenience with the letter.

Miserable, I looked into her eyes, trying to find the spark and reignite it.

Instead, she shook her head, went cold, and turned toward the police truck.

"Kamilah," I pleaded.

She didn't stop, so I told her the truth.

"He killed my brother." The words flew out and my breath caught in my throat. I was shocked at myself. Risking the mission and my freedom in the hopes that she'd understand me.

Kamilah stopped, quiet for a moment. She took a deep breath and turned back to me.

"I'm sorry," she said. "But this is bigger than your brother."

Kamilah got in the truck and they drove away, leaving me on a desolate hill between fire and night.

CHAPTER TWENTY-FIVE

What do they know about me?" Ortiz asked when I got back to the tent.

"Nothing. I didn't say shit."

Ortiz stared at me.

"The only thing they could know about you is what they can get off the La Cuenca roster," I said. "That we're on the same crew. I'm no snitch, you know that."

"But you've been made."

"I wouldn't do that to you, man. Trust." I used one of his favorite words and hoped it would help.

It didn't. Ortiz sighed, sat on his cot, and chewed his nails.

"You're like a brother to me," I added. I said it to manipulate him, but as the words came out, I realized I meant them. *Ortiz is a brother to me.* "And I've got your back. Because that's what brothers are for."

I almost choked on the phrase. It was what Caleb had said to pull me into my first job.

"You don't approve of how I make my money. Fine. But her brain is scrambled eggs because of him. This is the only way to make him pay."

"Good way to get shot, too."

I was back in the trailer, my bowl of mac n cheese almost empty, with Caleb across the table trying to convince me to help him take down Mom's meth dealer.

"It's a two-man job, Mace," Caleb had said. Before that night, he'd only called me Mace to tease me, because I thought it sounded tough. "You're the only one I can trust."

At fifteen, my chest swelled with pride at that. Not only did my brother consider me a man, but I was the only man worthy of his trust. My earliest memory was of Caleb keeping me out of his blanket fort. Now he was inviting me in.

"It's what brothers are for," Caleb said.

I couldn't refuse.

"Okay," I'd said.

I watched Ortiz, sitting on his cot, torn just like I had been.

Caleb's plan to steal meth from the cook and pin it on the dealer had gone straight to shit, and the dealer had cornered us in an abandoned oil field with a shotgun in his hands. Caleb tackled the dealer, stabbed him in the eye, and sliced his throat to stop the screaming. We took the body to a dusty field outside of town and spent hours digging into the hard-packed earth. The deeper, the better, we figured. We planted a cactus and did our best to disguise the burial plot. Stunned and scared, I stuck to Caleb like glue the following weeks, watching his back and helping him with his hustles. He liked having me around, and weeks became years. And here I was.

Because I said 'okay' to Caleb that night, I was caught between the cops and an arsonist-murderer. It was a shitty thing, to blame my dead brother for how my life turned out. But maybe he shouldn't have come to me with that first job. I could've refused him – it was my choice to join Caleb in this world. But would a good brother have asked me to?

Ortiz was quiet for a stretch. Then he said, "It's over."

"You really have lost your nerve."

"Whole thing was built on keeping it secret. No way you can get away with it now," he said.

He was right. It was one thing for Graham to know I was after him, it was another for Kamilah and her cop brother to catch Mason Jones posing as Pete McLean. Even if we could pay off the brother, Kamilah was too honest to stay quiet. And God knows who else they'd told.

Ten to one, I'd be caught if I took out Graham. Maybe not right away, but the odds were stacked against me. No one would know the context, that I'd wiped a murderer and arsonist off the Earth. I'd just be a murderous con.

Caleb wasn't perfect. But he pulled the alarm with his dying breath, saving my life. If I wasn't willing to risk 25 to life for avenging him, what kind of brother was I?

"So, I don't get away with it," I told Ortiz. "I get it done, and I run. Maybe your people can get me a little cash for the go…"

"You stupid motherfucker. What you do is you play along

with the cops, keep me out of it, and maybe this can all work out. All they got on you is impersonation and a few trips outside of camp. My peoples ain't gonna like it, but… this can be a win."

"Graham getting arrested isn't a win. He needs to be dead."

"Too late for that. Help the cops – as an informant, snitch, whatever the fuck, get Graham in bracelets. That's your out."

"You want me to fucking cooperate…" *Unbelievable.* Here was a gang member telling me to work with the police. Telling me to let my brother's murderer go peacefully to prison.

"Check yourself. This is me talking as your business partner now. You got made. I can't risk this coming back on me and my people. It's *over*. You got that?"

I nodded, but I had no intention of obeying. There had to be a way to turn the Richard and Kamilah problem into a solution.

"Gotta get a message to Serrato, they're gonna have to pull some soldiers back," Ortiz said, pulling out his phone.

"Can you hold off?" I asked, and he glared at me. "Just wait to let him know. I wanna get the best deal possible with the cops, and a cooperation strategy that keeps you safe. When we have that straightened out, then we'll let your boss know what's up. Deal?"

"Fine. Deal."

I wasn't going to do any of that.

Ortiz was only looking out for me. *Like a good brother does.* The thought roiled my already agitated guts. He'd been behind me every step of the way, risking his neck and putting up with my bullshit. And now I had more bullshit to add to the pile. *Son-of-a-bitch was supposed to be a pawn!* Nothing more. An ache constricted my chest. The mission wasn't over for me, but I couldn't see Ortiz in bracelets, on the run… or bloody at Graham's feet. The images doubled the ache, and I had to force myself to breathe deep.

The only way to keep Ortiz safe now was to leave him out of it. I had to finish this alone.

I undressed to my skivvies and splashed bottled water on my face. There had to be a way, a way to convince Kamilah and her brother that I was helping them while still finishing my mission.

A corner of an envelope poked out of my pile of clothes on the floor. The letter from Troy, the boy at the campground. I opened it up.

Dear Mr. McLeen,
Thank you for saving me. I was so scared but you took me away from the fire. When I grow up I want to be -

No.

Vision blurring, I folded it back up. The hand-written sentiments hollowed me out. A distraction I didn't need right now.

The beginnings of a plan were forming in my mind.

This phone belongs to Sean Wolfe, a firefighter who's working with Graham. He tried to kill me two days ago."

I showed Kamilah and Richard Wolfe's phone. We sat across from each other at a wobbly table in a Wal-Mart evacuee lot. A hastily-organized jumble of canopies, sleeping bags, and scared people. Reminded me of a swap meet, but way more depressing. It was unlikely we'd run into anyone who knew us at this unsanctioned camp.

"I know Sean. He seemed like a good guy," Kamilah said, and glanced at me. "Clearly I have terrible judgment."

In a flash, I remembered where I'd seen Wolfe's name – on Graham's Transfer Form from his LAC Unit Classification Committee. Sean Wolfe was the pro firefighter who recommended Graham for fire crew duties. A connection who got Graham on the fireline, but not to fight fires.

To start them.

Graham. A murderer *and* an arsonist.

A murderer and arsonist who shared my M.O. Like me, Graham came to the fireline with an ulterior mission. What'd he get out of it? He was a cold-blooded predator, not a mindless destructive force.

I couldn't tell Kamilah and Richard about this. I couldn't risk giving away my leverage as a con who had 'history' with Graham.

"What else do you know about him, Kay?" Richard asked Kamilah about Wolfe.

"Don't know why he'd do something like this." Kamilah shook her head. Another betrayal, another question. "He's moving on in a few months. Private sector job with the Spear company."

I held up Wolfe's phone, refocusing the conversation.

"There's a text from a number that has to be Graham's. It says my name, my crew assignment, exactly where I'd be two days ago – the day Wolfe tried to kill me. That's all it says, but I know a hit order when I see it." Kamilah raised her eyebrows and held her hand open for the phone. Craving contact but afraid she'd recoil,

I placed it carefully in her palm. She didn't react at all, just took it and studied the messages. I continued, "I'm sure there's some, you know, corroborating evidence on this thing, but I think —"

"If we arrest him, he clams up, lawyers up, and there's a good chance he squirms out of it for lack of evidence," Richard cut me off. "If you corner him, we can get him to talk."

"No shit. That's what I said last night. You wanna let me finish, Super Cop?" I flashed him a fake, cheery smile.

"Real cocky for a guy looking at 20-to-life if you fuck it up," Richard leaned forward, nostrils flaring.

"Boys," Kamilah intoned.

Richard whispered something to Kamilah.

"You're undermining *yourself*," she replied, not whispering, and turned her focus to me.

"As I was saying," I continued, "I think I can use this to lure in Graham with a text from Wolfe. I get him to talk, and you listen in somehow."

Richard brought out a flesh-colored pill-sized device. Looked the perfect size for an ear canal.

"Audio receiver-transmitter."

"What if Graham knows he's the one with Wolfe's phone?" Kamilah asked.

I smiled, encouraged by her concern for me.

"Wolfe was on the hook to kill him and biffed it," Richard said. "Doubt he's eager to tell Graham he failed and lost his phone, with the hit order on it, to the victim."

"It's only my life on the line. Why be cautious?" I agreed with him about the phone and was already planning to put my life on the line, but I wanted to stick it to this pig.

"You brought this on yourself," Kamilah snapped. "23 people have died because of the Patchwork Fire while you've been parading around as Pete McLean. You should be thanking my brother for the opportunity."

That hurt worse than a punch to the gut and left a lingering ache. She wasn't concerned about me. Just the logistics.

"Before we go any further, I need to know the nature of your relationship with Graham," Richard said.

I stopped myself from gaping at Kamilah. She hadn't told him. My deepest secret, the tiny, earth-shattering fact that had defined my life for the past year. If Richard knew it, he wouldn't trust me. She hadn't given up on me. Not completely.

Maybe she understood why I pretended to be Pete McLean, or was at least beginning to. If she could understand, she could forgive. Without my lies, the air between us would be clean. Maybe I could stand next to her as Mason Jones.

My chest turned to lead, weighing down every breath, because going through with my plan meant I wasn't done lying to her.

"Me and Graham, we're rivals," I told Richard.

Kamilah said nothing.

Richard stared at me, considering. Then he nodded and waved his hand.

"Okay, perp. Proceed."

"You got it, pig. It'll go like this. I send a text to lure Graham to the Tapo Mine. I'll have that transmitter on me, too small for him to find. Everything you're saying he did, I tell him I know about it. Ask for hush money. A little negotiation, a little fishing so he says what you need him to say."

"An admission," Richard said. "I know rules are a foreign concept to you, but they exist. You can't compel or induce him to do anything illegal. You can't get any information from him under duress." His voice went up to a condescending pitch: "That means —"

"I can't twist his arm. Don't talk down to me."

"Right. Probably learned all this in juvie," Richard said.

"Check your records, sizzlean, I was never in juvie."

"Boys!" Kamilah reproached, going full mama-bear. Then she looked at a weather report on her phone to change the subject.

"It's supposed to rain. Will that affect the transmission?"

"It shouldn't," Richard said.

"We could really use the rain," I said, looking in the direction of the Patchwork.

"We really could. Bump up the R.H., be a godsend for the containment efforts," Kamilah sighed.

"Seriously." How many people from Ash River were here in this lot?

Kamilah gave me a suppressed smile and it was the world.

Richard coughed and picked up the receiver-transmitter.

"And you consent to all this?"

"Yeah."

Fair's fair, I thought. They were using me, and I was using them.

Richard nodded, loaded the device in a gun-like instrument, and moved behind me.

"Hold still."

Pff! A sharp pain and a pressure behind my ear. He *injected* it beneath my skin. I thought it would just go in my ear.

"Ow."

"This does more than send and receive audio," Richard explained. "It's a human lojack. We're not just going to listen in. We'll see your every move."

I didn't consent to *that*.

Kamilah looked down, unable to meet my eyes.

A fucking lojack. That was going to make things interesting.

"Got some paperwork for you to sign," Richard said, "then it's back to camp to get ready."

I yanked the winch rope I'd stolen from a CalFire truck. Tough, very little give. Perfect. Alone in the tent, I uncoiled it to its full eight-foot length, and held it over the open back of my yellow fire jacket – too long. I cut it down to five feet with Sean Wolfe's multi-tool. I'd unstitched the blue lining of the jacket and now I peeled it back like a sheet. I sewed the winch rope to it, careful to distribute the coils evenly to avoid bulk.

Night had fallen, my next shift didn't start for six hours, and I had fifteen minutes before I had to meet Kamilah and Richard outside of camp. I'd taken my time with the creation and filling of the hidden layer. As I began stitching the lining back to the jacket, Ortiz raced in the tent.

I didn't bother hiding it.

He had a pinched expression – something on his mind – but couldn't help shaking his head at what I was doing.

"Part of my deal with the cops," I said.

"Yeah right."

Ortiz sat down next to me and played a video on his phone. "Doesn't matter," he said. "Whatever you're doing, forget it."

The shaky phone view was dark and grainy, but Graham's back was visible as he cut around a well-lit parking lot and behind a poorly lit concrete building with a rock wall façade and signs for *men* and *women*'s bathrooms. He wore a backpack.

"You followed him," I grunted.

Ortiz ignored the rebuke.

"This was tonight. Ten miles from here. One of those interstate rest areas," he explained.

In the video, Graham crept next to a dark wall. What seemed to be the farthest spot from the light and activity at the front of the rest area. He turned a flashlight on and set it on the ground to illuminate his doings.

Graham looked around, and thinking he was alone, he pulled up a green valve box cover and dug out a foot of soil by hand. No valves in there. From the hole, he pulled out bags. From the bags, Graham pulled out rubber-banded stacks of cash.

The camera – Ortiz – zoomed in on the cash. The bills were hundreds.

Graham flipped through them, making sure it was all there.

It seemed to be. Graham unzipped his backpack and added more stacks to the hideaway bags. Covered them back up, put the false valve box over it all, and stole off into the night. The video ended in the shadows of the rest area.

"He's squirreling money away, man. *A lot* of it," Ortiz said, stating the obvious.

Way more money than you'd get from the prison contraband business.

It clicked. Graham was an arsonist for hire. Someone was paying him a shitload to spread the Patchwork.

Kamilah said 23 people had died from the fire complex so far. First Caleb, then innocent people all over California. *He really is a monster.*

"Let's use this." Ortiz said.

"Okay…" I replied, though I knew where he was going with this.

"We got him! You show this to the cops, you got leverage. Got him on camera moving it, and they can do their forensics… physical evidence of a shady deal, Mace. That's what they're missing, right? No-shit evidence? That's why they need you."

"You don't even have a disguise. And you left camp without telling me?"

"I do stuff too, you know. My life doesn't revolve around you, and *you've* been on your own fucking program since day one." Ortiz shook the phone. "This'll give you leverage with the cops. Graham goes away and we come out clean."

"No," I said.

Evidence meant an arrest, and an arrest meant losing my last chance to end Graham.

That kind of cash could do wonders for a fugitive, though, and I'd be one before the night was over. There was only one rest stop within 10 miles – I'd seen it coming back from the campground. After it was done, that rest stop would be my first stop.

"I have a plan, and it's time for me to go," I said.

I threaded the last stitch in the jacket's lining, leaving it loose so it'd be easy to rip, stood, and put the jacket on.

Ortiz grabbed the multi-tool and blocked the way out. He flicked out the blade.

Just like when we met. Leg muscles twitched from a flood of adrenalin and my heartbeat pounded in my ears. I hissed a breath in and out, trying to keep the venom from my voice.

"I'm doing what you wanted. Cooperating. We got the evidence covered without that video." I didn't like lying right to his face again, but I was out of options.

"Stop! Enough bullshit. How many times you snuck off without telling me? Risking everything – including me?" Ortiz planted his feet, his face getting red. "You couldn't've done none of this without me. But I'm just a gofer, a dog to fetch the shit *you* need for *your* payback. We're supposed to be partners, you ungrateful fuck," he said, voice cracking.

My stomach wrenched and the acid fury imploded, leaving me hollow. Unable to meet his eyes, I took in his wide stance and ready posture. His knuckles were white from clenching the multi-tool, and the veins of his arms bulged.

If he'd gotten here five minutes later, I'd have been gone.

"I can't stop now," I confessed.

I ducked under the blade and tackled him, rolling onto his arm and pinning it to strip the multi-tool away.

Tunk! Ortiz whacked the aluminum cot pole against my head, exploding stars across my vision, but I grabbed the pole and wrenched it down on his face, then pummeled his kidneys until he was gasping. *Goddammit.* Why hadn't he got here five minutes later? A cancerous ache took root in my chest.

The leftover winch rope – I grabbed it and tied his hands. Then his feet.

"I'm trying to help you, you piece of shit. You're the one on the chopping block," Ortiz said.

"Yeah. And when they find you tied up like this, it'll keep you off it."

"The cops need to see the video."

I put a sock in his mouth and used the last bit of rope to tie it there. I pocketed his cell phone.

"Not until I'm done," I told him, and left, the ache spreading out, constricting every breath.

CHAPTER TWENTY-SIX

Graham's response appeared on Sean Wolfe's phone:

'omw'

"He took the bait," I said.

28 minutes ago, I'd texted Graham a message from the same phone.

'Money or I talk. Negotiation at top of Tapo Mine, 2300. Come alone.'

I stood with Kamilah and Richard on a hilltop facing the Tapo

Mine scar, next to the tech-filled listening post disguised with camo netting and vegetation. Haze from the Patchwork hugged the scar's sharp corners and the air smelled like burned wood. It was a gray night.

Beep. Richard activated the audio receiver-transmitter, and feedback screeched in my ear and from a pair of headphones plugged into their equipment.

"Jesus."

Richard turned a knob down and the screech died.

"Give me your axe and any other tools on you," Richard said.

I put on a show of concern, holding onto my Pulaski axe. It was important to keep up the ruse that I was reluctant and worried about my safety. "Showing up unarmed will throw him off. He'll know something's up."

"I never said there wouldn't be risks," Richard replied.

"What if things go south? Don't I have a right to defend myself?"

"Non-negotiable, Jones," he said, voice firm and eyes steady.

I handed over my Pulaski axe.

"He's got a point, though. Graham could be dangerous," Kamilah said. She knew damn well he was, but she continued to keep my secret.

"We'll be right here on this hill, watching and listening. Can get to you in about five minutes. But…" Richard fished in a bag and brought out a tiny pepper spray canister, "Last resort."

I nodded thanks. This could be useful, but I had my own last resort.

The two of them looked me up and down. I was in my yellow

pro gear. From a distance, Graham could think I was Sean, or if he had suspicions, another firefighter, not an inmate looking for trouble.

"Ready?" Kamilah asked.

"As I'll ever be," I said.

"Don't do anything stupid," she said.

I smiled at her – she didn't smile back – and I made my way down the hill and up the steps and ladders to the scar's top terrace. The haze-mist was tainted with ash, making it hard to breathe.

"Audio check," Richard's voice was a strange, tinny vibration that came from behind my ear, instead of inside it. He said it worked through bone conduction.

"I hear you, how am I coming in?" I asked.

"Loud and clear. We'll do another check with the target, copy?"

"Copy."

I walked to the designated spot – a rusted-out shipping container sitting atop the summit of the scar. It was in Kamilah and Richard's line of sight from their post and a safe distance from the sharp drops of the terraces. It was also all the way across the top level from the prefab where I'd set my trap. I glanced at their post, a green smudge through the ashy haze, and made a mental note to keep my eyes off it when he arrived.

I waited in the gray for 26 minutes until the scuffle of footsteps echoed off the rock walls and he appeared out of the murk, walking across a land bridge to the top terrace of the scar. First, the tall, muscular frame, then the short, reddish-brown hair, and finally the freckled face. He wore his inmate firefighting gear and carried a shovel over his shoulder.

He caught sight of me and made his way over.

My heartbeat thundered in my ears, that familiar panic shivering at the same time that hot power coursed through my head and limbs. Bile rose in my throat – Caleb was screaming with a knife in his back, bleeding out on the floor –

I took a deep breath and pictured the rocks giving way under him and then converging on his head.

The madness passed. It wasn't just imagining his end. This was it. I took down Ulrich, I could take down Graham. He was just one man. This time *I* was leading him into the trap. This time the authorities were on *my* side. This time *I* had the upper hand, and it gave me an icy confidence.

Graham stopped 20 yards away now and recognition flickered across his face. A grimace that became a sneer that became nothingness. A blank stare with dead eyes.

He was silent.

"Audio check for target," Richard's voice returned to my ear. "Ask him: 'You came alone, right,' and use those exact words so we know you copy."

"You came alone, right?" I asked Graham.

"I'm alone," he said. Our voices reverberated off the rigid surfaces of the scar.

"Copy. We're reading him via your implant," Richard said.

"You got this," Kamilah said.

"Let's go somewhere private," I told Graham, and nodded to the shipping container.

Graham nodded, but instead pointed to a frail shed.

"Suit yourself." I'd anticipated this.

Slowly, I let him lead us over to the shed. Its walls and a finger of the scar now blocked us from Kamilah and Richard's line of sight. They would not be able to see us enter or leave.

"Shovel," I demanded.

Graham, keeping a safe distance, tossed me the shovel.

"This stays outside," I said, leaning the shovel against the wall.

I nodded him inside, and we entered the shack, never within an arm's length of each other. There was a small round table with chairs in the corner. Graham examined the space, tapping the corner, sliding his hands under the table and chairs. Checking for bugs or weapons. There were no surprises. Here.

"Remember," Richard said in my ear, "draw it out of him. No inducement, no duress."

They'd get their confession. They wouldn't get Graham.

"Need to know you're not wired. Strip," Graham ordered.

I smirked at his misreading of the situation. "There's no crooked C.O.s here. No meth heads on the payroll. You're not calling the shots now."

"We need him to feel like it's safe to talk, Jones," Richard said.

"Shirts and skivvies," I told Graham. "You first. Then me."

He dropped his jacket, undressed down to his fire pants, boots, and wife-beater. The massive muscles on his arms displayed a burst of ink. Flames, eagles, knives, and on one shoulder the phrase '*Will To Power.*' He showed me his phone and then pocketed it again. No shiv or weapon in sight.

I followed suit.

"Keeping my pants on," he said. "Never pegged you for a faggot."

"Drop 'em and pull 'em back up."

Graham glared at me, but he did it, baring his legs and boxers. No weapons. He belted his pants back up.

I did the same. I had no weapons or wires there.

"Sit," I said.

We took seats across from each other at the table.

Graham checked the table and chairs again and said, "Talk."

My rapidly thumping heart threatened to burst from my chest. I'd prepared, I was ready, but first I had to get him to talk. I owed Kamilah and Ash River that much. Ending him would be easy. Getting an admission was the hard part.

"Different messenger. Same message," I began, referring to the text supposedly from Sean Wolfe. "Money or I talk."

Graham's eyebrows furrowed.

"You didn't go to the cops before. Why would you now?"

'Before.'

Shlick. Shlip. Splash. Slicing Caleb apart, leaving me in a lake of blood to die. Just 'before' to him. I almost missed his question. *'Why now?'*

"People don't care about the death of one con," I replied, voice cracking at the awful reality of Caleb's murder. "Twenty-three people? Two responders, twenty-one civilians, on the other hand... Hushing that is up a worth a pretty penny."

"What's that got to do with me?" Graham asked.

I repeated the circumstantial evidence Richard had given me on Graham.

"The arson investigators found the origin points of at least four patches and figured out when those fires were started. All but one of those was started during your crew's off-shift, all within one hour of your off-shift inmate count. The one that doesn't align with the crew schedule, that was a week ago. Started about noon the day you had a gate pass."

Doubt crept into Graham's eyes.

Finally. It was euphoric seeing him *realize* I had the upper hand.

"That's all what the pigs call circumstantial. I can say I saw it all. Eyeball witness."

"Had you all wrong," Graham said. "A long con for a payout? Thought your brother meant something to you. More than cash at least."

"What's he talking about?" Richard asked.

"He's goading you, Mason. Stay on track," Kamilah said.

"He's dead, and nothing I do can change that," I told Graham, echoing Ortiz's words. "My sentence is up next year and the job market is hell on ex-cons."

"He went out like a bitch anyway," Graham sneered.

Crack!

I threw the table up, knocking his chin and spilling him out of the chair and onto his back. I rolled the table over, pressing its edge against his neck from the other side.

"Tell me about the fires, motherfucker." Blood thundering in my ears, Richard and Kamilah's shouts through the implant became whispers.

"Godammit, Jones!"

"Mason, no!"

I didn't give a shit about duress.

Graham coughed and kicked, so I pressed harder. He stopped kicking and pushed back with his hands. With gravity on my side, I pushed down just enough to keep his hands busy and the edge against his neck.

"The fires," I demanded.

"Let up and I'll talk."

I kicked him in the stomach and he flinched. Finally, he was on his back. Finally, he was helpless and afraid for his life. A talented butcher but not unstoppable.

"You talk and I'll let up."

"I set a few fires," he rasped.

I got you. A thrill of triumph, then a wave of nausea. An inmate firefighter and CalFire heavy equipment operator were dead because of him, 11 innocent people burned alive in a firestorm because of him. And 10 more bodies on top of that – Kamilah had said the Patchwork had now killed 23 people.

"Keep going," I grunted, trying not to be sick.

"This guy wanted the fires to get worse. Uncontrollable. He offered a lot of money. You said it yourself. Job market is hell on ex-cons."

Piece of shit.

"We can't use this!" Richard shouted in my earpiece.

Didn't matter. They knew what kind of man he was now. The rest was up to me.

Graham only had one hand on the table – the other one swishing a knife out of his boot and toward my legs – I jumped back, the blade ripped my fire pants.

As he scrambled up, I whipped out the pepper spray and shot

a heavy stream right into his eyes. Graham shouted in shock and dropped the knife, hands going to his eyes. He shouted again in pain and I sprayed it right in his goddamn mouth. He coughed and I smacked him down with a chair.

Grabbing my fire jacket, I ripped off the false lining I'd sewn in, pulled out the winch rope, and hog-tied Graham. Cinching his hands and feet painfully together.

His face red and covered in snot, he shouted a steady stream of curses. Graham was finally powerless, and I stood over him. My own eyes started stinging and watering and my face was burning with heat. Second-hand spray. *Need to get out of here.*

I took his knife and dug it into the skin behind my ear, popping out the implant.

"Rat fuck," Graham said, leering at it with his wet red eyes.

"Sorry, Kamilah," I said, and I threw the implant to the ground.

They'd be here in minutes.

Eyelids twitching and mucus dribbling down my chin, I grabbed the rope and lugged Graham outside. Muscles throbbing from the strain. *Hefty motherfucker.*

I glanced around – the two were probably running down the hill at this moment.

"Try anything and you die," I said.

I attached the rope to his shovel, and keeping low, I dragged him through shadows, across the terrace, and toward my original trap – the guardrailed pit.

CHAPTER TWENTY-SEVEN

Graham twisted his massive frame and I dropped the shovel. His phone flew from his pocket and clattered in the dirt. I scooped it up and dove back on him.

"Don't fucking move!" I shouted, stabbing his foot to the ground with his own knife, making him bellow in agony.

"Hurts, doesn't it? Maybe I stab you nine more times like you did my brother."

Graham spit snot and rage at me.

Lightning flashed on the horizon and distant thunder rumbled, echoing across the scar. A warm trickle flowed from my ear down my back. I thought it was rain, then realized it was blood from carving out the implant.

I yanked out the knife, grabbed the hog-tie knot, and dragged him to the pit. He clawed and kicked, sending me against the guardrail with my own momentum. The guard panels gave just like I'd planned, and I tottered on the edge until I threw myself back on firm ground.

Graham's eyes flashed at the trap intended for him and he rolled away, popping the knot that bound his hands to his legs.

Kicked the shovel, tripping me.

Freed his hands and feet from the remaining rope. Barged into the prefab and found the sledgehammer I'd hid in the fridge and held it with his hands still bound. He barreled out of the prefab at me.

No. Wasn't supposed to go down like this.

I picked up the shovel and slammed the sledgehammer down.

The metal reverberation sent shockwaves, reviving the pain in my right hand. I shouted, dropped the shovel, and picked it back up with my other hand. *Not letting this get away from me.*

Graham pointed at my scarred hand and laughed, remembering. "How'd that happen?"

I roared and swung the shovel like an axe – fingers flew off his hand, leaving a bloody trail in the dirt.

Intoxicating. I was a furnace, my limbs made of fire.

You fucking piece of shit.

I smacked the flat of the shovel against the stumps, making him scream.

Like Caleb had when he dragged him by his foot with the shiv. All over again, Graham pinned my brother down and plunged the shiv in his back over and over. Savage focus in his eyes, animalistic power.

I was outside myself.

I saw me beating Graham with the shovel, curled up to protect himself, covered in snot and blood. Feral rage in my face, the wretched fear in Graham's eyes, knowing he was about to die.

I looked just like Graham the day he killed my brother.

I froze. Back in my own head.

Entire body shaking. Insides churning, like breakfast was coming back up.

Graham was cringing beneath me, bleeding in the dirt.

I held the shovel up, ready to bring it down on his head. Ring his bell so I could push him into the pit.

"Hands down! Stop moving!" I shouted.

Graham put his hands down, exposing his head.

Finish it, goddammit, I told myself.

Head lights lit the top terrace, casting grotesque shadows. The low thrum of an engine reverberated through the terraces. More echoes: a car door opened and closed; footsteps stomped toward us. They'd made it over here fast. I thought I had more time.

"Jones, what are you doing?"

I turned to see Captain Hallenbeck gaping at us.

The fuck is he doing here?

"Help me!" Graham said.

"Stay back, Captain!" I shouted as Hallenbeck approached.

"Jones, listen to me…"

"Just stay back," I said. I didn't care what it looked like. I needed to finish it and couldn't have Hallenbeck in the way.

"No," Hallenbeck said, taking out his first aid kit.

He knelt beside Graham, blocking the bastard with his own body.

I dropped the shovel and stepped back. I could never hurt Hallenbeck.

"He's not worth it, Captain," I said, disgusted.

"Like your bunkmate, Ortiz? The man saved your life and I found him tied up in your tent."

Must've found Ortiz and tracked me here.

Hallenbeck wrapped Graham's bloody hand with a roll of gauze.

"Hold on, keep pressure on it," he said, and took out his radio. "Allcon, this is –"

The predatory gleam returned to Graham's face.

"Captain, don't," I said, pleading now. He had no idea what Graham was capable of.

"You dug your own grave, Jones." Hallenbeck pressed the '*talk*' button.

Graham tightened the gauze on his hand and tied it off.

"Not me, Cap," I warned.

Hallenbeck ignored me and continued: "Allcon, this is Hallenbeck. Location is Tapo scar, Tapo Trail Road. We have two inmates out of bounds, one injured. Requesting immediate correctional and law enforcement support to –"

Graham snatched the sledgehammer and sprang to his feet, I grabbed the shovel – Hallenbeck scrambled to his feet –

"Hey, whoa!"

Whonk! Graham brained Hallenbeck and he crumpled to the floor. Graham ran away, limping. Hallenbeck was on his side on the ground, eyes stuck wide open, blood seeping through the hair on his head. The sight turned my veins to ice.

I could catch Graham.

Hallenbeck's body twitched. *Shit shit shit.*

I got down by the fallen firefighter's side.

No idea what to do, but I couldn't leave him.

Graham slid down the terrace ladders and ran off into the darkness. There was an orange glow on the horizon, one that hadn't been there before.

Footsteps stomping toward me again.

This time I was right. Kamilah and Richard.

They stared in shock at the bloody scene.

CHAPTER TWENTY-EIGHT

He's hurt bad, I don't know what to do," I said, voice shaking. Richard pointed his gun at me and I put my hands up.

Kamilah's eyes were dinner plates as she ran and knelt next to Hallenbeck. Felt his pulse, checked his breathing, examined the wound. She flashed a light in his open eyes and shook her head, expelling a wavering breath. Gently, she laid gauze on the wound in his scalp.

"Head wound, nothing we can do here," she said quietly, and spoke into her radio, "Firefighter down. Emergency medevac requested, Tapo Mine scar. Head trauma, patient doesn't have much time. Repeat, emergency medevac for firefighter at Tapo Mine scar."

Richard's lip curled in disgust.

"Kneel away from me and put your hands behind your head,"

he told me.

Next would come the bracelets.

Hands interlaced on the back of my head, I knelt facing Richard to study the area. A truck – Hallenbeck's – sat idling on the land bridge to the neighboring hill. Looked at Hallenbeck. He had stopped twitching. Bloody mucus seeped from his nostrils, and he was pale and still.

"Away from me, Jones!"

I turned away from Richard. Heard the clink as he took out the cuffs.

"Tapo, Dispatch. Rerouting a bird to your location for emergency medevac," the dispatcher said over Kamilah's radio.

"Copy," Kamilah said.

Thank God. Help was on the way for Hallenbeck.

There was nothing I could do for him.

I slammed backward into Richard, knocking him down. His gun landed next to him. I kicked it into the darkness and heard it clatter down to the terrace below.

"I'm sorry," I told Kamilah for the second time tonight, and ran to the truck.

I was in the truck and barreling down a dirt road before Richard even got up – he waved Kamilah off as he stood, and then I was around a bend and all I could see was dark chaparral.

Wasn't admissible, but they knew Graham was an arsonist. He'd be in the wind.

I needed to be in the wind, too.

First stop, Graham's money. No time to waste because it would be Graham's first stop too. He'd fled on foot. I'd get there first.

Crackling adrenaline smothered visions of Hallenbeck's blank face and Caleb's bloodied body. I let the sensations of my hammering heart and jittery limbs consume my mind, because it kept me from seeing those visions.

I pressed the pedal to the floor.

The money was buried under the faux valve cover behind the rest area, three bags, and I counted 250,000 dollars. A quarter million to set California ablaze.

It was just past dawn.

Maybe I wait for Graham here. Finish it.

Richard would question Ortiz first, and Ortiz, thinking he was helping me, would tell them about this place. There had to be an APB on me by now, and soon enough every cop in the state would be looking for me.

The adrenaline was wearing off. A night breeze cooled the salty sweat on my lips, and as the raw fight-or-flight energy left my system, unwelcome thoughts rushed in.

Sorry, Caleb. I failed.

Months of physical therapy, the fire crew training, the maneuvering and preparation, surviving his shiv and the burnover and Wolfe – all for nothing. *Now* Ortiz was right. It was over.

I needed to keep this head start.

Zipping the cash back up, I got on the interstate, then onto the first local road I could find.

Second stop, Nevada by way of Death Valley. US Routes and state highways only. The longest way out of Southern California, but the safest. The 15, 40 and 10 interstates would be packed with Vegas and Arizona-bound traffic – too many eyeballs, too many CHiPs.

Had to drive west through the damn Patchwork evacuation areas first.

An indicator on the dash glowed 'E' – I was going east.

"Shit, shit, shit!" I shouted, pounding the wheel, lighting my hand up with pain that made everything worse.

I flipped a bitch, tires squealing. *What fucking road is this?* Looked familiar, but it was a high-country road in California. They all look the same at night.

"How about a goddamn road sign? Fuck!"

Hallenbeck twitching on the floor.

Nothing I could do. I warned him.

The look on Kamilah's face.

Her fault. She kept my secret.

Ortiz, gagged with a sock, betrayal on his face.

All their fucking fault. Should've stayed out of my way.

Bullshit, I thought. *Enough of the bullshit.*

I was weak and stupid. I left SCC with every advantage. Surprise, the resources of an entire gang at my disposal, and a friend. Pissed it all away. Lost surprise when I chased after Kamilah, lost Ortiz because I was an asshole. Now an honest man's head was smashed in because of me.

I was one wayward thought away from a mental breakdown.

My hand shook as I turned on the car stereo and scanned through the FM band. Pop garbage, hip-hop garbage, alt-rock garbage, all fucking garbage – nothing to keep me from slipping into madness. Finally, something soothing and catchy came up, and I stopped it there. Turned out to be a Coca-Cola commercial, but I left it on the station.

The scar on my hand had Graham's blood on it.

I'm sorry, Caleb, I thought again. *I tried.*

Hadn't I?

Piece of shit had been at my feet and I'd been too weak to finish it.

The road carried me through a narrow mountain pass choking with steam and smoke. I remembered I had three goddamn phones – Ortiz's, Wolfe's, and Graham's – and took one out to see where I was.

Ash River Road. The Patchwork wasn't supposed to be burning this far north – the Tapo scar was supposed to stop it.

Out of the haze a dog loped across the asphalt, its face black and pink – badly burned. I braked but then it was gone, like a ghost, and it took the smoke with it.

Ahead stretched the grim expanse of a town that no longer existed. Black spires that were once trees, and rows and rows and rows of neat ashen plots where homes used to be.

It's not Ash River, I told myself, but there was the black-streaked mesa looming over the ashes. I slowed the truck, sighting even more damning details. Ventura County Fire Station 58, one of the few buildings still standing, and the scorched façade of the Falcon's Nest, the only piece of the restaurant that was left. Farther down the road, Ash River Mobile Estates was an empty black space.

Dark clouds hung low on the horizon, the murky streaks of a storm beneath them. The predicted rain had come, but not anywhere helpful. 50 miles outside the Patchwork perimeter.

A fire engine team hosed down the sooty foundations of a commercial building, weaving the hose around gnarly points of rebar that stuck out everywhere.

I pulled over.

Shouldn't stop. But this wasn't right. *How the hell'd this happen?* We'd spent four whole days clearing the Tapo Scar to prevent this.

Still in fire pants and a bloody wife-beater, I put on a CalFire windbreaker from the passenger seat and stepped out.

Everywhere, ash-covered cars pulled up next to ash-covered plots, and families poured out to look at the empty space. Moms and dads and sons and daughters, holding each other, looking at us, the responders, silently asking why.

I wasn't a responder, though. I was an imposter.

The flecks of yellow in the gray canvas pulled me like a magnet. A firefighter misted the commercial rubble, his whole body sagging.

"Anyone hurt?" I asked him.

"Not here, no. Had to a drag a few out myself, but far as I know we got all the civilians."

"I thought the northern edge was contained," I said.

"It was," the firefighter replied. "But the inmate crew assigned to this area never showed this morning. Missing inmate or something."

My chest tightened.

"Murphy's Law was a real bitch today," the firefighter continued, "because as soon as we got the birds dumping here, they got pulled away to medevac a firefighter."

Not possible. Not him. Not because of me.

"How does that happen?" I asked. "Aren't they supposed to have some set aside for emergencies?"

"Look around. What part of this Patchwork ain't an emergency?"

I was afraid of the answer, but I had to know:

"They say anything about the, uh, casualty?"

"Someone said he was a foreman for one of the inmate crews. Guess one of 'em attacked him." He sighed and shook his head, but my feet were already carrying me away.

The lead landscape went out of focus. Chest collapsing in on itself. The oxygen sucked away, like during the burnover.

It's my fault.

I drifted through ground zero and ended up holding onto a lone brick chimney still warm from the fire. The next plot over, a mother stood with her two young boys. The youngest one picked up a melted plastic T-rex, then tossed it with a shout. The older one hissed at him and tilted his head to indicate the mother, '*Not now!*' The mom stared at the rubble in shock, barely noticing them.

Didn't know if they were rich or poor. No way to tell, because nothing was left of their home. Just a mother and two sons.

Might as well be me and Caleb.

It wasn't supposed to go down like this. No one else was supposed to suffer. Just Graham.

All the pain and destruction started with *him*.

Started.

Graham had slashed and Graham had burned. But I had fanned the flames.

Eventually I found my way back to the car and back onto the road. The radio was playing a familiar 80's song.

'Gimme all of your lovin! Gimme all that you got!'

That was the song. The road trips to Aunt Jenny's – me and Caleb fighting in the back, Mom at the wheel listening to a bizarre mix tape of the Grateful Dead, Mariah Carey, and 80's hair bands. But there was a moment in the middle of this Def Leppard song when the purple nurples and pyramid punches stopped. Right on cue, in sync with the lead singer, Caleb and I would shout "*C'mon Steve, get it!*" and launch into the guitar solo, jamming the invisible strings, heads banging.

Now it really was a solo.

I'd never grieved for him. Not really.

Channeling it all into rage had been the right thing. Useful. Gave me focus.

The road got blurry, and the blur spilled down my cheeks, joining the snot dribbling as I sniffed, trying to keep it all in. I was going to crash, and maybe that wouldn't be such a bad thing, going lead-foot into a tree and calling it a day, but that would bring responders, could even start a fire, making things even worse for everyone on the line and the people threatened by the Patchwork.

I pulled over and cried.

A phone in the passenger seat vibrated and a text popped up on the lock screen. Sean Wolfe's phone.

I wasn't done. It was finally coming out.

But I rubbed my eyes with my sleeve and picked up the phone.

'Running out of time' the text said.

The lock screen showed **Two other missed messages.**

I opened the text thread and scrolled up.

'the $ or he dies – G.'

And the first message was a picture.

Ortiz, hands bound, face swollen and bloody from a beating.

G. Graham.

The snake had gone to the rest stop, and when his money wasn't there, he'd guessed why. Probably found out about Ortiz from Hallenbeck's reprimand at Tapo. So Graham tracked him down and rolled him up for leverage.

I dialed, waiting an agonizing four rings for Graham to pick up.

"You alone?"

"I don't have your fucking money," I snapped, thinking the lie could save Ortiz, then realizing it could doom him.

"You sure? That's the only reason your buddy's still alive."

"A trade," I stated.

"A trade," Graham agreed. "I'll send you the location when you confirm you have the money. No tricks, no cops. You come alone or he dies."

Graham hung up.

I couldn't bring back the brother I lost. But I could still save the brother I found.

I took a picture of the cash, sent it to Graham, and turned the truck around once again.

K amilah was where I thought she'd be. Gearing up for a trip to the central patch's newest line at base camp, which was intact but looked like it'd been hit with a gray blizzard.

When I approached, she hefted a Pulaski axe meaningfully and glared at me. Even simmering with rage, I was a moth to her flame. Fearless, brilliant, and good-hearted. I hoped that goodness in her heart outweighed the rage.

"Stay back," she said.

"Okay," I said, and I did.

"My brother's looking for you."

"I bet."

"There are four deputies in this camp, all close enough to hear if I scream."

"I saw 'em."

"Tell me why I shouldn't," Kamilah said.

"I want to…" *Grovel until you forgive me. Show you I'm not a monster. Tell you everything. Hold you.* "There's a lot I want to say," I sighed, "But nothing I can say will make any of this right. I should've listened when you said this is bigger than my brother. And because I didn't, the only friend I have is about to die. I'm here because I need your help."

"Others need it more. *Innocent* people." Her eyes bored into me, icy with disappointment, and it was everything I could do not to shrink away. I met Kamilah's gaze and she made a cynical gesture with the axe. "Like I could ever trust you again!"

"This is a chance to finish what you started, to stop the son-of-a-bitch behind the Patchwork. And it might be the last chance."

I explained about Ortiz, Graham, and the cash. She didn't have to take my word for it, and I showed her the texts, pictures, and stacks of hundreds. She squeezed her eyes shut for an achingly long moment.

"You think it'll be a simple exchange?" Kamilah was incredulous. "You expect him to keep his word? It's a trap."

"That's why I came to you. You're the toughest bitch I've ever known, and I can't do this alone. If Graham ghosts with the cash, we'll never find out who hired him to set fires. Help me save my friend and stop the Patchwork."

Thunk. Kamilah dropped the axe and crossed her arms, studying me.

CHAPTER TWENTY-NINE

The ash plots of Ash River baked in the sun, dry, but the gully that gave the town its name was rippling with brown-water rapids. A railroad tie flipped vertical beneath the water and splashed back to the surface – the muddy water had to be at least eight feet deep. A flash flood sent by the storm miles away.

A half-burnt, half-intact colonial house dangled over the edge of the river while rising water and chunks of wood battered its exposed foundations. The once-white house looked like a burnt skull, the windows scorched-black eyes, an entire side gone and open like a mouth.

He was a psychopath, but like me, Graham knew how to choose a trap. There was no way he was going to let me leave here alive.

I was here to save Ortiz, to do right by Ash River. I was unarmed. All I had on me was the money and Graham's own phone. Both were essential if this was going to work.

This had to work. I couldn't let Ortiz die because of me.

I set a bag holding 125,000 dollars – half – on the doorstep. An insurance policy. Shouldering the remaining bag of cash, I walked in the house, greeted by an overpowering smell of burnt wood. It creaked and rattled and shook, the water sloshing against the side facing the river. It was like climbing through a sinking pirate ship.

I heard him before I saw him.

"Upstairs," Graham said.

The paint along the stairway was cracked from heat, but the stairs themselves were solid. The house groaned and a crack widened in the roof. The foundations were disintegrating. If Graham didn't kill me, the house would.

The stairway went to a hallway, and the hallway got more mutilated as I went, charred ceilings and exposed drywall, and then I came to Graham in the master bedroom, a blackened shell of its former self. At his feet, Ortiz knelt with his hands bound. Behind them, a melted screen door opened to the burned planks of what used to be a balcony.

Ortiz followed me with one eye. The other was swollen shut inside a lumpy, purple face crusted with blood. Feverish rage flared, roaring in my ears, and I stopped in my tracks, rattling a breath in and out to stop it from overtaking me.

Graham stared at me with calm, dead eyes that I wanted to rip out and shove down his throat. I had many, many regrets, but they didn't stop the acid hate from burning through my veins. What if ending him was the only way to make it stop?

Ortiz looked at me and I knew his thoughts. *'You actually came. Don't fuck this up. Please don't fuck this up.'*

"I'm sorry," I told him, hollow with shame.

"Don't talk to him," Graham said.

Graham held a gun in his good hand. On his other hand were two duct-taped stumps where fingers used to be. It gave me a thrill of satisfaction – *I did that* – until that damnable image intruded in my mind – me standing over a bloody and broken Graham just like he'd stood over Caleb.

Focus.

In the bad hand, Graham gripped a wand device with his remaining fingers.

"What's that?"

"Bug scanner. Walmart," he said.

"You think they'd still let me snitch?" I said, incredulous. "I tried to kill you earlier tonight. I'm done with that."

"Just put your hands up so I can do it."

"Put your gun down first," I said.

We stared at each other, willing the other to go first, ready for a trick.

Crack!

Graham whipped the muzzle to aim at me at the same the house trembled and split open wider above us – the source of the sound.

We both looked up at the widening crack and shared a grim smirk. Whole thing almost went to shit because of this crumbling house.

If he shot me, then he would gun down Ortiz, take the cash, and run. Only reason he hadn't already is because he thought I had an ace up my sleeve – another bug.

I went first, putting the cash on the floor behind me.

Graham put the gun down on the floor behind him and moved toward me with the bug sweeper, limping from where I'd stabbed his foot. Another thrill, another jarring vision of Mason the monster. I tensed as Graham waved the device over me. He could whip out a hidden blade and gut me in a split-second.

I could deck him while he swept the device and try to beat him to the gun. If he had a hidden weapon, he could take it out and kill me or Ortiz. Even if he didn't have a hidden weapon, he was too fast and too strong.

This time, I actually was unarmed.

My life was worth the risk. Ortiz's wasn't.

Graham finished his sweep, finding one device. His own phone.

"That's yours," I said.

Graham tapped the screen, confirmed as much, and pocketed it. This time, I actually was sans-recording device.

"No bugs. I do have insurance, though," I explained, and hefted the bag of cash. "This is half. Other half is close by. I'll tell you where once we're safely out the door."

"That wasn't the deal," Graham said, glaring as he put down the bug-sweeper and picked up his gun.

"For the best. We both have a rough history when it comes to making deals."

Graham waved the muzzle near Ortiz's head.

"Let's do it, then."

"One second," I said.

I gave Graham a wide berth and moved onto what was left of the balcony – a few sooty planks extending over the turbulent brown water barreling down Ash River. I held the bag over the stream.

"Call your boss and tell him you're done," I said. "I don't care who it is. Like I said, I'm done snitching." I motioned to Ortiz. "But I need to know he's safe, and that the people in these towns are safe. You don't make that call, I don't give you the money. You shoot Ortiz, I drop the money. You shoot me, I drop the money. No more fires."

"This is a bad fucking idea, dude," Ortiz groaned.

"Listen to your friend," Graham replied. "You drop it and I kill you both. You're not ready to die over this."

"I'm in constant pain from the wounds you gave me, I ruined my deal with the cops, and the only family I had is dead. A bullet would be a blessing," I said.

Graham stared. I seemed to be getting through.

"Call your boss, tell him you tied up the loose ends," I motioned to Ortiz and myself again, "and you're done setting fires. Do that, both bags of cash are yours, and we all go our separate ways. Everyone wins."

Graham had to see the sense in that. With the heat on him for felony escape and assaulting Hallenbeck, it was smart to cut ties with his arson-loving employer.

The house shook *hard* – Ortiz, hands bound and on his knees, fell over, while Graham fought for balance and I tottered over the floodwaters.

"These foundations are on borrowed time. Better hurry," I told him.

"Fine," Graham said, taking out his phone.

"I saw your recents, your call history. You're not gonna bullshit me on this." The recents list had been made of calls entirely to 'E.M.'

Graham showed me the contact – E.M. – I nodded, and he dialed it.

"He won't answer," Graham said. "I just call it, hang up, and he calls me back from a burner."

"Then leave a fucking voicemail."

We waited for the dial tone to go to voicemail as the house creaked and the floodwaters rushed. Finally, a digital assistant gave the voicemail prompt, followed by a beep.

"You got yours, I got mine," Graham said as the voicemail recorded. "We're done. No loose ends here. Good doing business with you."

Graham put away the phone, and I nodded again.

I hoped that would do it.

He tucked his gun in his pants and motioned for the cash.

I tossed the bag at his feet.

Graham unzipped the bag and shook it around to make sure all the stacks were there. They were.

He grunted and untied Ortiz.

"We're done here," Graham said.

I skirted around Graham. Ortiz stood stiffly and joined me where the door opened to the hall.

"Go ahead," I told Ortiz, letting him in front, and I faced Graham as I backed into the hallway, "The rest of the money is on the doorstep. Wait 'til we're gone."

I turned the corner and Graham was out of sight.

Zzzzip!

A rope whisked behind the exposed drywall in the charred hall – *ker-thunk* – and an attic stairway dropped down from the ceiling, bringing half the blackened attic with it, knocking Ortiz down and blocking our exit.

Graham's trap.

"Stay down!" I yelled, and Graham marched into the hall, gun aimed at my head.

Something snapped and there was a rapid clicking and a loud pop of Graham's gun – the bullet punched through the air as it went past my head – Graham dropped his gun and fell forward, two wires trailing out of his back.

Tased, right as he was pulling the trigger.

Kamilah and Richard walked up behind him, both wearing ballistic vests, Richard holding the taser. As planned, they'd used a ladder to come through a window in the master bedroom. The crumbling house had done a good job concealing their arrival.

"Stay down and put your hands on the back of your head," Richard ordered. To Kamilah, he said, "Get the phone."

Kamilah crouched next to Graham, took the phone from his pocket, and put it in a Ziploc bag.

"Will that do it?" I asked.

"It's enough," Richard said.

The house rattled, half of it drooping toward the river. Richard stumbled, hands on the wall for support.

Graham tore out the taser barbs and dashed for the gun, getting a hold of it as Richard got his footing.

The house rumbled and this time it didn't stop, the crack in the roof opening wide, the walls splintering and the attic stairway disconnecting from the ceiling – clearing the way.

Kamilah, Ortiz and Richard were in the hallway like ducks in a barrel, ready for Graham to gun them down. Richard cracked shots off at Graham, but the shaking house skewed his aim, and the killer took cover in the master bedroom.

I shoved Kamilah toward the exit. They needed cover. My back would have to do.

"The house is falling apart. Go!"

"You don't have vests, we do," she said.

"Not for your head. Go, I got the rear."

Richard fired off down the hall to keep Graham at bay a few seconds more, then put Kamilah and Ortiz in front of him and ran for the door.

A tight pressure point hammered into my neck and then my upper back as they ran out the door. I was right behind them.

Until the house lurched and the stairs broke apart beneath me. I smacked the wall and grabbed the railing to stop my fall, but it snapped off and I crumpled on the steps.

Burning – like a red-hot poker stabbing my neck and back, seeping slippery warmth.

Timbers cracked, the foundations groaned, and the house split in two. The half facing Ash River slid into the surging floodwaters.

Graham. He'd been thrown off the stairs onto the first floor and was stuck under a beam in the doomed half of the house. Veins popping, he clung to a length of shorn drywall on the safe side. He couldn't hold it. In seconds the floodwaters would take the half-house and him with it. The muddy water was splashing and battering him with debris.

Richard and Kamilah had what they needed, having captured the Ortiz-money exchange with a directional microphone and taken the phone as evidence. Enough to find his employer.

No reason Graham had to survive this.

Ash River was gone, nothing left but ashes and skull-houses like this one, and how many others gone in other towns? Gone too, the people who died fighting the patchwork quilt inferno Graham had created. Hallenbeck's smashed-in face.

It was all there, an inferno in my blood.

Blood – mine? – trickled down my right arm, winding around the scarred tattoo on my hand. The muscles in it were tearing apart all over again as the shiv was plunged in and Caleb was face down in a pool of his blood and Graham's boots squeaked in the blood as he ran away after he flayed my brother's back after Ulrich cracked him on the head with his baton after the fight after Caleb had said '*We can make it right*' and Graham had replied '*No, you can't.*'

All this pain and hate started with Graham. With his death, it could end forever.

Let him die.

For Caleb. For Ash River. For Hallenbeck.

But Hallenbeck was my fault. Ash River too. An eruption of blood and fire caused by my obsession with *this* blood-spiller, this fire-starter. When I had him at my feet at Tapo, I'd become a destroyer just like him. How many people would suffer, how much more would burn if I let that take over me? *And Caleb…*

My brother deserved to be remembered. He didn't deserve to become fuel for the destroyer. *Enough.* Enough of the flames hollowing me out from the inside. I wanted the feeling in my chest I got from returning Troy to his parents, to be a man that saves lives instead of ending them.

I crawled through the wreckage of the stairs and pulled Graham up and away from the maelstrom.

For me.

The doomed half of the house collapsed into the floodwaters with a shudder and a hiss, the last bits of structure breaking apart and the entire first floor sinking underwater as it sailed downstream.

I felt for the red-hot stingers in my neck and back and my fingers came away crimson. Bloody bullet holes. The one on the neck going straight through the muscle running down the shoulder, the one on my upper back had no exit hole.

I dragged Graham to the front door and out onto the firm ground of the front yard. Kamilah, Ortiz, and Richard waiting for me. I was so tired.

Graham staggered to his feet and sneered at me.

"That was a mistake," he said.

I punched him in the face, sending him sprawling on his back. Done with him.

I took in Kamilah's beautiful face and Ortiz's friendly one.

So tired.

Their faces slipped away, along with the world.

CHAPTER THIRTY

The hospital, again. The tubes and wires clinging to my body and the sterile smell clinging to my nostrils. Nurse Mike had left the blinds open, so I could see the sun fighting through scattered gray clouds.

I'd said no to opioids. Things were clearer now, and I needed to keep them that way. With a little help from ibuprofen and ice packs, I lived with the pain.

My right hand was filled with pins and covered in bandages. The surgeon said I'd probably get full use back, but that it'd be painful for the rest of my life.

There was one thing I had to do before I could heal. I finally grieved for Caleb without interruption.

Shredding the air guitar and harmonizing to the Def Leppard song, beating me up just to show me he could, walking me to school to show my bully Trent Sutter I was not to be fucked with, me watching green with envy as he sacked the Bakersfield quarterback, getting me to help him fuck over Mom's meth dealer, racing Audis with fresh VINs down Van Nuys Boulevard, blocking the alley as he brass-knuckled a snitch, him watching me put a new tattoo on Rubio and proudly saying it was 'really sick.'

Remembering him as more than a reason to pay pain back with pain, to trade destruction for destruction, to embrace hate in the name of brotherly love. Remembering Caleb as a man. Good, bad, and everything in between.

I let it all out, blowing my nose when I was done but leaving the tears to dry on my face.

And it was quiet.

I pulled the medical tape off my right hand. The ink of the unfinished night sky was a warped shadow, split in half by the white scar from Graham's shiv and intersected by a pink, new scar from the surgeon's scalpel. Together, the scars made a curvy Y shape. *Like a tree.* A vision of a tattoo formed in my mind. The scar tissue itself would push out any ink, but I could ink millimeters next to it, outlining it, shaping it with new branches and knots in the wood. Extending the tree beyond the scar, I'd add a burning cavity at its base, gnawing away at its insides. Just like the one that had mesmerized me after the burnover.

I'd had my own furnace blazing inside. The tattoo would be a reminder not to give it fuel.

Like in prison, time in the hospital stretched on and on. It was seven hours until I got my first visitor. Richard, who was not the Martin I wanted to see.

He pulled up a chair next to my bed, and I elevated the head rest to meet his eyes.

"You been watching the news?" Richard asked.

"No," I said, "the only thing I wanna know about is the Patchwork." My insides knotted waiting for an answer.

"70 percent contained."

I released a deep breath, beyond relieved.

"I ask about the news because there've been some developments. Thanks to the evidence we got in the hostage exchange, we were able to make an arrest. Erik Marshall."

E.M. The initials in Graham's phone.

"Why'd he wanna set California on fire?"

"He's an executive with the Spear Company. Trying to turn a profit off the housing crisis. California's other never-ending problem. No affordability, availability, all that. Even before the Patchwork. The Spear Company had a billion-dollar housing contract dead in the water because of building regulations –"

"He was squeezing the state," I realized out loud.

Richard nodded.

"And last week Sacramento relaxed those regulations because of the massive population displaced by the Patchwork," he said.

"Burned down thousands of homes, ruined lives, killed people. For a building deal." My stomach turned and my mouth flooded with saliva. I was on the verge of throwing up.

"You're surprised?"

"No," I sighed.

I'd known people like Erik Marshall since I was fifteen, when I joined Caleb's world. Mom's meth dealer, the double-crossers on the Benz job, our frequent employer Quincy Reed. The selfishness of it was just hitting me in a way it hadn't in years.

"And it worked."

"We'll see if it sticks. Sacramento loves their regulations. My concern is making the criminal charges stick. That goes for Graham, too. D.A. is building a case on him. Might as well hear it straight from me, first, so here's what –"

"It's okay," I cut him off. For half a second, I wanted to know. More out of habit than anything. There was a glimmer of heat in the pit of me, but I let it go. "I don't want to know. I'll make the statements I need to make, testify… but he's not worth keeping tabs on."

I was done with Graham.

"Fair enough," Richard said. He cleared his throat, "As for you, I did my best with the D.A. given… everything. The events at Eagle View Campground, what happened at Ash River."

The con in me said I deserved a break for saving Troy, for not killing Graham. That it wasn't my fault. The Pete McLean in me knew better. Deserting my crew in Ash River's time of need, wearing the turnout gear of the brave to pursue murder.

"The charges?" I asked, ready to accept them all.

"One count of felony escape."

I was floored. It was more than I could hope for.

"'Course, you'll want to discuss it with your lawyer."

But I won't be getting a better deal than that.

"The docket's pretty full. Your arraignment won't be for a few months."

"What happens to me until then?"

"With some persuasion from Kamilah, I got you cleared back to La Cuenca. Can go as soon as you're physically fit, might even be able to stay if you plead guilty. Play your cards right, maybe get time served."

"Are you kidding me? That's... amazing." I couldn't believe I was saying this to a cop, but, "thank you."

"It's good for the state. She says you have a knack for the work."

He stood to go.

"Is she... does she know I'm here?"

"She knows. I'd prefer you let it be, stay away from her, tell you not to hurt her... but you already did. And my sister does what she wants." Richard shrugged and brought out an ash-smudged envelope out of his jacket. I recognized it immediately. "Found this in your tent. Believe it belongs to you." He smiled and met my eyes, and for a single second there was a kinship between us. Then he adjusted his belt and gave me a business-like nod, "I'll be seeing you."

Not a bad dude, as far as cops go.

When Richard was gone, I finally read Troy's letter all the way through.

Dear Mr. McLeen,

Thank you for saving me. I was so scared but you took me away from the fire. When I grow up I want to be a fireman like you. Then I can save people too. My birthday is not for a while but will you come? There will be cake and probably a pinyata. It would mean a lot if you could be there.

I wish I knew more what to say. I am thankful for you.

Sincerely,
Troy Cooper

My throat stopped up and tears splotched the page. I folded up the letter before my leaky eyes could speckle it any further.

Thank you, Troy. I took it as a blessing of my decision to save Graham. To smother the furnace and starve the destroyer. It was a charge to become a man like the one Troy believed in. Even though I was a fuckup, a fake hero, and God only knew if I could ever live up to that charge. I thought of the real hero I'd sent to death's doorstep with my rage.

I needed to see him.

I decided nurses are the best people in the world. Jenny put me in a wheelchair and took me two floors down and across three wings to see Hallenbeck.

"He's stable," Nurse Jenny said. "Swelling has gone down. If his condition stays the same, they'll bring him out of the coma soon."

"Thanks, Jenny."

"I'll let you keep him company for a bit. Be back in about

fifteen minutes," she told me, and slipped out.

His head was wrapped in a clean bandage, and his face was mottled with yellow, purple, and brown bruises. But alive, thank God.

I wheeled closer. An ache spread down the back of my throat and I needed to look at everything in the room but him. I forced my gaze on him and said,

"I'm sorry."

"Never where you're supposed to be," said a voice behind me.

I turned the wheelchair to Kamilah. My heart leapt into my throat. She maintained that stony Kamilah poker face, but my nerves tingled all the same.

"You here for me or him?"

"I don't know Hallenbeck," she said.

For me. My pulse skyrocketed, but I didn't know how to reply, and an awkward silence stretched for an eternity. Kamilah drummed her fingers on her thigh.

"How are you feeling?" Kamilah asked.

"Light," I said, voice catching from dry mouth, "You know? Lighter than I've felt in a long time."

"That's good," she said, expression softening, moving closer to me.

Again, I didn't know what to say. *Don't mess it up.* I settled on a small, grateful smile and waited for her next move. This was so awkward.

"Indubitably," I said, unable to wait any longer.

Kamilah smirked and my chest fluttered. Then she turned serious.

"I gotta get going. Just wanted to make sure you're, you know."

"Yeah."

"Heal up," she said, and started out.

Is this it? She walks out and I never see her again?

"I see how it is," I teased, "I was in the sweet spot, scars-wise, and now I have a few too many."

Kamilah cocked her head, brow furrowed in confusion, and then she remembered the text, smiling. "That's totally what it is," she replied, playing along.

"Will you come see me at La Cuenca? Nice little spot, for an inmate camp." I had to try. She probably just needed some space.

Kamilah stopped at the door.

"You did a good thing," she said. "But that doesn't make you a good man. That's a choice you have to make day-in and day-out. Maybe… someday, I don't know…"

Kamilah didn't finish her thought. She looked down at her feet, her eyes glassy.

I wanted to hold onto that '*maybe someday*,' but I knew better. Kamilah was letting me down easy, trying to tell me she deserved better.

She does deserve better.

Kamilah walked briskly over and kissed me on the forehead.

"Good luck, okay? Take care of yourself," she said, and walked out the door.

I doubted I'd ever see her again, and I had no sorrow left to mourn the loss of the most amazing woman I'd ever know.

I was done with Graham. I'd grieved for Caleb, finally.

I felt light was because I was empty. I didn't have Caleb to lean

on or the rage over his murder to drive me. I didn't have Kamilah
to ache for or Pete McLean to impersonate.

What am I supposed to do now?

The ground crunched under my boots, a mix of baked
soil, burnt vegetation, and ashes. Overhead stretched a
boundless, deep-blue sky. I didn't know the sky could be
so blue.

Two months after Kamilah kissed me goodbye, I hiked into the
black of the defeated Patchwork. Crew 9 was working an erosion
control job on a scorched hilltop overlooking a clear stream that fed
Ash River. The goal was to prevent another mudslide, and all the
damage it could do downstream. I had yet to fill the emptiness and
it followed me like a shadow.

I reached the top of the hill, and as soon as the crew members
saw me, the razzing began.

"Honor grad," Damarius said ironically, as he lifted a railroad
tie with Baby Einstein.

"This fucking guy. Get any action from the hospital nurses?"
Skeevy Steve asked.

"Give him space, guys. Bad Luck Brian here's liable to get you
shot," Vito said.

Damarius, Skeevy Steve, Vito. Other crew members placed
sediment barriers and planted saplings. Lt. Nelson, the acting
foreman, nodded at me in greeting. The gang was all here. I was a
puzzle piece falling into place.

Ortiz chopped up some dead bushes close by, but he didn't

look over.

"I heard he soaks up them bullets. Like a magnet," Skeevy Steve said.

"That what you heard? I wasn't hospitalized because I got shot, I was hospitalized because I ran into that rabid beaver of yours," I quipped. "You said its teeth were orange, but they were pretty damn red by the time I passed out from blood loss."

Skeevy Steve smirked while the rest of the crew chortled. I studied the back of Ortiz's head, trying to see if that'd at least got me a smile. His sweaty neck gave nothing away, and I kept my distance. He needed time.

"How's Cap?" he asked, turning and swaggering up, his eyes narrowed.

Or not.

"Better. Awake. He told me to tell you to keep an eye on me." Ortiz grunted – half amused, half annoyed. He crossed his arms, waiting for me to continue. I had to make things right. It wasn't just about me anymore. "Your shot caller, Serrato. He can't be too happy Graham is still alive."

"Shit happens," Ortiz said with a neutral tone.

"If you can get me some face time with him, I'll explain everything. I don't want any of this falling on you."

"Never had a problem with that before." Ortiz scratched his chin and studied me.

"I was a real piece of shit and I took you for granted," I burst, sincere, "I'm sorr– "

"Trust. Don't get all sappy."

I kept quiet. It seemed like the right thing to do.

"Graham's connects are under a microscope, and that's freeing up real estate for my peoples. If Serrato ain't liking that…" Ortiz looked at me, "… you and me, we'll figure it out."

"Trust," I said, and tapped his shoulder with my fist. I doubted it'd be that simple. But he had my back, and I had his. *From now on.*

Ortiz grinned and tossed me my Pulaski axe.

The empty feeling faded. That's what I was supposed to do now. The work.

The only thing I had to think about today was clearing the black. There was something pure in that. I took a moment to listen to the burble of the water, to watch the rippled sun reflect from the stream, and then plunged my axe into the dead tree at my feet.

ACKNOWLEDGMENTS

Writing is hard. If I could do anything else, I would. That's why I'm very thankful for the feedback and support I received from friends, family, and colleagues while writing this novel. My developmental editor Carly Hayward was instrumental in getting me to rip Mace's heart out of my head and onto the page. I'm very grateful for her guidance. To the readers of my interim drafts – Kevin Sheridan, Jack Bentele, Anna Abate, and MJ Gardner – I couldn't have completed this book without your feedback. Thank you!

I owe a huge debt of gratitude to those who've read my past work and helped me improve my writing. This includes my fellow students at the USC Cinema School, my professors there, and the members of the Burbank Barnes & Noble Writers Group, especially Julie Beers. Their feedback and encouragement kept me afloat in times of doubt. A big thanks as well to my writing mentor, Mark Shepherd, for the good advice, good conversation, and good beer.

I pestered my siblings Elise and Justin DeCapite frequently about word choice and phrasing, and their prompt and helpful responses prevented quite a few procrastination delays.

Major props to those who helped me across the finish line: Lex Schultz, with their eagle-eyed proofing, and Connie Fan, with her marketing insight.

This book is dedicated to my parents. Unlike Mace Jones, I was lucky enough to be raised by two dedicated, caring parents, and they have always supported my pursuits.

This story was inspired by the real work done by inmate hand crews, and I hope fire professionals, inmates, and correctional personnel can indulge the creative liberties I've taken with this novel. Any errors regarding this world are my own. To all those fighting wildfires, thank you for everything you do, and stay safe.

ABOUT THE AUTHOR

Anthony DeCapite served in the Marine Corps as a Combat Videographer, deploying to cyclone-stricken Bangladesh and to the remote islands of the southern Philippines. The real-life humanitarian crises he experienced during his service continue to influence his work. Anthony went on to graduate from the USC Cinema School's Writing for Screen and Television Program and is now an author and screenwriter. He's also a writer-producer at the Institute for Creative Technologies, where he creates games, short films, and futurist fiction for military training and research. He lives in Los Angeles with his faithful dog Sammy.

anthonydecapite.com